M000190575

DANGEROUS SLEUTHING

I paused at the corner of the building. My blood ran cold. Twenty yards away a hooded figure was crouching behind the oak tree, directing a pinpoint light into the office where Walter and Lola did business.

The figure was of medium height and medium build, but I couldn't make out if it was a man or a woman, the hood pulled low over the intruder's face. I peeked around the corner to get a better look and my jacket scraped against the brick of the building. I froze. The individual stood and looked my way. I held my breath and leaned into the wall, making myself as flat as possible. Then the person backed away from the theater and ran down Main past the Windjammer and disappeared. I considered my options: I could get my car and try to follow, I could run after whoever was casing the theater, or I could go home and call Bill in the morning. But by the time Bill made a move on the possible attempted break-in, this person could be anywhere.

I stepped around the corner and peered down Main again. The street was empty except for a lone pickup truck that rattled past the theater. What if the person had cut down a side street and vanished into a backyard, or hopped in a getaway vehicle that had been stashed several blocks over, or had a companion waiting somewhere?

I felt vulnerable on foot, but in my Metro I could scour the streets off Main and look for any sign of the prowler. I spun on my heel to dash to my car. A burst of light blinded me. It took a moment before I realized what it was. Someone was deliberately shining a powerful utility flashlight in my face. I raised my hands to block the light and felt a thud from behind. A heavy object connected with the back of my head and a burst of colors detonated in my brain. I saw stars. And then black . . .

Books by Suzanne Trauth

SHOW TIME

TIME OUT

Published by Kensington Publishing Corporation

Time Out

Suzanne Trauth

LYRICAL UNDERGROUND
Kensington Publishing Corp.
www.kensingtonbooks.com

To the extent that the image or images on the cover of this book depict a person or persons, such person or persons are merely models, and are not intended to portray any character or characters featured in the book.

LYRICAL UNDERGROUND BOOKS are published by

Kensington Publishing Corp.
119 West 40th Street
New York, NY 10018

Copyright © 2017 by Suzanne Trauth

All rights reserved. No part of this book may be reproduced in any form or by any means without the prior written consent of the Publisher, excepting brief quotes used in reviews.

All Kensington titles, imprints, and distributed lines are available at special quantity discounts for bulk purchases for sales promotion, premiums, fund-raising, educational, or institutional use.

Special book excerpts or customized printings can also be created to fit specific needs. For details, write or phone the office of the Kensington Sales Manager: Kensington Publishing Corp., 119 West 40th Street, New York, NY 10018. Attn. Sales Department. Phone: 1-800-221-2647.

Lyrical Underground and Lyrical Underground logo Reg. US Pat. & TM Off.

First Electronic Edition: January 2017
eISBN-13: 978-1-60183-721-9
eISBN-10: 1-60183-721-6

First Print Edition: January 2017
ISBN-13: 978-1-60183-722-6
ISBN-10: 1-60183-722-4

Printed in the United States of America

ACKNOWLEDGMENTS

Thanks to my family and friends, who have graciously supported my every new adventure.

1

It's not always true that "all the world's a stage." Sometimes it's a boxing ring. Right now I had a ringside seat at the Windjammer restaurant in Etonville, New Jersey. A charming little town sitting in the shadow of New York City, it was named after Thomas Eton, one of George Washington's army officers during the American Revolution.

I downed my second glass of seltzer as I watched Benny, the bartender, give a quick swipe to the sticky surface of the glossy wooden bar.

"You missed a spot," I said, pointing to a dollop of barbecue sauce. I pushed my empty glass in his direction.

Benny raised an eyebrow. "Eagle eye. Hey, what's going on next door?" He jerked his thumb in the direction of the Etonville Little Theatre. "I heard there was a real hubbub here at lunchtime today."

Geez. Probably from the dotty Banger sisters. The two elderly women were the gossip mavens of the town. "Lola came in with Antonio. The two of them disagreeing over something. Then Edna stopped in for carryout and Abby tore into her," I said and lowered my voice. "And I'm not even talking about Henry."

Lola Tripper was the reigning diva and acting artistic director of the Etonville Little Theatre, which was deep in the throes of rehearsing its fall play—*Arsenic and Old Lace.* Antonio Digenza was the guest director trying to create order out of the bedlam of the community theater's rehearsal process. Edna May—dispatcher for the Etonville Police Department—was sharing the leading lady duties with Abby Henderson, manager of the Valley View Shooting Range. They were playing the Brewster sisters. Abby was on probation at the theater, due to unprofessional behavior during the ELT production of *Romeo and Juliet*, but she had finally accepted the fact that she was less a teenage Juliet and more a matronly sister.

Henry was my boss, the owner-chef of the Windjammer, and in a sulky mood since his cross-town archrival, Italian restaurant La Famiglia, received a four-star review in the *Etonville Standard*, again, last week.

"Mercury must be in retrograde. Everybody's touchy and having it out with someone. I'm trying to remain neutral. I feel like Switzerland," I said.

I am Dodie O'Dell. Manager of the Windjammer restaurant, BFF to Lola, and her moral support when she's overwhelmed, which she is with just about every ELT production.

"Hi, Dot." Honey bounced out of the kitchen.

I gritted my teeth. I hated being called Dot. Only my great aunt Maureen could get away with that. And she was gone now, so there was no one left to torment me. Except Honey. Benny sniggered and dipped his cloth in soapy water, attacking the bar stain. I turned my attention to Honey—named for her hair, she claimed. As if. It was really mousy brown.

"Uncle Henry wants to know if you have the specials inserts printed for tomorrow." She inclined her head and studied me.

Honey, twenty-two, had been a fixture in the restaurant for the past month, presumably learning all aspects of restaurant management from the kitchen to the dining room, and taking a "gap-semester" away from college. More likely her university was taking a semester break from Honey. She was majoring in Packaging—who even knew there was such a thing—and had nonstop ideas on how to improve the Windjammer's "dissemination presence." Honey had become a pain in my butt, but apparently Henry was making up for some past transgression committed against his brother. Or else he had a long-range plan for his niece? I shuddered. The two of us could not occupy the same space indefinitely.

"I'll pick up the inserts from the printer on my way in tomorrow." I smiled. No sense picking one more fight; tensions in the restaurant were riding high enough.

"Oh, and I don't, like, get this theme-food thing." She propped one hand on her skinny hip, her voice doing that upward sweep that made it seem as if she was asking a question with every sentence.

I counted to five. "What don't you get, Honey?"

She scratched her head. "Who wants to eat stuff like egg creams and nishes?"

"It's k-nishes."

"Whatever. I mean, like, the hotdogs aren't too bad but the other stuff? I'd say ditch it and let's have chicken fingers and mozzarella sticks."

I counted from five to ten. "Honey, the whole point of *theme* food is to match the *theme* of the play. *Arsenic and Old Lace* takes place in Brooklyn in 1940, so we're having New York food from that time." I waited while she processed this.

"Hmmm," she said, acting all important. "I still think chicken fingers are, like, more interesting." She flounced off.

My great aunt Maureen would have said Honey was about as useless as a solar-powered flashlight.

"She's related to Henry?" Benny muttered out of the corner of his mouth.

"We've got five days until the food festival. Henry's not thrilled with my choice of menu."

Theme food to accompany each production of the Etonville Little Theatre had been my idea last year and so far, so good. *Dames at Sea* and seafood, Italian fare for *Romeo and Juliet*, beef bourguignon for the French farce. I was pretty impressed with my choice for this show: Nathan's hot dogs, Italian ices, egg creams, soft pretzels, black-and-white cookies, and, of course, knishes. But Henry was smarting from his competitor's recent success, and none of my theme-food dishes were exactly haute cuisine. Never mind. People would flock to the sidewalk kiosks and gobble down the throwback food.

"But at least he's agreed to play along. I just hope Lola's scuffle with Antonio cools down before next weekend. I need the staff and cast out in full costume to make the event festive. Smiling. Looking like this theater thing is a lot of fun."

"Good luck with that," Benny said.

The front door opened and Lola strode in, eyes blazing. "Benny, set me up with a chardonnay and keep them coming."

"Hey, girlfriend, what's up? Rehearsal's over already?"

Lola shook her head and took a healthy gulp of her wine. She closed her eyes. "I've been dreaming about that sip for two hours."

Sip? She must really be rattled.

"I had to get out of there. Or I might have killed someone."

"Like the director?"

"I had no idea he was so ..."

"Obnoxious?" I said.

She pointed her index finger at me. "Yes! Obnoxious! I thought it would be, you know, nice to hire a theater professional. Elevate the artistic profile of the ELT."

"And give him a place to stay."

She grumbled. "I didn't know he'd married a twenty-something."

"Or insist she be cast as the ingénue." I was into theater lingo ever since I helped manage *Romeo and Juliet* last spring.

Antonio Digenza was a fiftyish, fiercely handsome, egotistical theater acquaintance from Lola's days as an off-off-Broadway ingénue herself. Though she'd never admitted it, I had the impression that, until she found out he was married, Lola might have been crushing on the director. Widowed for ten years, her recent love life had consisted of an on-again, off-again dalliance with Walter Zeitzman, the past artistic director who was currently in the doghouse for playing fast and loose with the box office till. No wonder he was cast as the play's criminal element.

"Still, it was nice that you welcomed Antonio and Tiffany into your home."

Lola dismissed her generosity. "Saved the theater money. You know the ELT budget."

The theater's finances were usually stretched to the point of transparency.

"Besides, we have a history." Her face took on a dreamy look. "I remember nights after long rehearsals when Antonio and I would get together to share a bottle of cheap wine and work on lines. Or at least my lines." She smiled at the memory.

I could imagine what Antonio was working on. Even though Lola had been married at the time.

Lola caught herself. "But with Tiffany around ..." She sniffed and swept her long blond hair behind one shoulder. Lola was forty-four but looked thirty—sophisticated, compelling—and certainly not the mother of a college sophomore. Which she was.

"Tiffany's his wife," I said.

"And a terrible actress." Lola motioned to Benny to top off her glass. "They argue constantly. I didn't mean to eavesdrop last night, but I heard Antonio yelling at Tiffany because she apparently misplaced her cell phone and used his."

"What was the big deal?"

"I don't know. He said she had no business getting into his personal affairs and how did she know his password anyway? And she says..." Lola shifted her pitch upward, mimicking Tiffany's. "*Like, duh, the password's your name and you use it for everything. TONY.*"

"Hard to think of Antonio as a Tony," I said.

"I've never heard him use that name. Anyway, I can't imagine what he sees in her."

I can, I thought, as I pictured the redheaded bombshell in her leggings and tight-fitting sweaters. "What's he done tonight?"

She waved her hand. "Oh, you know, the regular. Bullying actors, canceling rehearsals, then disappearing—"

"Disappearing? Where to?"

"Who knows? At first it was just once a week. Then twice a week. But he was gone Friday and then again last night. He said he wasn't feeling well."

"Wow. That's odd. Don't you have a 'disappearing clause' in his contract?"

"I don't think the board anticipated this. The contract was a handshake." Lola scratched a dark mark on the bar. "They trusted my judgment." She took a swallow of her wine. "I hope I'm not in trouble."

I could see Lola's point. Antonio was the first guest director, and out-of-towner, that the Etonville Little Theatre had hired in its twenty-five-year history. Walter usually directed all of the productions. Before him, those duties were handled by the drama coach at Etonville High, until his eyesight got so bad that one night he fell off the stage and landed on an oversized female member of the cast. He broke her arm and she squashed his ego. Walter stepped in.

"Maybe he's just getting anxious? Or needs to clear his head?"

Lola frowned. "I wish it was as simple as that. Usually he comes back by midnight, but yesterday he left midafternoon and didn't get back until this morning."

Yikes. This was a little more than pre-opening jitters.

"What does Tiffany say? I mean she is his wife. She must know—"

My cell clanged and I checked the caller ID. "Hi, Carol. What's up?"

"Just checking in about your hair appointment tomorrow."

Carol Palmieri, my second BFF, was the owner of Snippets, Etonville's popular hair salon and rumor central. If you wanted to know what was going on in town—who was romancing whom, whose house was in foreclosure, who'd fallen off the diet wagon—you spent an hour or so at Snippets.

"Is nine a.m. still good?" My auburn hank of shoulder-length hair needed a reprieve from its ponytail. A trim would do the trick. I usually took my afternoon break between three and five, but with Honey in the restaurant, I was wary of staying away too long and had been skipping my late-day breather.

"That's fine. I've got a new shampoo girl and I'm breaking her in tomorrow."

Lola motioned for my cell. "Hang on for Lola." I handed her the phone.

"Carol, are you going to stop by the theater and talk with Antonio about hair for next weekend?" Lola asked.

Carol was the hair and makeup specialist for the Etonville Little Theatre. No one did an updo like Carol.

"Thursday night at nine? That's fine. I'll try to keep Antonio in the theater until then," Lola said with a smidge of sarcasm. "Never mind, Carol. I'll explain later."

Lola clicked off, downed the rest of her wine, and bravely headed back to rehearsal. I moved to my favorite back booth where I did restaurant business, and faced a stack of bills.

Two hours later, the bills were paid, the last customer had departed, the floor was mopped, and the receipts bundled for deposit. Henry had gone a half hour ago with Honey in tow; I think they were crowding each other's social life, but he was determined to take his uncle responsibilities seriously.

I turned out the lights, locked the door, and stepped into the autumn night, chilly for early October in New Jersey. Next to summer, fall was my favorite time of year. The crispness of the air, the clear night sky, and the faint smell of burning wood. Somewhere in the neighborhood a fireplace was getting a workout. I gazed upward, trying to locate the North Star at the end of the Little Dipper's handle. Stargazing at night had been one of my pastimes before Hurricane Sandy made short work of my beach life two years ago and sent me up north to Etonville.

I trotted to my red Chevy Metro, one of the last vestiges of my previous life in southern New Jersey. It had over 90,000 miles but still purred like a contented cat. Which reminded me, I had offered to feed my neighbor's kitten, Sammy, while she was visiting her daughter in Ohio. Though I'd fed her this morning, I should probably stop in and check on her just in case—

"Hi," said a voice behind me.

I jumped, dropped my keys, and my heart thudded in my chest. I whipped around.

"Didn't mean to scare you." Bill Thompson leaned down to retrieve the key ring, forcing his shoulder muscles to tighten across the back of his uniform shirt. You'd think I'd be used to his former-football-player physique by now. But no, those rippling muscles did a number on my pulse. He placed the keys in my palm, his fingers brushing my hand.

"What's Etonville's police chief doing on the street so late? Chasing bad guys?"

Bill's quirky grin turned up the corner of the left side of his mouth. "More like chasing paperwork."

"Been there, done that tonight."

He rubbed his eyes. "I've been chained to my desk for the past three hours, so I decided to stretch my legs."

The glow of the street lamp lit up his sandy-colored brush cut, blonder now as a result of the summer sun. The police department was a fifteen-minute walk down Amber Street and up Main to the Windjammer. A little more than a stretch. "You had a busy August."

He scraped the toe of one shoe back and forth like an embarrassed kid. "Yeah. My two-week vacation—"

"To see family in Vermont, right?"

He stared at me, his face a question mark.

"Snippets."

"No privacy in Etonville," he said.

I laughed. "I guess not."

"Then there was our conference. The Association of—"

"—Chiefs of Police. Right. Also Snippets."

He shook his head. "And you were?"

"Down the shore for a week. Feeding fries to the seagulls, getting buried in the sand . . ."

He grinned. "Sounds like illegal activity to me."

"It was nice to see the boardwalk rebuilt after Hurricane Sandy."
He turned serious. "I can imagine."

We let the silence settle between us for a moment. I could sense, rather than see, his laser-like blue eyes on me. "Guess I'll head home. Knowing you're on duty makes me feel a lot safer," I said dramatically. "Anyway, you must be getting cold."

"Nah. I used to play in Buffalo with bare arms in zero degrees."

"The Bills, right," I said.

"Speaking of which. Did you talk with Henry about our picnic?"

Bill had agreed to coach Etonville's Youth Football team for the nine- to eleven-year-old crowd. Saturday after next he planned to treat the kids to Henry's cheeseburgers and fries after the game, win or lose.

Between the food festival this weekend and the football picnic the following weekend, the Windjammer was going to be busy the next couple of weeks. Henry was lukewarm about both events—he was more a stay-home-and-cook kind of chef—but I had convinced him that catering to the town was way more Etonville-friendly than a four-star review in the *Standard*. Honey agreed, mainly because she could practice packaging skills with cardboard, Saran wrap, and Styrofoam. "No problem. We'll have the food on the field by the fourth quarter."

"If the kids make it that long. Last Saturday we were losing thirty-five to nothing after three quarters, and the official called the game." He shook his head. "The NFL was nothing like this."

I unlocked my door and eased behind the steering wheel. "I'll write up the invoice for the burgers."

"Drive carefully."

I nodded and put my Metro in reverse. Bill's figure on the sidewalk grew smaller as I cruised down Main Street. I mused over our relationship . . .

Relationship? *Is that what we have?* I wondered. I coasted past the Etonville Little Theatre, dark at this hour, and Coffee Heaven, an old-fashioned breakfast diner with a handful of red booths, a soda fountain, and a few modern coffee items on the menu. Caramel macchiato was my obsession.

I paused for the red light at the corner of Fairfield and Main Streets. Bill and I'd had a nice moment together after I'd stepped into the investigation of the murder of my good friend Jerome and orchestrated a sting to catch the killer. He was initially a little resistant to my participation, but eventually came around. He even squeezed my hand on opening night of *Romeo and Juliet* . . . But then came summer. And his vacation. My vacation. The police chiefs' convention. Now it was fall.

I stepped on the accelerator and started to turn right. From out of nowhere a distinctive white Mercedes tore past me, barreling down Fairfield at what had to be seventy miles an hour. In a twenty-five-mile-per-hour zone. I jammed on the brakes instinctively.

That was weird, for midnight on a Monday in Etonville. What was even weirder was the occupant of the Mercedes: guest director Antonio Digenza. I'd recognize that face and beret anywhere.

2

I'd slept fitfully. I couldn't get Antonio out of my mind. Why was he driving like a maniac at midnight at the opposite end of town from Lola's, where he was staying during the rehearsal and run of the show? A pattern of disappearances from the ELT, plus this late night excursion. Hmm.

Snippets was already humming when I opened the door at nine. Carol's salt-and-pepper curly head was bouncing up and down, the phone in one hand, a comb in the other. She motioned for me to head to the sinks at the rear of the salon for a shampoo. I worked my way past cutting and color stations, to the back wall where silver side-by-side sinks were occupied by the Banger sisters. I had no idea what their first names were; no one ever referred to them individually. They were always together—same flowered blouses, same brown walking shoes, same gray permed hair in little ringlets.

"Morning ladies," I said.

The new shampoo girl, a tiny thing with rings up her ears, in her nose, and poking out of her tongue, wrapped towels around their wet heads. They looked up.

"Oh, Dodie. You poor thing," said the first sister.

"You are taking it so well," said the second.

I looked at them blankly. "What?"

They glanced at each other, then back at me and clucked sympathetically. "Who would think Henry could replace you with his niece?" said one.

"Replace me? No, she's just here—"

"We heard that she intends to change the menu—"

"—and redecorate."

"Who said that? Has Honey been talking?"

"Okay, ladies, time for perms." Carol positioned her forty-year-old compact frame next to the sisters for leverage and helped hoist them to their feet. The new shampoo girl escorted the Bangers to empty chairs.

"Do you know what they were saying?" I asked Carol as she whipped out a cape and prepared to snap it around my neck.

Carol shook her head.

"Someone has been spreading a rumor that Henry is firing me and Honey's taking over my job," I fumed. "As if."

Carol stopped mid-snap. "Henry did that? Why—?"

"No, Carol. It's just gossip," I said patiently. "But still. I wonder if Honey has been talking out of turn."

"She was in here yesterday chatting it up with Rita."

"The shampoo girl with—"

"The tattoo."

"By the way, how's the new one working out?" I asked.

"Imogen?" Carol shifted her gaze to the young woman, who was currently taking selfies with the Banger sisters. "It's so hard to find good help."

"Amen to that," I said as Imogen sauntered over and flipped on the warm water.

Forty-five minutes later, I stared at myself in the wall mirror behind Carol's back. My chestnut-colored hair, a gift from my maternal grandmother, now barely skimmed my shoulders and complimented my father's contribution—green eyes. My bangs were half an inch shorter. I felt lighter, freer. I wiggled my head a bit and watched my hair sway back and forth. I studied my reflection. Maybe I'd drop by the police department later with the invoice for Bill's picnic food. I visualized his deep blue eyes crinkling in the corners when he caught sight of me, new hairdo, silk blouse, some makeup . . .

"What did Lola mean last night about keeping Antonio in the theater?"

"It seems that he's been disappearing lately." I made eye contact with Carol in the mirror. "And no one knows where he goes or why. I think Lola's getting frantic."

Truth be told, I was getting a little frantic myself. If things didn't settle down between Lola and Antonio, the food festival could turn into a disaster.

"I heard that his wife is having a 'thing' with one of the cast members," Carol whispered.

"A 'thing'? What kind of a 'thing'?" Now I *was* getting worried. "I heard Tiffany's difficult and can't learn her lines, but a 'thing'?"

"And that Antonio's assistant . . ." Carol paused to think.

"Carlyle. I've seen him around the Windjammer. What about him?" He was a thin, prissy-looking guy who I'd heard was a part-time bookkeeper and lived with his mother in Queens.

She tilted her head toward me confidentially. "He's going to quit because no one listens to his ideas."

I grumbled. "Where do people get this stuff? I mean, sure, there are a few bumps with the production, but—"

Rita was gesturing to Carol from reception. "I have to scoot," Carol said and unsnapped the cape, sending a cascade of cut hair to the floor. "You should pop over and see the chief now." She let out a vigorous laugh, winked, and hurried away.

OMG. I hoped Bill and I weren't a topic of conversation with the Snippets crowd. I paid my bill and was halfway out the door when I remembered. "By the way, could you ask Pauli to call me? I want to do some updates on the website."

Carol beamed, a proud mother. "Of course. Did I tell you he's taking a computer class online? He's so into it."

Pauli was my seventeen-year-old IT guru who did everything from creating a website for the Windjammer—despite Henry's reluctance to enter the twenty-first century—to introducing me to password hacking, in the interest of solving a murder. The kid was a genius in the Internet universe and I had corralled him to help with the food booths Saturday.

I waved good-bye. I had about forty-five minutes before I was needed at the Windjammer. Time to stop home and change into my best green silk blouse and stretchy black pants. Today I intended to take my afternoon break, regardless of Honey.

Benny whistled from the bar as I stepped through the entrance to the restaurant. "Nice."

"I needed a trim," I said, trying to act indifferent.

"Is that makeup I see? What's the occasion?"

I set sheets of paper printed with the lunch and dinner specials on the bar and dropped my bag into the back booth. "I wear makeup," I said.

Benny set to work polishing glassware. "Uh-huh."

I did wear makeup, usually just a little eyeliner and a touch of color to my eyelids and lips. But today I'd included my cheekbones and eyelashes. There was a chance I was looking a little hot.

And then Honey walked in the door.

"Can you believe it? I found these in the trash behind the Shop N Go." Honey was carrying a stack of brown cardboard boxes, so tall her face was hidden. "It's like insane!"

The girl was obsessed with packaging. I took a few off her hands and her glowing face appeared. "Honey, we have boxes out back by the dumpster. Why bring these from the Shop N Go? What are you going to do with them?"

There went the hand on the hip and that look. "Dot, I need to practice with this size if we're going to set up a delivery service."

"A delivery service? Did you run this by Henry?"

"Uncle Henry agrees with me," she said and stuck her chin in the air.

I replaced my boxes on hers and her face disappeared again. Honey stomped off to the kitchen and I went to work on the menu inserts.

Lunch specials included Henry's barbecue rib sandwich, a three-napkin meal, and a new experiment: watermelon and mint salad, with some onion, olives, and goat cheese thrown in for good measure. It was a refreshing addition to the menu, kind of a poetic transition from the warm, lazy days of summer to the cooler, brisker tempo of autumn.

The verdict was mixed.

"What's that minty taste?" one of the Banger sisters asked after nibbling on a bit of the salad.

"Mint," I said.

"Oh." She nudged the watermelon salad to one side; her sister did the same. They nodded their newly coiffed heads in unison.

"I like it," Abby Henderson said, gobbling the watermelon. "These watermelon balls remind me of marbles. I used to play Chinese checkers as a kid before I started going to the range."

That would be the Valley View Shooting Range she managed.

"Okay," I said. "How's rehearsal going?" I hoped for some inside intel.

Abby opened her mouth just as the front door opened. Edna May, her theatrical archenemy, stood on the threshold, stony. "I told Lola casting Edna opposite me was asking for trouble. She just doesn't have the chops," she griped. "She's only done one real role."

That would be the Nurse in *Romeo and Juliet.*

"And she only got that because the real Nurse's granddaughter had a baby in North Dakota."

"Uh-huh. So . . . besides that, how's—?"

Edna sashayed past us on her way to the register to pick up a carry-out order. "Abby," she said frostily, nodding her head.

"Edna," Abby said, equally coolly.

Geez. This town.

At three o'clock I left the restaurant in Benny's hands and made him promise to keep an eye on Honey. I had just spent the last two years getting the Windjammer organized, efficient, and full of regulars; I didn't want Henry listening to her ridiculous ideas on menu, décor, or packaging.

It was a beautiful fall afternoon, the sky a clear blue, the sun warm on my face, and the temperature hovering at seventy. A perfect shore day. I could feel my toes burrowing in the sand and hear the screech of seagulls wheeling overhead. And then I felt sad. If you were born and bred in South Jersey, as I was, this time of the year made one nostalgic for the long, hot summer days. But I was a northerner now.

I strolled down Main, resisting the urge to take a brief detour to Coffee Heaven for a caramel macchiato. Instead I turned left onto Amber Street, passing Betty's Boutique, which featured exotic lingerie à la Victoria's Secret. Nestled between the boutique and JC's Hardware was a one-story, redbrick building dating from the founding of Etonville in the late 1700s. Bill's black-and-white vehicle occupied the "Reserved for Chief" parking space.

I pulled on the door handle and as it opened I nearly collided with Antonio. "Sorry!" I said, one hand going to his shoulder to prevent my face meeting his. Not that that would be the end of the world. Stunning brown eyes set wide in a bronzed face that sported higher cheekbones than any man had a right to, a square jaw, and the hint of a dimple. His black V-neck sweater and tight jeans made him appear twenty years younger than his actual age. He removed a beret, which on many men might seem pretentious. On Antonio it was a symbol of continental sophistication.

"Oh! Hello . . ." He stared at me, as if my face was a code he was trying desperately to crack.

"Dodie. O'Dell. From the Windjammer?"

"Oh, yes. Sorry. I'm a little . . ."

The thought must have eluded him, but Antonio still managed a fabulous smile. The one he probably reserved for all of the young ingénues.

"Wild time for you with the show."

"Of course," he said.

"Right. I saw what kind of a hurry you were in last night."

His demeanor altered abruptly. "Last night?"

"You know, at the corner of Fairfield and Main? About midnight? You were in your—"

He stiffened, glancing over his shoulder. "You must be mistaken. I was working late at the theater," he said irritably.

"Sorry. Guess you have a body double."

I laughed to ease the tension. Antonio nodded curtly, slapped the beret back on his head of untamed dark curls, and left the building. I knew I was not mistaken. It *was* Antonio last night. And the theater was dark when I drove past. *Why not tell the truth?* What was he hiding?

Inside the Municipal Building I paused in front of Etonville's ego wall: decades of trophies for winning teams, certificates of merit from the state police, and photographs of citizens accepting awards for honorable achievements. In the center was a photo of previous Police Chief Bull Bennet and a thirty-pound bass. Next to it was a shot of current Chief Bill Thompson shaking hands with a reporter from the *Etonville Standard* after solving the murder of Jerome Angleton, ELT member and my personal friend, last April.

I smiled, remembering how exhilarated the town was at the capture of Jerome's killer. Bill was certainly happy in the picture. I considered the distance between us in the months since.

I swung my purse onto my other shoulder and continued down the corridor.

"Dodie!" It was Edna at the dispatch window, a headset covering her brownish-gray bun. "Loved the rib sandwich at lunch. Tell Henry." Her appetite was legendary.

"Will do." I stopped. "Edna, was Antonio at rehearsal last night. Till the end, I mean?"

A 911 call came in. She punched a button. "Etonville Police Department." She listened, her expression shifting from alert and ready to impatient and exasperated. "Mrs. Parker, haven't I told you not to call 911 every time Missy runs off? Okay, okay, I'll call Officer Ostrowski." She clicked off, punched a second button, and waited for Ralph to respond. "Ralph, we got a 10-91 over on Belvidere. Yep. It's Missy again. 10-91. Missing cat." She listened for a moment. "Well, take your donuts with you. 10-4." She hung up.

"I can see you're busy so I'll just—"

Edna removed her headset and leaned forward. "You heard about his disappearing act?" she asked.

"Lola told me."

"Everybody's on edge," she said.

"I guess." No mention of her feud with Abby. "What about last night?" I asked.

"Nope. Not last night. We finished rehearsal about nine thirty and he was there until the bitter end."

I wondered.

"But Carlyle gave us notes. Antonio went to the office."

"All set for Saturday? You know the cast is going to be a huge part of the food festival."

Edna brightened, chuckling. "You should see the dress they've got me in. Big hoop skirt, frilly blouse . . . adorable!"

"Can't wait to see it. Got to check in with the chief," I said.

Her console lit up and she snapped the headset back in place. I moved on and paused at the outer office where Officer Suki Shung was typing on a keyboard surrounded by three monitors. I'd gotten acquainted with Suki—a Buddhist and martial arts black belt—during the murder investigation back in April. She was enigmatic and calm, but professional in every way possible.

I showed her my sheaf of papers. "I need the chief's signature."

She nodded solemnly.

I knocked on the door to Bill's inner sanctum.

"Enter."

I opened the door and peered in. I hadn't been in here for four months. Since the murder investigation, actually. Things were still the same: NFL paraphernalia—a Bills ball cap and a team picture from his time in Buffalo—and the faint whiff of furniture polish. His desk was tidy, stacks of papers and files neatly arranged around its perimeter.

"I have the invoice for the football picnic," I said, and stepped in.

Bill looked up from his laptop keyboard and a smile creased his face. "Good."

He removed his uniform jacket from a reception chair and motioned for me to have a seat. I couldn't help but notice his flexing biceps.

"Busy day?" I smoothed my silk blouse and sat.

He ran a hand over his spiky hair. "Speech writing. I got suckered into introducing the mayor at the New Jersey Conference of Mayors dinner next month. He's getting a community service award."

Mayor Bennet was the former chief's brother. There was no love lost between Bill and Etonville's top executive, but maybe this event would square things and convince the mayor that Bill was here to stay, that he was finally getting into the rhythm of small-town policing after his stint with Philadelphia law enforcement.

"Good luck with that. I have enough trouble writing menu descriptions. 'Savory squash and pungent pickled beets.'"

He laughed and paused. "So. The invoice."

I handed it over.

He inspected the form. "Looks good to me. Burgers, fries, and sodas. Setup at eleven thirty a.m. The game starts at nine and we'll be done by noon, one way or the other." He signed the form and pushed it across the desk. "Will you be accompanying the delivery?" he asked casually.

"Well, I am the manager . . ." I said equally casually.

"Come early and watch some of the game, that is if you can stand to see the home team soundly beaten." His hypnotic blue eyes twinkled.

I twinkled back and tossed my hair off one shoulder. Was this an invitation? Like a date? Of course it would be a date accompanied by a crowd of nine- to eleven-year-olds in too-big helmets and orange jerseys.

"I just might. I'm kind of a sucker for losers," I said.

Bill cocked his head. "Really."

I was walking on air as I left the Municipal Building. I had an almost-date with Bill. So I decided to treat myself to a caramel macchiato from Coffee Heaven. I pushed open the door to the tinkling of bells announcing a patron.

"Hey, Dodie," Jocelyn, the waitress, called out as I slid onto a stool at the counter. "Caramel macchiato coming up."

I liked that about life in Etonville. Almost everyone knew your name and your coffee preference.

She grinned. "Been visiting the chief?"

And your business.

"Just getting paperwork signed for a football-and-burgers event," I said.

"Going to be busy this weekend in Etonville, with the food festival. You know, I've never had a knish," she said.

"It's a fried pastry with potatoes and onions."

"And you eat 'em with egg creams? What is that? Like eggs whipped up in cream?" she asked.

"Egg creams are just carbonated water, chocolate syrup, and milk."

Jocelyn looked puzzled. "No eggs?"

I shook my head.

She placed my caramel macchiato in front of me. "That's like saying *Arsenic and Old Lace* has no arsenic and no lace," she said, waiting for me to respond.

I was stumped. "Right."

I mentally created my to-do list as I made my way back to the Windjammer, sorry to have to spend the rest of the day indoors. My conversation with Jocelyn had reminded me I needed to confirm the schedule with Henry. Thursday was the delivery of the ingredients for the egg creams and "elderberry wine," in a nod to the drink featured in *Arsenic and Old Lace*, which Benny would be serving; Friday was stocking the hot dogs, condiments, Italian ices, and pretzels; Saturday morning Henry would be preparing the knishes. A huge weekend for all of us, but a real windfall for the Windjammer. I was congratulating myself on juggling all of these balls as I arrived back at work.

I had no sooner stepped into the restaurant than Benny gave me the eyeball.

"What's up?"

"You better get in there and quiet things down," he said in a hushed tone.

We were between lunch and dinner and there were only four customers in the place, but they had already perked up; an argument was in progress in the kitchen.

I shoved the swinging doors. At a counter in the corner, Enrico, Henry's *sous-chef*, and his wife, Carmen—one of our waitresses—were chopping onions and peppers for a sausage dinner dish, their heads down, pretending not to hear. Henry and Honey stood toe-to-toe, arms akimbo.

"You can't take off this weekend and that's final," Henry said between clenched teeth. "I don't care if it is the annual Pumpkins and Pirates Festival."

I had an image of rambunctious, one-eyed buccaneers hurling orange globes with their swords. "Hi." I took the delivery clipboard off a hook on the wall.

"I need everybody here." Henry stared at me as if the food festival was entirely my fault.

It was, actually.

Honey was silently fuming, either out of arguments or unwilling to let me see too much of the confrontation with Uncle Henry. "But, like, I'll have to cancel tickets to the concert," she sputtered, and slammed out the back door.

It was a dramatic exit that only led to the dumpster and an herb garden that kept the kitchen stocked in aromatic plants. I counted to five. Honey reentered, marched through the kitchen, her back rigid, and exited into the dining room with a "humph." Henry heaved a sigh and went back to his homemade tomato basil soup.

This weekend was going to be a lot of fun.

3

Two days to go until the food festival. I hadn't seen Lola since Tuesday; ELT rehearsals had probably sucked up all of her time and energy. Benny and I shared closing duties most nights and this was his night on, so at eight o'clock I decided to swing next door once the dinner rush was over. I simply wanted to confirm that the cast would be costumed and ready to mingle with the patrons on Saturday. I was staking a lot on this weekend—Henry's goodwill, the reputation of the Windjammer, and a continued relationship with the Etonville Little Theatre. Not too much pressure.

The lobby of the theater was empty, as expected, but I could hear the rise and fall of voices in the house. I opened the door quietly and slipped inside. The scene was ugly. Edna and Abby, who played the sweet, daffy Brewster sisters in *Arsenic and Old Lace*, stood sullenly staring out at Antonio, who was quarreling with set designer JC— from JC's Hardware—about the construction of a window seat that held dead bodies; while Carlyle, Antonio's know-it-all assistant, was demonstrating how to walk up a flight of stairs to Walter, former artistic director and kingpin of the ELT, who smoldered; and Tiffany, the director's buxom wife, took provocative selfies with Romeo, her leading man. He'd played the actual Romeo last spring and the name just stuck. Were the "thing" rumors true? Lola was sitting in the front row, biting a fingernail, next to Penny, who was holding the promptbook.

Penny Ossining, the ELT stage manager for twenty-five years, worked the early shift at the post office. She wasn't one of the most efficient members of the theater, but she was loyal, dedicated, and armed with a clipboard and whistle.

Edna saw me standing at the back of the theater and swung her arm in a wide arc.

"Stay in character, please!" Antonio hollered.

Which caused the rest of the cast to look up. Abby nodded her head in Edna's direction as if to say *See what I mean?* and Lola jumped up.

"This is a closed rehearsal," Carlyle yelled.

"Dodie is a member of the ELT and welcome anytime," Lola said firmly and walked up the aisle to join me. I could see that she'd had it.

Carlyle shrugged and went back to ordering Walter around while Antonio took a break from arguing with JC in order to mesmerize a teenage crew member—even younger than Tiffany—with a dazzling smile and a hug.

"Oh, Dodie," Lola whispered, "this show can't open too soon for me."

"That bad, huh? The set is looking good." The walls were covered with faux flocked burgundy wallpaper with period-looking light fixtures.

"True. But Antonio has alienated the entire cast and most of them are ready to quit."

"Not before Saturday, I hope. I need them front and center at the food festival. Where's Chrystal?" The ELT costumer.

"She's down in the shop. I'll call her." Lola whipped out her cell phone and punched in numbers.

Penny blew her whistle, startling the cast and crew. "Take ten," she commanded.

"Chrystal will be right up," Lola said and hurried off to intercept Antonio.

"Hey, O'Dell," Penny said behind me, tapping a pencil on her clipboard.

"Hi, Penny," I said.

"I've got the sign-up sheet for Saturday."

"You do? For the food festival?" I knew I sounded a little bit pathetic and overly grateful. "How many have committed?"

Penny pushed her glasses up her nose, checked her clipboard, and chuckled. "Eight if Walter agrees to do it. He might have to show a house."

Walter was a full-time real estate agent in addition to being the former ELT head honcho.

"And if Edna and Abby both come. Not sure about Tiffany. She's got an 'appointment.'"

It wasn't the entire cast, but eight was still respectable. I needed to speak with Chrystal, check Penny's sheet, and then head home for a glass of wine and the latest thriller in the Cindy Collins Mystery series. I was addicted to them.

"Probably won't matter much anyway. Gonna rain Saturday. Later, O'Dell." Penny blasted her whistle.

Penny was only half-right. It rained early Saturday morning, leaving a slick sheen on the streets of Etonville, but by ten o'clock the sun was poking its head above banks of clouds and promising to keep the day warm and bright. The booths had been delivered yesterday afternoon and Benny, Enrico, Carmen, and I had worked until 11:00 p.m. setting them up. Honey had had a pass, due to a sudden bout of hay fever. We had a permit from the town to close the block of Main that ran past the Windjammer and the Etonville Little Theatre, so we set up a tent and placed rented tables and chairs in the street. The crowds could flow out, sit and eat, or stroll from kiosk to kiosk, munching. At least that was the plan.

By eleven thirty Saturday morning we were ready. Henry had a fryer and steam table set up to produce the knishes; Enrico was responsible for dispensing the hot dogs; Benny and Carmen busied themselves behind a portable bar with kegs of beer, a soda fountain, the makings of the egg creams, and the wine. Honey was miserable, sitting behind the freezer with the Italian ices. Pauli, being a good sport, was selling soft pretzels and black-and-white cookies. I intended to keep an eye on the booths, the patrons, and the actors.

To suit the occasion, I was in full 1940s dress. Chrystal had raided the costume shop for me and I was feeling pretty fierce in a vintage black cocktail dress with padded shoulders, a long slim skirt, and a red belt that cinched the iridescent fabric. I was topped off with my own version of a period hairdo: Ava Gardner waves and a touch of Lauren Bacall's off-the-face pompadour. As a kid, I'd spent many an evening curled up on the sofa with my mom watching old movies. I'd look right at home with the cast.

"Where do you want me?"

I looked up from the warmer, where I was placing several dozen pretzels, into Lola's frowning face. She hugged her digital camera to her chest. I'd had a brainstorm: While eating their Brooklyn food, patrons could get their pictures taken with cast members. Lola had agreed to act as photographer.

"I set up a bench in front of the theater." I pointed over my shoulder.

Lola nodded listlessly. "Okay."

I studied her expression. "Another bad night? I hope Antonio didn't stay out—"

Lola waved away my question. "No. He was actually pleasant last night. Kind of a personality transplant."

"What, then?" I asked.

"I don't know . . . I just feel like this whole thing is doomed. Maybe it's time for me to take a break from the ELT."

"Lola," I said calmly, "pump the brakes. You have a show opening in two weeks. This isn't the time for extended soul-searching. You gotta snap out of it," I said with tough love.

She nodded grimly. "I know."

"So let's have a good time today." I gave her a big, phony grin.

The door to the theater opened and out they came: the two Brewster sisters, barely speaking, Romeo, a couple of gangsters, and two cops. All in period dress, looking slightly uncomfortable at being in costume off the stage, as though they had been caught in skimpy swimwear on the street. Only Edna was having a ball in her Victorian hoop skirt, fancy blouse, gray wig, and a large lace collar that stretched from high on her neck to mid-bosom.

Penny trailed behind with her clipboard.

I hurried into their midst as customers started to appear in front of the booths. "So. Mingle and smile," I said to the cast. They looked at me like I had two heads. "Let's give them a taste of Brooklyn," I offered. A few actors plunked down on chairs and one of the cops yanked the collar of his uniform to let in some air.

Penny stuck a pencil behind one ear. "Just get out there and sell tickets."

That they understood. Lola positioned herself with the camera, and the cast members scurried off to sample the food.

"Thanks, Penny," I said.

"No problem, O'Dell. You got to know how to talk to actors."

She straightened her shoulders and headed for Enrico and the hot dogs.

The crowd was growing and the roadway was filling nicely. We'd run ads in the local newspapers of neighboring towns. It looked like it worked because I saw a number of people I didn't recognize.

I watched as customers meandered from one station to the next, sampling the food and drink, chatting and laughing. I could feel the tension lifting from between my shoulder blades. Maybe everything was going to work out. I crossed my fingers and scanned the crowd. The Banger sisters were driving Henry bananas, trying to decide which knish they wanted. Carol, waving from the pretzel stand, was keeping Pauli occupied when he wasn't chatting it up with Imogen from Snippets. I recognized Mildred Tower, Etonville Public Librarian, and there was Jocelyn dipping her tongue into an egg cream, even though there were neither eggs nor cream in it. It looked like much of Etonville had closed down today so that everyone could enjoy the food festival. I was feeling a warm spot in my chest that could have been either gratitude to the town or thoughts of Bill, triggered by one of the costumed policemen. I knew he had a game today in Creston, a neighboring town four miles away, but I assumed he'd be back in time to stop by and taste-test some food. Officer Ralph Ostrowski was on duty, happily stuffing his face.

I glanced at the entrance to the theater, where Lola was patiently seating two giggling teenage girls on either side of Romeo, his arms around their shoulders. He kissed their cheeks, they laughed, she snapped their picture. I watched as the threesome ambled off.

Walter exploded from the theater in a fedora and double-breasted suit, glared at everyone walking around, as if they were to blame for his apparently foul mood, and finally let his gaze land on Lola. He tramped to her side, bent down, and, quietly but vehemently, discussed some issue. Lola turned her back on him. Probably had to do with Antonio. Or Carlyle. I couldn't hear what was being said, but body language was clear. Walter was furious and Lola was fed up. It was the only skirmish interrupting an otherwise lovely afternoon.

By two o'clock I'd eaten a hot dog, two knishes, one black-and-white cookie, and half a pretzel. My stomach was on the verge of rebelling when I saw a commotion in the middle of the block. It was Antonio, arriving in his own version of a 1940s costume: a wide-lapelled, pin-striped, single-breasted navy suit; hair slicked back to keep his curly locks plastered to his head; and a bright red tie. On his arm was Tiffany, in a short, tight black skirt, a sexy knit top, and three-inch spike heels. Definitely *not* in costume.

Antonio was waving manically, smiling and nodding to actors and townspeople alike, as if he were running for office and every vote counted. His gait was a little unsteady, possibly from tipping a few before his entrance? Tiffany was stone-faced, her eyes searching the crowd. Looking for her leading man? They made their way to a table in a secluded corner of the tent, where Tiffany deposited her purse and promptly took off. Antonio adjusted his tie, ran a hand through his hair, and strode purposefully to the food booths, plastic cup in hand. *So he has been drinking.*

"Antonio," I said, greeting him and steering him toward the knishes, where Henry slaved away, his forehead shiny from effort and the warmth of the day. "You need to try one of these."

Antonio's face was flushed, his breath coming in short bursts. He dropped his congenial persona. His eyes grazed the swarm of people eating and rambling, as if he were expecting to see someone. Obviously not his wife; she was out in the open, two booths away, licking an Italian ice while Romeo looked on, smiling. Antonio refocused his gaze, his amiable-face embracing me. "Dodie, yes?" he said, taking my hand.

"Right!"

He took the plate Henry handed him; three hot, fried knishes lying in state, and proceeded to move from booth to booth, good-naturedly piling on the food: a hotdog, pretzel, and cookie. He paused at the bar.

"What can I get you?" Benny asked.

"Well . . ." Antonio loosened his tie and coughed.

"We have beer and 'elderberry wine.' Really it's a Merlot, but the play . . . you know." Benny laughed. "And cream soda."

"Of course. Lovely. All the Brooklyn cuisine. I'll sample the wine." He handed Benny his cup to be refilled.

Antonio balanced the full plate and wine as he wove through the crowd, stumbling a bit before he sat down at his table. He dove into the knishes, seemingly hungry and ready to make short work of the cuisine. A number of people, including actors, stopped by and Antonio held court, chitchatting, as though all were best friends and he had not badgered them only hours ago. A young costume-crew member grinned stupidly at him and he put an arm around her waist, whispering something in her ear. She giggled. Then he vanished from sight, lost in a crowd of humanity. Amazing, the way these theater people could hide their true feelings.

"Yep. Pretty amazing."

I whirled around. Penny was stuffing the last bite of a pretzel into her mouth. "How did you know what I was thinking?"

She chewed and talked. "O'Dell, didn't you learn anything with *Romeo and Juliet*? I'm the stage manager. It's my business to know everything." Off she went.

Maybe she wasn't as dense as she sometimes appeared to be.

I started to gather up plates and cups and generally spruce up the scene. Lola was busy snapping pictures of the two cops and Jocelyn. Antonio was trying to appear interested in something Edna was saying. He shook his head, smiled at her, and she relocated to the Italian ices.

Then he unbuttoned his shirt collar, his face red. He struggled to breathe. Wow, that elderberry wine was really getting to him. He coughed, grabbed his throat, and fell forward on the table. Oh no. Everything was going so nicely. People were having such a good time, and now Antonio had overdone the vino and passed out. Or maybe he was choking on a piece of food?

I ran to his side, motioning Benny to follow me. "Have you ever done the Heimlich maneuver?"

Benny shook his head vigorously. "Never."

At Antonio's back, I jiggled his shoulder. "Antonio? Can you talk?" His face was resting on his plate of pretzels, his arms dangling limply at his sides. Completely unresponsive. "Uh-oh. Help me get him to his feet."

A little girl several tables away from us, pointed and giggled. "Look, Mommy, that man's face is in his food."

Geez.

"Benny, let's stand him up." I needed to get my arms around his chest to do an abdominal thrust and dislodge whatever had apparently caused him to stop breathing. I grabbed one shoulder, Benny the other, and we lifted his torso off the table.

"He's like dead weight," Benny said, grunting.

I was about to encircle his chest when Antonio's head snapped back—his eyes had bugged out, staring, shocked. A piece of knish hung out of his mouth. Speechless, Benny let go and Antonio's head dropped back down on the table.

My hand shaking, my heart pounding, I put one finger on Antonio's neck. There was no pulse. "Call 911!" I yelled.

Edna plowed through the hordes. "What do we have here?" Her gray wig sideways, she bent down to glance at Antonio's gruesome face. "Oh my. Oh my. Oh my." She snapped from startled bystander to professional dispatcher and punched in the numbers. "Suki? I'm at the food festival. We have an 11-41. Right away." She mouthed "ambulance" to me.

I took deep gulps of air to calm myself.

"It's a 10-54," she said to Suki. "Possible dead body," she said to me.

"Possible?" My voice slid up the scale.

Edna spoke into her cell, "Make that a 10-55," and clicked off. "Medical examiner case."

4

"You better find Tiffany," I babbled to Benny, and draped a plastic tablecloth over Antonio's body. No one should be on view with that facial expression. It had to be a heart attack.

I glanced up as Benny ran off. I'd been so concentrated on Antonio that I hadn't noticed the gathering bunches of festival attendees pressing steadily forward. Word had skyrocketed through the crowd faster than the speed of light.

"Was that the director?"

"Is he sick?"

Officer Ostrowski appeared and spoke briefly with Edna, then to the crowd with authority. "Okay, folks, let's back up and give him some air."

It was too late for air.

"Do something," one of the Banger sisters screeched and grabbed hold of an actor costumed as a cop. "You're an officer of the law."

The kid freaked. "I'm not a real cop. I'm just acting like one."

The other sister glared at him. "Shame on you!"

The bogus officer backed away into Lola. "I think some guy died," he said, and ran off.

Lola's eyes grew round. "Is that true, Dodie?"

I pulled her aside. "Oh yeah. You're not going to believe—"

A piercing wail split the racket of the assembled onlookers. It was Tiffany discovering her dead husband. She collapsed theatrically over his body, then, as Benny attempted to get her upright, she threw herself into his arms and clung to his neck for dear life. Benny caught my eye. "Help me!" he signaled.

"Antonio?" Lola whispered.

I nodded my head. "Can you . . . do something with Tiffany?"

Lola, in a daze, rescued Benny and walked Tiffany inside the Windjammer for privacy.

I whipped out my cell. "Hello? Bill?"

"Hi, Dodie. Can't talk now. Can you believe it? We're only behind by twelve points with ten minutes to go and—"

"Are you coming to the food festival?"

"Just as soon as the game is over." There was a rustling on the line. "Send in Petey," I heard him say to someone. "Let's see if he can tackle."

"Bill?" A frantic note had crept into my voice.

"What?" he asked.

"There's been a death."

"Where?"

"Here. At the festival. Antonio, the director," I said urgently. "Probably a heart attack."

"Have you called—?"

I heard the sirens of the ambulance and fire department. "They're here. Edna called it in."

"Oh boy." I could see him running a hand through the spikes of his brush cut, sitting at various angles to his scalp. "A heart attack, right?"

"I think so." I paused. "I hate to interrupt the game. I just thought you should know."

"Thanks for calling," he said.

I wasn't so sure he was grateful.

"I can be there in about half an hour."

Relief flooded my veins. "Good." Somehow with Bill on the scene, things would seem less bizarre.

I stuffed my cell into my back pocket. Henry was beside himself. "Somebody said it was food poisoning?" He was white as a ghost.

"No, I think his heart stopped suddenly."

An elderly gentleman overheard us. "Probably caused by spoiled hot dogs. Or something in the knishes."

"There was nothing wrong with the—"

"Dodie, maybe the eggs in the egg creams were rotten," Jocelyn said helpfully.

"There were no eggs in the . . ." I shook my head. "Never mind."

Etonville had begun to reveal its inner wacky. Again. Just when I was getting used to this place, it caught me off guard: The gossip machine would be going full tilt by tomorrow and there was nothing I could do about it. Forlorn, Henry shook his head.

I touched his arm. "It couldn't have been the food. Look at all of these other people who've been eating all afternoon. No one else is even sick."

Just then the elderly gentleman dropped a half-eaten knish in a trash can. "I don't feel so well."

"This sure puts a damper on things," Lola murmured. "Hard to celebrate a show opening when its director is no longer on the scene."

We had parked ourselves next to the pretzel and cookie station to stay out of the way of the ambulance and fire truck, which had arrived ten minutes ago, lights flashing. Several minutes later the county medical examiner appeared in a black van.

"Right." Not to mention the fact that the food festival was scheduled to be a two-day affair; but with the rumors about food poisoning swirling everywhere . . .

I felt depressed and sad, for Henry, me, the ELT, and Tiffany, of course—who was playing the grieving widow to the hilt.

"That's the best acting I've seen her do," Penny muttered in my ear.

I started. "Really."

"Word is they were overdue for a divorce," she said and shoved her glasses up a notch.

Carol was right. "So she and Romeo were having a 'thing'?"

"Romeo?" Penny snorted at the idea. She leaned in between Lola and me. "More like Carlyle."

"Carlyle?" Lola looked shocked. "Are you sure?"

Penny looked about to deliver her standard lecture on how she was the stage manager and stage managers knew everything, when a familiar gold BMW pulled in behind the ambulance.

Bill, still in his Youth Football orange sweatshirt with *Tigers* emblazoned across the front, strode to the secure area where Antonio was being attended to by the medical examiner. He spoke briefly to Ralph, who had managed the crowd by installing crime scene tape, even though this was only a crime scene if you counted the fact that I still had fifty pounds of hotdogs and two hundred pretzels to sell.

At the end of the block, the actors were gathered around the Italian ices, sporadically staring at the table where Antonio's body was being transferred to a gurney, and huddling among themselves, gesturing and squabbling.

Lola observed them for a moment. "I know this might sound inappropriate, but what are we going to do about the show? Who's going to direct?"

"Carlyle?"

Lola moaned.

Where was Carlyle anyway? Walter was in the center of the group of actors. Probably fomenting rebellion.

"Would you consider—?"

"Walter? I don't know if I can go through that again." She paused. "At the beginning everyone was so excited about a guest director."

"No sense beating yourself up now. You couldn't have predicted that Antonio would have a heart attack."

"So you don't think it was food poisoning?" Lola asked.

"I don't think you keel over that suddenly." The medical examiner shook hands with Bill, closed a black bag, nodded a few times, and walked back to his van.

Bill watched as Antonio was loaded into the ambulance, which made its way slowly down Main Street. The remaining festival patrons packed up their families and belongings, pointedly leaving any remaining food on tables and in trash bins, and headed for home.

The sun was sinking lower in the sky and the food booths and equipment cast silhouettes on the street. "I'd better see if I can do anything for Tiffany," Lola said. "It was a terrific event, Dodie, until . . ." She smiled sadly. "What should Penny tell the actors about tomorrow?"

"Let me check with Henry. He was in such a dither half an hour ago."

"I'll call you in the morning," Lola said and moved off.

I surveyed the remains of the festival. We'd need to wash tables, stack chairs, and package food. Honey would love that. Was there any point in even setting up for Sunday? I was mulling over my predicament. Maybe Etonville would forget about the food poisoning rumors and return tomorrow eager to eat, laugh, chat, and take pictures with actors.

"It probably wasn't food poisoning." Bill took off his ball cap and scratched his head.

I spun around to face him. "It wasn't?"

"I heard about the gossip," he said.

"I didn't think it was, but you know Etonville and how everyone likes to talk and create stories even when there isn't any cause."

"Uh-huh. I know Etonville." He looked off in the direction where the ambulance had disappeared, frowning.

"Was it a heart attack?" I asked.

"Well, something stopped his heart. Exactly what, the ME's not sure. They'll take blood and tissue samples."

Henry, with a sulky Honey in tow, no doubt still peeved over missing the Pumpkins and Pirates Festival, emerged from the Windjammer, looking nervous. He nodded at Bill. "So, what did the medical examiner have to say?"

Bill scrunched his ball cap. "He has to run tests. Nothing definite at the moment. Probably a heart attack."

Henry shook his head. "I had the feeling this whole thing was not going to end well. We'd better forget about tomorrow."

Honey smiled, did her hip thing. "Dot, maybe you'd better pack up all of that extra food. Like, I can't imagine where you're going to put it."

I knew one place I'd like to put it.

"Look, if it's any consolation, the medical examiner doesn't think it was related to anything he consumed," Bill said.

"That makes sense. Too many other people ate the same things Antonio ate, and they're fine." I tried my best to be encouraging.

"Well . . ." Henry said.

I turned to Bill. "Is there any reason we can't have the festival tomorrow?"

He shrugged. "I don't see any."

Of course, I wasn't sure how the actors would feel about participating without their director. But even without actors in costume, we could sell food, right? We just had to get beyond the food poisoning theory and act like everything was back to normal.

Bill gave me a reassuring nod. "Say, what about some carryout for me?"

Henry appeared relieved that someone was actually asking to eat his food. Honey snapped to attention and unlocked her hip. "Like, I could do that. I know just what packaging to use." She ran inside the restaurant and reappeared with three small boxes and a roll of Saran wrap.

"I could use a beer," Bill said and followed Henry to the bar.

I could have used an entire six-pack.

5

The Windjammer staff scrubbed the booths and tables, closing up shop by nine. I was so exhausted I fell into a deep sleep and didn't budge until the clang of my alarm clock forced my eyes open at 8:00 a.m. I tumbled out of bed and jumped in the shower, letting the warm water ping off my face as I remembered yesterday's catastrophe—Antonio was dead.

I toweled my hair, ran a blob of gel through the damp tresses, and slid into a pair of jeans and a white sweater. No costume for me today. Then I called Lola.

"We're on," I said. "Can you spread the word to the actors? I'm not sure how many people will show, but I think we should be ready in case—"

"Oh, Dodie, what a mess. Tiffany has been acting strange."

"Understandable under the circumstances—"

"First off, she drank a glass of wine and then she polished off two gin and tonics."

I whistled. "Guess she's really broken up. Maybe all of that wailing wasn't an act."

"I made an effort to comfort her. But she just went into her room and started talking on the phone. I couldn't make out the conversation."

"But you tried, right?"

"Well, someone should keep an eye on her," Lola said solemnly.

"Maybe she was contacting Antonio's family."

"I don't think he had much family. I don't remember him mentioning children or parents."

"Did she at least sleep? She's going to need her wits about her to face a funeral director."

"That's the worst thing. She took off right after the call. Just got in the car and drove away. I asked where she was going, but she just shook her head and ran out the door." Lola sighed.

"When did she get back?"

"I don't know. I waited up until midnight, then I passed out. Her bedroom door's still closed and the car's in the driveway."

"Where will she have the funeral? New York?"

"Dodie, I'm just not sure about anything. I'll offer to help her with arrangements. But who knows what she'll want."

I hung up after convincing Lola that she was doing the best she could to handle Tiffany and begging her to get a few actors out on the street again. I had just enough time to grab a caramel macchiato at Coffee Heaven and arrive at the Windjammer by ten. I squinted into the sunlight; it would be another pleasant fall day, a brisk breeze lifting the hair off the nape of my neck.

Luckily the Windjammer was closed on Sundays, so I wouldn't have to listen to Henry gripe about losing customers while the food festival was still on. I walked from my parking space on Main, through the tables and booths, to the entrance of the restaurant.

I put my game face on. "Morning, all," I said cheerfully.

Henry was putting together the ingredients for his knishes and Benny was taking inventory of the beer kegs and wine stock. "Nobody's going to come to this today," Henry whined.

"Don't be such a gloomy Gus." I glanced at Benny, who shrugged. "Let's be positive. Maybe the food poisoning rumors died out overnight." Both Henry and Benny stared at me skeptically. "Okay, so let's just hope for the best."

Honey stomped in the door, dropped her purse on the bar, and confronted me, glaring. "Dot, if, like, I was managing a restaurant and somebody died while eating my food, the least I would do is close up for a day."

Her voice swooped up on the last sentence as if she was asking me for permission to lock the door and close the blinds. I guessed the Pumpkins and Pirates Festival was still running this afternoon, too; Antonio's death must have given Honey hope that she'd have the day off.

"Honey, a little respect for Uncle Henry's efforts here?" I said with as much sweetness as I could muster. I was determined to outlast her sulky disposition. Next semester could not come too fast for me.

Once Enrico and Carmen arrived, we restocked the booths and

plugged in equipment. Unlike yesterday, when noon saw a trail of actors and clusters of Etonville families and friends, today saw only a group of tired Windjammer staff, a warmer than usual late fall morning, and fading hopes that the food festival would survive yesterday's tragedy.

"Like, how long do we have to wait for people?" Honey asked, sticking her head inside the portable freezer to cool off.

Henry turned off the steam table. "I'm giving them till one o'clock."

"One? That's not enough time. The Methodist church has an eleven o'clock service and the Episcopalians aren't finished till noon."

Henry gave me a grudging nod. Let's face it—he knew, I knew, today was probably going to be a bust.

And then I spied Lola parking up the street, followed by Penny.

"Okay, now we're cooking," I said metaphorically.

Strictly speaking we were not out of the throwback-food woods yet; Lola was here to take pictures with, hopefully, actors who had yet to arrive. I appreciated the fact that Lola and the cast were depressed about Antonio, but maybe participating today would help lift their spirits. And mine.

Carol dropped Pauli off—he took his place with the pretzels and cookies—and Edna, in full costume, emerged from the theater and onto Main Street, ready to get her picture taken with whoever appeared. The two fake cops were wary, lest they accidentally be called into action, mistaken for the real thing again. Tiffany was not present, of course, and neither was her Romeo. All in all, not a great showing.

"How's Tiffany doing?" I asked Lola.

"I don't know. I was in the shower and she disappeared again. No note. Nothing." Lola eyed the skimpy cast turnout. "I'm sorry, Dodie, I called everyone. Most of them had excuses. Some of them just didn't want to have to think about the show without a director."

As if on cue, Walter, in his gangster getup, waltzed out of the theater. Carlyle followed him.

"Uh-oh," Lola said. "This could mean trouble."

"Maybe they've called a truce?"

Lola blinked. "I can't imagine that."

Walter nodded to Lola and he and Carlyle headed for the bar. Carlyle was a mystery. What had made him commute from Queens to Etonville? Loyalty to Antonio? Or maybe Penny was right . . . a romance with Tiffany.

"I'd better see what's up," Lola said and hurried away.

"Hey, O'Dell," Penny called out.

"Hi, Penny. Have Walter and Carlyle made up?"

Penny snorted. "Walter's just buddying up to Carlyle because now that Antonio is . . . you know . . ."

"Dead," I said.

"Yeah. Everybody figures Carlyle is in charge."

"So you think he'll direct the show now?"

Penny gazed at me, the world-weary ELT stage manager. "O'Dell, that's not how these things work. It's a board decision," she reminded me.

"Got it." I knew it was more a Lola decision.

Penny nudged her glasses and tapped her clipboard. With only a handful of actors to keep track of, her day would be a short one. "Gotta get to work."

Our day was a short one, too. We hung around longer than one; in fact we made it to two o'clock. By then everyone was grouchy and only too eager to head out. We'd served a dozen people and most of them avoided the knishes, settling for bottled drinks and pretzels. Even the Italian ices were taking a beating; surprising, given the temperature of the day. I had to face the facts. Nobody wanted to take a chance that the medical examiner was wrong about Antonio's cause of death.

I inspected the crowd. Honey was Snapchatting, the two cops were texting, and the Banger sisters had planted themselves at a table with a good view of the entire area, just in case someone else died. They didn't want to miss a thing.

I had to admit it was time to call it a day.

I gave Henry the universal sign for wrapping up, and he nodded grimly. I'd hear about this tomorrow.

"Excuse me."

A warm, friendly voice interrupted my pity party and I turned around. "Yes?"

"I'm looking for Antonio Digenza." A woman removed her sunglasses, her hazel eyes set deep into her face.

My heart thumped. A friend of Antonio's who hadn't heard about his death?

"Perhaps I should introduce myself. I'm Brianna Kincaid." She had short silver hair, designer sunglasses, and a smart, olive green suit. Way too chic for the food festival. Probably Antonio's age but with a very youthful persona.

"Hi. I'm Dodie O'Dell." I shook the hand she offered. It was cool and dry. Mine was clammy. "Antonio's . . . not here at the moment." I couldn't handle this alone. Where was Lola? I shaded my eyes and searched the front of the theater where she was last seen sitting on the bench, tapping her foot, waiting for customers. "The artistic director might be able to help you. I guess she's taken a break. Would you like to wait for her inside the Windjammer? It might be more . . . comfortable."

Her eyes flicked in the direction of the restaurant. "I'm fine here. I was on the edge of town getting gas and the attendant mentioned the festival." She paused, replaced her glasses. "What a lovely idea."

"Thanks." I had to put a stop to this innocent conversation; Antonio lay dead in the county morgue!

"Brianna . . . may I call you Brianna?"

"Of course."

"I'm so very sorry. I'm not sure how to tell you this, but there's been an unfortunate . . ." Incident? Event? "Antonio is no longer . . . with us."

She laughed. A deep, full-throated hoot. "How like him. To quit a show weeks before it opens. I know this is just a community theater, but a commitment is a commitment."

"Brianna . . ."

"Of course Antonio sometimes has difficulty with commitments," she said wryly.

Out of the corner of my right eye, I saw Lola approach, brushing her blond hair off her shoulder. I saw Henry out of the corner of my left eye, motioning to me to hurry it up. I felt squeezed. "Here's Lola now."

"Hello," she said, assuming Brianna was a new customer who represented one more potential warm body in an ELT seat.

"This is Brianna Kincaid," I said. "She was asking about Antonio?" I underlined his name.

Lola shot me an "uh-oh" look and stammered, "Are you a friend of his?"

"His wife." She sent Lola and me a magnificent smile.

"Ex-wife." Brianna massaged her empty glass.

We sat in my back booth inside the Windjammer. I'd whispered the situation to Benny, who'd promptly passed the word to Henry. They'd left us alone as they cleaned up the remains of the food festival, hauling equipment, wiping down the steam table, moving the portable bar. Pauli and Honey stacked the tables and chairs.

Lola and I sipped coffee. Brianna claimed she needed something stronger, so Benny poured her a double shot of bourbon, which she'd downed in one gulp.

"Would you like another?" Lola asked.

Brianna shook her head.

We'd broken the news of Antonio's death as gently as possible, then hurried her inside the Windjammer. She had cried, not uncommon for an ex-wife, especially one who seemed as emotionally attached to her ex-husband as Brianna. But in keeping with her sophisticated demeanor, she pulled herself together, drank her liquor, and pressed us on details.

"He was eating knishes when he died?" she asked me.

"Well, yes, but I don't think they had anything—"

Brianna frowned. "He was told to avoid fried foods. I understood he was on a strict diet."

I was about to defend the festival menu when Lola chimed in. "That's true. I tried to fix him dinner a few times, but he insisted on handling his own meals. Now Tiffany was another matter. She'd eat anything I cooked."

The name of Antonio's current wife hung in the ether.

"Yes. Tiffany." Brianna's lip curled.

Whoa. I slid my eyes in Lola's direction. Nothing ventured, nothing gained. "Did you know Tiffany?" I asked.

"I met her. Once. I couldn't imagine the two of them . . ." Her eyes filled.

Better to change the subject. "So Antonio had heart issues? High blood pressure, or an arrhythmia, or something?" I asked.

Brianna nodded. "Probably, but he avoided doctors like the plague."

"Antonio did complain of not feeling well a few nights ago. He left rehearsal early," Lola added.

Brianna shook her head. "If he'd only taken better care of himself. To die so young . . ."

"The county medical examiner will run tests," Lola said gently. "They'll be able to determine exactly why he died."

Brianna dabbed at her eyes with a Kleenex. "It's all so unbelievable . . . and shocking."

We nodded sympathetically. "At first we thought it might have been something he ate, but he was the only one at the food festival to . . ." Lola shrugged.

"He had the elderberry wine, too," I said. "We were using ideas from the play. It was really Merlot."

Brianna looked amazed. "What was he trying to prove? Eating knishes and drinking red wine? Antonio disliked red wine," she said.

"When I knew him in New York, he pretty much drank anything," Lola said. "Of course that was fifteen years ago."

"Were you married to him then?" I asked Brianna.

"No. We met and married in Los Angeles. By 1998 we'd drifted apart. We divorced and I came back East," Brianna said simply and checked her watch. "I should go."

"Are you okay to drive?" I asked.

"I'm fine."

Brianna offered no further information about her living situation or Antonio. We watched her scoot out of the booth and withdraw a card from her purse. "If you don't mind . . . if you hear anything more . . ."

I nodded and took the card. "Sure. Take care."

After she'd left, Lola said, "Now I need a drink."

I ran my thumb over the embossed letters of Brianna's business card. *Flowers by Kincaid, Rumson, New Jersey.*

6

Lola and I chewed over Brianna's appearance, along with a couple of Henry's special burgers, before I closed up for the night. Henry, Benny, Enrico, and Honey had all lit out by seven; I agreed to turn out the lights and lock up.

"Strange." Lola dabbed her mouth. "Brianna said Antonio never went to a doctor. But one night when we were talking about vegetarian diets, he said he was told he had the heart of a twenty-year-old. Who would have told him that if he'd never gone to a doctor?"

"Maybe he got healthy after he divorced Brianna? I guess there's more to Antonio's backstory," I said.

"I knew he'd been in Los Angeles before New York. But then he just disappeared. Thirteen years later he's emailing me and wanting to get back in touch."

"When was that?"

She thought. "Maybe a year ago. That's when I got the idea of having him as a possible guest director." Then she winced.

I picked up Brianna's card. "She's certainly done well for herself. She has her own business."

"Funny that she called herself Antonio's wife at first," Lola said. "Of course, I had no idea he'd been married and divorced when I knew him in New York."

"Maybe she never got over him."

Monday morning, bright and early, I brewed a cup of coffee and opened my laptop. I Googled "Flowers by Kincaid." The website was attractive and easy to navigate. You could find what you wanted. I had become a website connoisseur since Pauli had created an Internet presence for the Windjammer. Which reminded me, I had to give him a call.

Flowers by Kincaid had links for gift baskets, special occasions, same-day delivery, and great deals—a variety of autumn flowers arranged in baskets and bowls. Nice. The prices, for the most part, seemed reasonable. There was also a home page picture of Brianna and her staff, all of them smiling, ready to serve. Brianna looked as poised as she had yesterday hearing about the death of her ex.

I rested my fingers on the keyboard, then downed the last of my coffee. On a whim I deleted "Flowers by Kincaid" and typed in "Antonio Digenza." Up popped a handful of links that included either "Antonio" or "Digenza." Several had to do with classical composers and musical content. I added "+ New York" and got a number of hits: Digenza Towing, Digenza Bakery, and an appellate court case for an E. Digenza and two other defendants.

I scrolled down the links and on page two there were theater reviews for Antonio's shows from 1998 and 1999 and one for a 2000 off-off-Broadway production. The play—some bedroom farce I'd never heard of—received a good reception but only ran three weeks. It featured a young actress named Lola Trotter. She'd gotten an excellent notice. There were other reviews from 2013. But nothing else. Unusual in this day and age, when every aspect of one's existence was often blared front and center on the web and social media. I needed to check some other sources. But first I needed to get to the Windjammer and mend some fences with Henry.

The coffee was already percolating when I stepped through the door. Benny hadn't arrived yet, but Carmen was setting tables.

"Good morning, Miss Dodie," she said in her thick accent.

"Hi, Carmen. Henry's . . . ?" I pointed to the kitchen.

"*Sí.*" She lowered her voice. "He is little bit *disgustado.*"

I barely passed high school Spanish, but I got the gist.

I pushed open the swinging door to the kitchen. Enrico was chopping carrots for Henry's homemade cream of carrot soup; Henry was sautéing onions. "Mmmm. Something smells delicious."

Henry grunted. Enrico smiled.

"So we're doing the fried trout in herb butter sauce for dinner. With the walnut salad, right?"

Henry nodded and kept stirring the onions.

"Guess I'll do some inventory." I grabbed the clipboard off a hook by the door. "I'm sorry about the food festival. I think we might have sold out Sunday if Antonio hadn't . . . you know."

"So we're stuck with dogs, pretzels, and Italian ices. Not to mention potatoes and ground meat for the knishes," he said.

"Let's feature the Italian ices for dessert some night and I can take the hotdogs, pretzels, and cookies to the soup kitchen in Creston. It's tax deductible."

Enrico handed his pot of carrots to Henry.

"Honey can pack it all up. She'll love fooling around with the boxes and tape. By the way, where is she?" I asked.

"I gave her the day off," Henry said.

"Good idea."

He looked up. "We both deserved a break." He tried not to laugh. "All three of us."

I snickered quietly and headed to the walk-in freezer.

The lunch special was Henry's take on Mexican grilled cheese: *queso Chihuahua*, minced chorizo, and crushed taco chips. It sounded funky but was really a killer menu item. He'd only served it a few times in the past, but the word went out—get here early on those days.

I checked the dining room. Tables set, Benny installed behind the bar, and Carmen waiting for the onslaught. Except it never happened. The lunch "rush" consisted of a small group from South Jersey who were visiting Revolutionary War sites—Etonville's cemetery, established in 1759, was on the map, along with the Eton Bed & Breakfast; three construction workers repairing telephone wires on Route 53; and Edna, who'd stopped by to pick up a takeout order of the special sandwiches for the Etonville Police Department.

I rang up Edna's order.

"Not too busy," she said, turning her head to scan the dining room.

"I guess Etonville is eating in today." I handed her change.

Edna leaned over the counter. "It's a shame people in this town are so stubborn. The medical examiner said Antonio died of cardiac arrest. Not food poisoning," she said emphatically.

"He did? It's official?"

Edna stood up straight. Her face said it all—*oops.*

"Your secret's safe with me," I said.

She grinned sheepishly. "I overheard the chief on the phone. He distinctly said 'You're sure? Cardiac arrest?'"

"Wow. Well, that's good news. I mean not for Antonio."

"See you, Dodie. I've got to get these back to the department." Edna embraced the brown bags and said good-bye.

By three o'clock, I couldn't stand the Windjammer atmosphere: Henry was morose, Benny was working on a crossword puzzle, Carmen was cleaning tables no one had eaten at. I had to get out.

"Benny, I'm taking my break. Be back in an hour."

Outside I inhaled deeply. On a day like this I craved the sun and sand, running on the beach until I couldn't catch my breath and the sweat rolled down my face. *Maybe I'll just stroll around town, down Main to Amber, and stop in Betty's Boutique and see what's new in the lingerie world.* I could also drop in JC's and buy a new furnace filter. After all, winter was coming.

Who was I kidding? There was only one place I wanted to go. I bypassed Betty's and pushed open the outer door to the Municipal Building. The hallways gleamed, as usual, and eau de Lysol lingered in the air. I knew Bill wasn't responsible for keeping the building shipshape, but somehow everything seemed spiffier and more efficient since his arrival.

Edna was hard at work, one hand on the mouthpiece of her headset, the other surreptitiously holding her play script. Running lines with herself, no doubt.

"Quiet in here," I said.

Edna slid her script under the counter. "Ralph's got an 11-66 on Anderson Street and Suki is checking out an 11-24 near the highway."

I stared at her blankly. I knew she loved her codes, but it was difficult to follow along.

"That's a defective signal light and an abandoned vehicle," Edna said.

"Okay. So is the chief in? I just wanted to—"

Edna buzzed his inner office. "Dodie's here." She listened, then nodded. "10-4. You're cleared. And those sandwiches? De-licious. Etonville missed out today," she said.

"Thanks, Edna. We appreciate your support."

She picked up her script again. "Roger that."

I had no real reason to barge in on Bill; I just wanted to get confirmation about the cause of death. Not that I didn't trust Edna, but the sooner the official report was announced, the sooner the return of the Windjammer's clientele. I knocked on his door.

"Enter," he said.

I stuck my head in. "Hope I'm not disturbing you."

His lopsided grin appeared. "Has that ever stopped you before?"

"Oh. We're being funny today." I was playing it cool, but my heart bounced around like a Mexican jumping bean.

"Just practicing my presentational skills."

"Right. The introduction to the mayor. How's it going?" I asked.

"Let's just say no one's going to choke on their appetizer laughing at my jokes."

Which of course reminded us both of Antonio.

Bill became serious. "Sad about his death. But heart attacks can happen to anyone at any time." He paused. "I had an uncle who ran marathons, never smoked, no red meat. And he dropped over dead at forty-nine." Bill shook his head. "You never can tell."

"So it's official?" I asked hopefully.

"Well, the ME filed a preliminary report. Cardiac arrest as the cause of death. It will take a few weeks for the lab results from the blood and tissue samples, but he doesn't expect to find anything unusual. I guess that means I need to give a statement to the *Etonville Standard*." He nudged the local paper in my direction.

The headline blared GUEST DIRECTOR SUCCUMBS AT FOOD FESTIVAL. There was a picture of Antonio, black turtleneck, luxurious curly hair, brilliant smile. He looked to be about thirty. I skimmed the article; it summarized the events of his passing. Antonio, in full costume greeting the townsfolk of Etonville, was eating knishes and drinking elderberry wine when he was suddenly stricken. And, of course, the paper made sure to mention that folks were leery of attending the festival Sunday due to suspicions about food poisoning. Trust the *Etonville Standard* to fan the flames of innuendo.

"The sooner you talk to them the better. Our lunch service was noticeably smaller. And Henry's getting a little frantic."

"I understand. I'll call them this afternoon. His grilled cheese was out of this world." He looked at his waist. "Probably not too heart-friendly, speaking of dropping over dead."

I laughed. "I think you're safe. You get a lot of exercise running around ... 10-78s and 11-14s and 20-20s."

"Edna's rubbing off on you," he said with a smirk. "But I'm going to be busier in the next month. Serving as a consultant to the Creston PD." A hint of pride sneaked into his voice.

Creston was a decent-sized city, population 20,000 compared to Etonville's 3,284. It had a variety of middle-class and upscale neighborhoods and buzzed with chain stores and fast food places. Also crime, apparently.

"I guess congratulations are in order."

"Nah. It's just that they've been handling a bunch of upmarket residential robberies in the last month and they requested some help. I worked on a special task force years ago in Philly. A band of jewel thieves targeted million-dollar mansions in Society Hill."

"Old-fashioned cat burglars?"

"Burglary and theft. They managed to hit a dozen homes before we caught up with them."

"I read something about this in the *Standard*. Creston's not exactly Society Hill, but there've been three or four break-ins?"

"More like six or eight. All the same MO."

"Good luck," I said.

He checked his watch. "Thanks. Actually I need to get to Creston for a meeting. Was there anything else ... ?"

Oh yeah, I thought, as the afternoon light behind his head brought his chiseled face into sharp relief. But all I said was, "Not really. Well, maybe one thing."

He looked up from his briefcase. "I know that look. You're getting the itch to play detective again."

"I just wanted to let you know that Antonio's ex-wife showed up at the festival yesterday."

Bill looked interested. "Yeah?"

"A nice woman. Really broken up over his death. I guess there was still some ... feeling there."

"Unlike many divorces," he said.

Did he speak from personal experience?

"Right. Well, she said Antonio probably had heart issues, didn't watch his diet, and hated to go to doctors. Like he didn't take care of himself."

"As I said, they can—"

"—happen to anyone," I finished for him. "I'm glad the medical examiner has confirmed the cause of death, but . . ."

Bill took his jacket off a hook. "But what?"

I shook my head.

"Come on." He tapped his index finger against the brim of his cap.

"Okay. I was thinking that something didn't feel right, you know?"

"Like what?"

"It's probably nothing, but Antonio told Lola he had the heart of a twenty-year-old and was careful about his diet. She also told me Antonio had been disappearing from rehearsals and once he stayed out all night. And then he nearly drove into me at midnight last week at the opposite end of town from where he was staying."

Bill sat back down. "It's not a crime to drive around other parts of town, and given the stories I've been hearing lately about the ELT rehearsals . . ."

"Edna?"

"Edna. I'd probably take a powder and disappear, too." He laughed.

"I guess so."

"I know you have an overactive imagination. But this time, I think you're barking up the wrong tree."

Was I wrong? Was I imagining a problem where there wasn't one? Of course my great aunt Maureen always said even a stopped clock is right twice a day. Still, whenever something unexplainable bothered me, these tiny hairs on the back of my neck were like a radar system, alerting me to pay attention. They'd lain dormant for the past few months, but since Antonio's death I could feel them come alive.

Bill patted me on the back. "I have to get going. See you Saturday at the game?"

"Sure," I said.

Out on Main, I could still feel his hand on my upper back. It was just a pat, but still, contact was contact.

7

The sky overhead turned gunmetal gray and the wind picked up. I made it back to the safety of the restaurant just before a downpour drenched everything and everyone still on the street.

Benny was on the phone with his wife; she'd been downsized from the box factory in Bernridge and was now working at Georgette's Bakery, supplier of Windjammer's baked goods. They had a five-year-old daughter and, in his spare time, he drove a UPS delivery truck. Benny was usually grateful for any extra shifts I could offer him. Tonight that seemed like a good option. Usually I hung around until dinner was over, but what was the point? With only a handful of patrons in the restaurant, I wasn't needed and Benny could spend the later part of the evening doing crosswords and listening to Henry kvetch.

"Hey, want to work late?" I asked when Benny ended his call.

"You bet," he said eagerly. "The kid is home with an earache and the wife is grumbling about her job search. The Windjammer's the safest place to be tonight."

I punched in Carol's cell number.

"Hi, Dodie. How are you holding up?"

I could hear the whoosh of running water and the whirr of hair dryers. "Fine, I guess."

"The word here is that no one's eating at the Windjammer and you might have to call the health department."

"What? No! In fact you can announce that the medical examiner confirmed Antonio had a heart attack. It's going to be in the *Etonville Standard* tomorrow morning. That's one piece of information I hope you spread around."

"Will do. That's good news!"

I heard a glint in her eye. "What?"

"My new shampoo girl—"

"The one with the earrings?"

"Imogen. Yes. She has a neighbor whose cousin works at a doctor's office in Bernridge. She was on duty a few days before Antonio died."

"And?"

"He had an appointment to see the doctor. Maybe he was already ill. Maybe he had heart problems nobody knew about. Or maybe he had food poisoning already and something he ate just pushed him over the edge."

Huh? "The medical examiner said—"

"Cardiac arrest, I know." She lowered her voice. "But people around town aren't buying it."

"There goes business."

"I'm sorry, Dodie. Anything I can do to help?" Carol asked.

"Could you ask Pauli to call me? I've been texting but no answer back," I said.

"That kid! He lost his cell phone. I'll give him the message. Meantime, do you think you should shut down the Windjammer? Just until this blows over?"

"Talk soon." I clicked off and downed two aspirin to combat the headache that I could feel coming on. I assumed I had gotten used to Etonville when the rumors swirled around the death of Jerome Angleton and nearly waylaid the investigation. But there had also been positive aspects to the town's gossip mill. People had noticed other people doing things that eventually helped crack the case wide open. One just had to take the positive with the not so positive. I decided to speak with Lola and see if she'd heard the Snippets rumors.

At seven o'clock, I stood under the awning that covered the door of the Windjammer and waited for a break in the rain; after two minutes the steady thrum of the water hitting the canvas softened to a gentle patter as the rain became a drizzle. I dashed next door to the theater and ran into the lobby. Two actors were sitting in a corner running lines; two others were drinking coffee and, from the look of their tetchy faces when they saw me, exchanging opinions on the food festival's liability for killing off their director.

"Is Lola around?" I asked, trying to look businesslike.

One of the guilty gossipers jerked his thumb in the direction of the theater.

"Thanks." I entered quietly, not wanting to disturb whatever dramatic moment was being created.

I needn't have bothered. It looked like nothing was being created, except maybe frustration. Walter and Carlyle stood onstage, facing each other, arms folded across their chests identically. Lola sat, head in hands, in the front row. Penny was stretched out on a sofa downstage, and a bunch of actors wandered around upstage, whispering until their voices grew too loud and Penny shushed them. To my shock, Tiffany was perched on a chair next to Romeo, who sporadically put a comforting arm around her.

"We can't start run-throughs this week. We haven't worked through Act Two yet," Walter said, and tugged on his brown-gray beard. It was a gesture I recognized from the past whenever he was stymied in the process of getting a show on its feet.

"Antonio scheduled the run for this week and then work-throughs next week," Carlyle shot back. "We should honor his plans." Carlyle sneaked a peak at Tiffany, who shrugged indifferently and walked off the stage, Romeo close behind.

Walter scowled. "But he's not here, so maybe we need to make our own decisions."

It looked like a stalemate. They both turned to Lola. "Let's give the actors a break and maybe we can sort this out," she said hopefully.

"I'm going for coffee," Carlyle said. "Tiffany?" He looked around for her.

"I'll be in my office." Walter tramped off.

"Take ten," Penny yelled and hauled herself up and off the divan. "Hey, O'Dell."

"Hi, Penny." I slid into Lola's row. "Whew. You've got your hands full."

"Rehearsal's a hot mess," Penny said at my back. "Lola, you want coffee, too?"

"No thanks."

Penny disappeared and I dropped into the seat next to Lola. "Who's in charge?"

"They both are. Codirecting," Lola said.

"Is that wise?"

"Probably not, but it was the only way to guarantee the show gets up. Walter has more experience, and of course some off-off-Broadway credits, like Antonio, but the cast is a little turned off by his attitude. Carlyle has never directed on his own, but he has the actors' sympathy. Now, anyway, being Antonio's assistant and all."

"What's Tiffany doing here? Why isn't she in mourning with family in New York or wherever?"

"I encouraged her to take the night off, take the show off, for that matter. We'd find someone to replace her. But she insisted on coming."

"I'm afraid to even ask . . . is she making funeral arrangements?"

Lola lowered her voice. "And that's another thing. They're releasing the body tomorrow, so she's free to proceed. I offered to help, you know, call people. But her family's in Oregon, and anyway they don't really know Antonio. Apparently, Tiffany doesn't think he had many friends who would come."

There was at least one other person who would want to come.

"So, what are you saying?" I asked.

"She wants to hold the service here. Bury Antonio in Etonville," she said.

OMG. Another funeral service run by the Etonville Little Theatre?

"I know what you're thinking," Lola said. "But this time no eulogy by Walter, just a simple remembrance and burial. At least that's what Tiffany said she wanted."

Last April, Jerome Angleton's funeral had been an ELT extravaganza, orchestrated by Walter, complete with Shakespearean quotations and Elizabethan costumes.

"Should I notify Brianna? I guess it's Tiffany's call. But she seemed genuinely grief-stricken."

Lola twisted a lock of her hair. "I hate to bring Brianna up again. I mentioned her name last night and Tiffany had a meltdown."

"Maybe better to leave her out of the picture. Let me know if there is something I can do."

"I'd suggest a repast at the restaurant, but under the circumstances . . ."

"Right," I said.

I'd arranged with Pauli to meet me at the Windjammer after school to talk about updates to the website. We'd been online since

April and there had been only one major glitch—in an effort to be proactive Pauli had listed Things To Do and Places To Go in Etonville and inadvertently offered free publicity to Henry's nemesis, La Famiglia. I'd managed to smooth things over by brokering a short-term reconciliation between the two eating establishments: They both participated in my theme-food nights for *Romeo and Juliet*.

But their goodwill took a hit when La Famiglia received its four-star endorsement, and I gave up on détente: The cold war was once more underway. I had to up the ante and plump up the website.

"Hey, Dodie."

I lifted my head from an inventory sheet where I was weighing vegetable choices—asparagus, broccoli, and kale—and took in a familiar sight: a hank of brown hair drifting over an acne-spattered forehead, a black hoodie, and a laptop. "Hi, Pauli."

I cleared papers from the other side of my booth and Pauli slid onto the bench opposite me. "Thanks for your help with the food festival."

"No problem," he said. Then with a frown, "Kinda freaky with that guy . . ."

"Dying. Yeah, I know." The *Etonville Standard* still lay on the table. "At least they published the truth about his death."

The paper's follow-up article was below the fold, had no pictures, and briefly quoted the medical examiner's official language: "All indications point to an acute myocardial infarction." Still, business had been slow all day.

Pauli swiped one hand across his forehead to reveal his whole face. "I didn't eat the knishes."

"Right." I motioned to Benny to bring Pauli a Coke and he opened his laptop. "So the website."

We stared at the Windjammer page and took a moment of silence to appreciate our efforts from the spring: pictures from the herb garden, a link for menus, and an online reservation system. We had talked about using reviews, but they were only three stars and would pale in comparison to La Famiglia.

I got down to business. "We need to add some pizazz, you know?"

Pauli nodded seriously. "Totally. Because, like, people still think the guy croaked of food poisoning."

Out of the mouths of babes.

His eyes gleamed. "I did some research."

In seconds he had called up a series of restaurant websites. We scrolled through them for ideas. Pictures of the staff, gift cards, photos of various dishes, and news about past and upcoming events. Some even had blogs.

"This is great, Pauli," I said. "We can definitely do the photos and I could write up a description of previous theme-food events for a news link."

Pauli slowly munched on chips.

"But maybe I should skip the food festival."

He nodded.

"And I can do a blurb on community outreach for the football picnic this weekend." I wasn't ready to commit to a daily or even weekly blog about the Windjammer, but a few short notes would be fine. "So we'll have a staff photo and a gallery of pictures of Henry's signature dishes and an events link. How does that sound?"

Pauli slurped down the rest of his Coke, already making notes on his laptop.

I smiled at his youthful enthusiasm. Nice to be almost eighteen—he had a birthday coming up soon. I was feeling older than my thirty-four years. Was it spending time on the beach this summer and seeing all of those tanned, hard bodies that made me feel as though—

"Is that okay?" Pauli asked.

"Sorry?"

"I can take pictures later this week. I have to finish up my online class tonight."

"That's right. Your mom mentioned it. Digital forensics?"

"Yeah." His face glowed. "Like we're studying the basic tools and procedures. Seizure of equipment, forensic duplication process, hardware recognition—"

"Whoa. Seriously?" I said.

"Like yeah." He stirred the ice in his glass with the straw. "We also study ethical stuff."

I knew what he was referring to. His ability to find a password and hack into Jerome's email account had made a huge difference in putting away a bad guy. Still, it was our little secret; ours and Lola's and Bill's. Even Carol had no idea about the extent of her son's technical skills. "Pretty soon you'll be able to investigate devices legally," I said quietly.

He grinned. "Next I'm going to take a class on Internet searches."

I started to gather my inventory sheets. Time to get back to work and time for Pauli to report home for dinner. "Pauli, can I find someone on the Internet even if they don't want to be found?" I had an itch about Antonio. Why didn't he have a bigger web presence? Even Henry had a handful of references and he was allergic to anything on the Internet.

Pauli shrugged nonchalantly. "Sure. There's all kinds of databases. You don't need much information to get going." His nonchalance abruptly changed to vigilance. He slid his eyes around the restaurant. No one was paying any attention to us. "Do you have another . . . like . . . thing for me to do?"

"Shh," I said.

"Remember the first rule of digital forensics?" he asked.

"Confidentiality," I said.

He nodded wisely.

"Got it."

Pauli stared behind me. "Hey," he said and pulled his hood over his head.

"Hey, yourself." Honey tossed her straggly locks behind one ear and stuck her chest out an inch or so. "Wassup?"

Pauli, too shy to respond, jammed the laptop into his backpack.

"We're working on the Windjammer website. Pauli's a computer whiz."

He blushed and Honey appraised him anew. "Huh. Maybe you should include like a delivery service. You know, prepackaged food we take to wherever."

Pauli beamed. "That's a good idea!"

"I've got some packaging videos on Instagram." She smiled teasingly at Pauli. "Bet you can use something on the website."

Pauli grinned stupidly. I ground my teeth. Honey was determined to box up Windjammer food.

"FYI, Dot. Uncle Henry wants to see you in the kitchen. Something about a mistake in the meat delivery. Toodles." She fluttered her fingers at Pauli's shining face and strutted out the door.

Geez.

"So, uh, Dodie, let me know if you want me to work on . . . whatever," he said.

I rose, ready to do battle with Cheney Brothers food distributors. "Will do."

"'Cause, like, eventually you can find everybody on the Internet." Pauli shuffled off.

I shivered even though the day was warm and the Windjammer slightly stuffy. My little hairs stood up straight and saluted.

8

I sat in the theater next to Lola and watched the ELT's "circle of light." This was Walter's way of forcing the cast members to trust each other. Every actor entered the middle of the circle and took turns falling into the outstretched arms of the rest of the cast, who, it was assumed, would catch the actor. I'd taken a turn during *Romeo and Juliet* and ended up on my backside. My takeaway? Don't trust the cast.

Walter was pontificating on the Etonville Little Theatre being a "family" and the importance of breathing as the actors released themselves into the arms of their "comrades." I was skeptical. I breathed, and look where it got me. Carlyle appeared bored; needless to say he didn't trust anyone.

Penny sounded her whistle when the exercise was completed. "Take five. Then we do a speed-through."

The actors cringed. Carlyle pouted. "Can't someone get that thing away from her?" he asked Lola, who was hunched over a rehearsal schedule.

"Maybe we should cancel the run-through on Friday and push everything back until next week. Tomorrow night we should sit everyone down and run lines," Lola said.

Carlyle's attention drifted away to stage right, where Tiffany was lounging in an easy chair.

"How is she doing?" I asked.

He turned his head to face me. "How would you feel if you lost your husband without warning?" He angrily stomped onto the stage and put an arm around Tiffany.

"Wow. Was it something I said?"

"Carlyle's being protective of Tiffany," Lola said.

Did Lola know what Penny apparently knew? "Do you think there's something going on between them?"

"Tiffany and Carlyle?" she asked. "No. He was just Antonio's assistant. And a good friend."

Maybe.

"So, Lola, I was doodling around on the Internet, you know, Googling Antonio."

I had her full consideration now. "You were?"

"I couldn't find anything on him before 1998. You worked with him in 2000, right? I saw the review. Nice notice."

Lola acknowledged the compliment. "Antonio did his best, but the rest of the cast was pretty uneven."

"You'd think there would have been something about his earlier work in the nineties and later stuff between 2000 and 2013."

Lola shrugged. "Is that important?"

"Just made me curious, that's all."

Lola lowered her voice. "Dodie, do you think there's something else about Antonio we don't know?"

"I'm not thinking anything . . . yet."

"Well, at least the medical examiner confirmed cardiac arrest. You have to feel relieved about that," she said.

"I wish it made more of a difference. The town is still suspicious about the Windjammer. If something doesn't change their opinions soon, we could be out of business."

"Seriously?"

"Maybe." I might have been exaggerating a bit.

Penny blew her whistle, whacked her clipboard against her leg. "Let's go. Everyone onstage."

"So the funeral is all set for Friday?"

Lola nodded. "We sent an announcement to the *New York Times* and the *Star Ledger*. In case any actors he's worked with over the years want to come."

"Who's doing the eulogy?"

"Walter offered, but I nixed that. So Carlyle stepped up."

"Good thing."

"This feels like déjà vu all over again," Lola said. "If we're going to have a funeral with every production, I'm going to invest in a black wardrobe."

"I've got to get back to work." I'd come over after the so-called dinner shift, but even Henry's herb-crusted pork loin couldn't tempt the palates of Etonville. I glanced at the stage, where Walter was physically maneuvering actors into various locations on the set. "What on earth is he doing?"

"Walter insisted he wanted a speed-through tonight. I assumed he meant everyone sitting around a table and doing lines as fast as they could."

No one was sitting around a table. Edna and Abby were stationed by the front door, Walter took his place at the top of the stairs, Tiffany stood outside the front door waiting for her entrance, the cops were hanging around the window seat, Romeo sat at the dining room table, and one of the gangsters was killing time in the "basement."

Penny tooted her whistle. "Get your rears in gear. On your mark, get set"—Penny blew her whistle again—"go!"

The actors looked at one another, confused, hesitant, and Walter shouted, "Let your creativity flow. Move wherever it feels right."

"What about the blocking?" Penny asked, and held up the prompt script.

"Don't get hung up on blocking. You need to make your movement organic. Improvise. Just keep flowing and speaking. Take it from the top!"

"From the top," Penny repeated, blasting her whistle.

Carlyle held his ears and hunched down in a theater seat as the cast began to drift slowly around the set, spitting out lines and trying not to bump into one another.

"Walter's supposed to be the one who knows what he's doing," I whispered.

Worry lines deepened on Lola's forehead.

And then the rehearsal went from problematic to plain idiotic. Edna tripped on her rehearsal skirt and ricocheted off Abby, who recoiled in surprise and landed in Romeo's lap. Romeo yelled an expletive and Walter rushed down the stairs. "Decorum, Romeo! Keep it going! Speed up the lines."

Romeo propelled Abby off him as the cops decided to climb in the window. Tiffany stuck her head in the front door. "What's going on?"

"Stay in character!" Walter barked.

The actor in the basement opened a trap door. "Is this my entrance?"

"No!" the cast cried in unison and he disappeared.

Carlyle marched to Penny and grabbed her whistle. He blasted his lungs out. Everyone stopped. Edna, out of breath, collapsed into a chair. Abby hiked up her skirt and sat on the stairs, the cops perched on the window seat, Romeo threw his rehearsal fedora on the floor, and Tiffany ran off to the green room.

"Another one of Walter's bright ideas," Lola groused.

Walter, maintaining his dignity, called, "Penny!"

"I'm on it," she said. "Take—"

"The rest of the night off," Lola said firmly. She stepped to the stage. "Walter, we need to talk."

I headed back to the Windjammer.

"Don't forget to wear something nice on Friday," I said to Henry and Honey two hours later as they walked out the door. "Staff picture."

Henry wasn't enthusiastic about the photography, but I'd convinced him that anything we did now to spruce up the website could only help business.

"Like, we're actually going to have our faces on the website?" Honey asked.

"Uh, yeah," I said.

"Dot, like, maybe I can be holding some boxes? For my packaging portfolio?"

Geez.

I filled out a deposit form, tucked the day's receipts—such as they were—into my purse, and flipped off the overhead spotlights in the dining room. Shadows played around the walls and tables. I usually never minded being the last one standing in the Windjammer. In fact, it was nice at the end of the day to have a quiet moment in the restaurant alone. But tonight it felt eerie, as if someone was watching me.

Ridiculous, I told myself. I walked outside and zipped up my jacket. The night was nippy but clear. Stars glittered and the moon was a perfect crescent. I was lucky today and had caught a parking space directly in front of the Windjammer. Of course, that meant feeding the meter all afternoon, when I remembered. As I grabbed the door handle I saw something lodged under the left windshield wiper. Nuts. The Etonville meter maid was at it again; she had nailed me. Tickets were thirty dollars.

I yanked it out. I was expecting a sturdy piece of card stock; instead I was holding a flimsy slip of lined paper with writing on it. I stepped under the street lamp and held it up to the light. In block letters it read: LEAVE ANTONIO ALONE.

I had trouble sleeping. I rose early, made my coffee, and studied the note, which I'd deposited in a plastic baggie, although my fingerprints were undoubtedly all over it. It was a five-by-seven sheet of white paper, the letters half an inch tall, as if a kid had printed it. I spent the morning mulling over this turn of events. Was it a hoax? A threat?

I needed to talk this through with my BFFs. It was my day off, so I did my laundry and straightened the house, a simple job since I lived in a five-room, 1930s bungalow; perfect for my needs. Then I invited Lola and Carol over for an early dinner before rehearsal. We'd all been so crazy busy recently that we hadn't had a girls' night out in New York or gone to a movie. I knew Carol would bring some Italian dish, as she always did whenever I hosted them for a meal. I decided to use my great aunt Maureen's silver, and cloth napkins, and I set the dining room table for the three of us.

I had baby greens for a salad and a gallon of lemon ice that I'd liberated from the Windjammer freezer. Which reminded me, I had planned to drop off the leftover food from the festival to the soup kitchen in Creston. I checked the wall clock. I had a few hours before either of my guests would show up. I tucked the note in my bag, grabbed my keys off the hook by the back door, and pulled on my denim jacket.

Outside, my neighbor was back from Ohio and washing her brand-new car. I looked at my red Chevy and considered: It deserved a wash, too. Maybe later. I waved to her and she gestured with her chamois. Someday I'd have enough money saved to buy a new car, but that might mean a change in jobs.

Never mind. I touched the dashboard of my Metro. We were good friends and had seen each other through some serious scrapes. I headed down Ames and turned onto Fairfield as I calculated exactly how much I'd saved since my arrival in Etonville. Not much. I turned into an alley off Amber that led me to the loading dock of the restaurant. It was two o'clock and lunch would be nearly over.

"Hi, Enrico," I said as I entered the back door and headed for the refrigerators.

He looked up. "Miss Dodie? It's your day off," he said, his chocolate eyes opening wide.

Carmen called him her brown-eyed baby. "Just here to pick up the leftover festival food."

Enrico looked over this shoulder. "Go quick before Henry comes."

"Bad mood, huh?"

"His meat loaf was no comfort today," he said sadly.

"Got it." I had no time to play cheerleader for Henry. "Give me a hand."

Enrico and I loaded the fifty pounds of hotdogs, two hundred pretzels, and a case of the black-and-white cookies into my car. Honey poked her head out the back door. "Like, what's going on? Dot, you should tell Uncle Henry that—"

"Sorry, Honey. Got to go." I ripped out of my parking space next to the dumpster.

I was three minutes from the Municipal Building. I had a good reason to see Bill—dropping off the note. And I had a good excuse to beat a hasty retreat—the food packed into my backseat—in case it felt like I was overstaying my welcome. Though Bill and I were on friendly terms, I was cautious about barging in on him too frequently.

"Hi, Edna," I said and hurried past the dispatch window.

Edna took off her headset. "Dodie! The chief's not in."

I stopped. "Oh. Do you expect him back soon?" In other words, was he taking a break at Coffee Heaven or on a 10-something call.

"Don't know. He was gone when I came on duty."

"Okay. Thanks, Edna."

"Officer Shung's in, if it's urgent," she said.

I hesitated. "Nothing that can't wait."

She replaced the headset glumly. "Some rehearsal last night."

It wasn't like Edna to get down in the dumps. I felt sorry for the whole cast. They'd been working hard and didn't deserve to have the show collapse around them.

"You know how Walter gets this close to an opening. A little . . . frenetic," I said.

"I've been tweeting my relatives in Pennsylvania. I may have to uninvite them." Her board lit up and she punched a button. "Etonville Police Department."

I could always drop off the note to Bill tomorrow.

I wound the window down and headed onto State Route 53. The wind whooshed into my front seat and sent my hair in a swirl around my face. I felt free and removed from the food-festival fiasco for the first time all week. I dialed up the volume on my radio and sang along to Katy Perry.

I slowed down as I entered Creston and followed the GPS—I called her my Genie—on my cell phone. Left on Banks, right on Maywood, and I found myself in a part of town I'd never visited. The houses were old 1920s-style Craftsman bungalows, mostly two-story with upstairs dormers and tidy yards, sided in earth tones—yellows, browns, and greens. I cruised down Maywood and stopped in front of a Lutheran church.

Inside the door marked Annie's Place, I found a jolly woman who identified herself as the kitchen manager and offered to find someone to help me unload the car. They were only too happy to receive the food; it made me feel better about all of the leftovers.

Ten minutes later, I made a U-turn on Maywood and drove back to the center of Creston. I passed a familiar jewelry store, a café I frequented when I needed an out-of-Etonville break, and a doctors' professional building that offered the kinds of medical specialties unavailable in Etonville. I paused at a red light, humming to the radio, and looked to my left: the Creston Police Department. It made me think of Bill's involvement with the series of robberies in town. I wondered how that was going and if he was here.

As if my mind had the power to make things materialize, Bill stepped out of the building with another officer. They shook hands. I imagined he was smiling with that familiar lip curve.

The light changed and I had to make a decision. My route home was straight ahead, but Bill was to my left. It looked as if his work was done and he was leaving, so why not stop by and say hello? I turned on my blinker and slowly spun the wheel, aiming for the curb. I pulled in and put the car in park. I looked down to get my lipstick from the console and when I glanced up, Bill and the officer had been joined by a woman: thirties, striking, short brunette hair, a hot business suit, and three-inch heels. OMG. I scrunched down in my seat, far enough to hide my face but not so far that I couldn't see the events unfolding.

She placed a hand on Bill's arm and he smiled. This time I could see his lip turn up at one end. The three of them chatted awhile longer, then the officer returned to the department and Bill kissed the woman on the cheek. I had never seen or experienced Bill Thompson being that affectionate with anyone. Much less me. My heart dropped in my chest. When he got in his car, I waited ten minutes to be sure he was gone before I edged down the street, went around the block, and got back on State Route 53. Depressed.

"I can't believe this," Lola said, staring at the note in a baggie. She took a forkful of baked ziti.

Carol had outdone herself. The edges of the casserole were crunchy and the melted mozzarella thick and gooey. Just the kind of comfort food I needed tonight. It would have been an all-day affair if I'd attempted to cook. Carol kept a half dozen of these dishes frozen and ready for last-minute emergencies. I picked up the Cabernet bottle to top off our wineglasses; Carol and I had no particular place to go this evening. I was planning on hunkering down, and Carol had one of her hairdressers closing up later.

Lola, on the other hand, had a line rehearsal to attend—one that didn't include actors bouncing around the stage as if the theater were a pinball machine. She placed a hand over her glass. "Wish I could," she said.

"What are you going to do about the note?" Carol asked, helping herself to another serving of ziti.

"I guess I'll give it to Bill tomorrow."

"If it is a prank, I don't think it's very funny," Lola said. "And if it's a threat? That's serious business."

I twisted the stem of my glass.

"Dodie? Are you okay? You seem a little out of it," Carol said.

"Just thinking." And I was, only not about someone warning me to forget about Antonio, but about the mystery woman that Bill had so freely kissed publicly. I shook myself mentally. "Carol, I should tell Bill about Imogen's neighbor's cousin."

"Good idea. Maybe someone should speak with her." Carol paused, swallowing her wine. "Speaking of Bill, did you know he's got some interesting things going on in Creston?"

Did I ever.

Carol leaned across the table like a conspirator. "One of my colorists said that Edna said that he's working on a case there."

I was sure he was.

9

I understood why Lola was frazzled. In addition to keeping the Etonville Little Theatre on schedule for an opening in ten days, she had had to put together a funeral very quickly. We sat in the back row of Ristaino's Funeral Home; me in my black skirt and dark blue jacket, she in a black suit and pearls that set off her blond hair and gave her a dignified, other-worldly presence. If I didn't know better I would have taken her for the grieving widow. It was 8:30 a.m., a half hour before the viewing was open to the public. I had agreed to keep Lola company when she brought Tiffany to see Antonio's body. We watched her sitting in a chair in the first row of seats, almost as if she had no idea what she was supposed to do. It was to be a simple service here, followed by a burial in St. Andrew's Episcopal cemetery.

"I hope this comes off okay," Lola murmured, twisting a lace handkerchief.

"Things will be fine." I patted her knee, which reminded me of Bill patting my back.

"It's just that I had no idea what Antonio would have wanted."

"Tiffany wasn't any help there?" I asked.

Lola shook her head. "Not really. She claimed she didn't know Antonio that well. They'd only been married a year."

"Wow."

"She left everything up to me."

The minister arrived and approached Tiffany. "I guess I'd better get 'onstage,'" Lola said, and joined them.

So Tiffany didn't really know Antonio's background, his family, his history. He might have been part of the witness protection program for all she knew. But then again, what did any of us know about the people in our lives? What did I know about Bill? He was a former

NFL running back who served on the Philadelphia police force before arriving in Etonville. He was a wine connoisseur and appreciated great food—at La Famiglia, unfortunately. Was that all I knew? Oh, and of course there was the brunette in Creston on the steps of the police department.

A rustle of activity at the front of the room tugged at my attention as Mr. Ristaino opened the doors and mourners filed in. Lola had wisely left Tiffany in her chair and positioned herself to greet people as they entered. She was all composure and poise. I admired Lola's ability to play whatever role she was handed. Leading lady? She was there. Artistic director? No problem. Funeral arranger?

OMG. At the head of the line was Brianna, looking as smart as Lola, in a muted gray suit and black neck scarf. The two of them could have been sisters. Brianna greeted her as if they were good friends and made a beeline for the casket, kneeling, then laying a hand on Antonio's chest. She had to notice how good Antonio looked. The undertaker had done an amazing piece of work; Antonio's skin was rosy and his lips were in a slightly condescending smile—just as he'd looked in rehearsal. Brianna blotted her eyes, nodded at Tiffany, and walked back toward the foyer. I craned my head to see where she'd gone, but the room was filling up and she disappeared into the crowd.

The membership of the ELT was well represented: the entire cast of *Arsenic and Old Lace,* of course, scenery and costume crews, Chrystal, even JC from the hardware store.

The Banger sisters were present; word was they loved a good funeral as long as it wasn't one of theirs.

"Pretty good show, O'Dell," I heard at my back.

I was becoming accustomed to Penny appearing out of thin air and responding to my thoughts. She landed in a seat next to me. "Where's Walter?" I asked.

Penny pushed her glasses up a bit on her nose. "He'll be here. He likes to make an entrance."

"Not in costume, I hope." I remembered his Elizabethan cape and frilly shirt, à la *Romeo and Juliet,* for Jerome's funeral.

Penny cackled softly. "Nah. He and Antonio were . . ." She crossed her index fingers to form an X.

"Right. Well, now he's gotten what he wanted. He's directing the show."

"Codirecting," she corrected me. "Too bad about Antonio. He was getting to like Etonville."

"Small-town life? He'd miss New York City," I said.

"Well, he was thinking of moving out here."

I stared at Penny. Where did she get her information? This was not the standard Snippets gossip; this sounded as if she and Antonio—

"We had a few conversations, eye to eye."

"You mean . . . heart-to-heart?" I asked.

"Whatever." She poked my shoulder and jerked her head toward the front of the room.

Carlyle had entered, pausing to glance first at Antonio, then at Tiffany, as if unsure about which direction to take. He opted for the living and advanced on Tiffany. She stood up for the first time and threw herself into his arms. It was an awkward moment and the place was suddenly silent.

"Told you," Penny muttered.

As if on cue Walter strode into the room. The ELT membership pivoted their heads toward him, acknowledging their leader's presence, and resumed their quiet murmuring.

For half an hour townspeople streamed in, many of whom had probably never met or even seen Antonio; but he was an honorary member of Etonville, having worked at the theater, and that was good enough for the citizens of the town. I recognized most of the crowd, but there were ten or twelve people who looked unfamiliar. Actors Antonio had worked with before, no doubt.

At nine thirty, the minister rose and signaled the start of the service. He asked everyone to take a seat and began with a prayer and general request for the repose of Antonio's soul. Heads bowed reverently. There was a Bible reading, the singing of "Rock of Ages" by Mildred Tower, choir director of St. Andrew's in addition to Etonville librarian, and a short sermon on the struggles of this life versus the peace of the next. It was Antonio's "time."

Maybe Antonio's "time" had come a little prematurely, I thought.

The minister motioned to the front row. Carlyle stood up and crossed to the coffin, placing one hand on its polished wood, the other holding a three-by-five note card. He cleared his throat.

"Antonio was my friend, my mentor, a shining star in the theater firmament . . ." His voice broke.

There was a collective gulp in the room. He took a breath. We took a breath. And waited.

"Now we need to figure out how to go on without him . . ."

Did Walter toss his head a little dismissively?

Carlyle continued, summarizing their bond (like brothers) and recounting lessons Antonio had taught him (how to run a rehearsal, how to deal with troubled actors—squirming from the ELT bunch—and how to have a successful relationship). This last caused a minor stir. A few eyes slid in Tiffany's direction. What an odd thing to say, considering Carlyle's closeness with Antonio's wife.

Carlyle wrapped it up and the reverend asked if anyone would like to say a few words. I fervently prayed that the crowd was too moved to speak. I hadn't even gotten to "Amen" when Walter rose.

"Watch this," Penny whispered.

Walter stood majestically, the resurrected Artistic Director of the Etonville Little Theatre. He turned and studied Antonio as if in conversation with the dead man, then faced us, allowing his gaze to take in the whole room.

"I didn't know Antonio well, unlike Carlyle, but I do know theater."

Some ELT members nodded in acknowledgment.

"And so to honor both him and his place in our Etonville family, I would like to lead us in singing an ode to his life that I'm sure Antonio would appreciate." Walter thrust a piece of paper into Mildred's hands. She blinked and looked at the minister, who shrugged helplessly. This was Penny's cue. She pulled out a stack of papers she'd been hoarding in her stage manager's bag and hurriedly passed them out to the gathering.

Walter found his first note and began slowly, "'There's no business . . . like show business . . .'" he sang dramatically, his baritone full and rich. Mildred added her soprano tentatively as Walter signaled for the gathered assembly to join in. Up front Lola looked stupefied, Carlyle furious, and Tiffany numb. It was too late to question the wisdom of Walter's choice of hymn. One by one mourners looked at each other, then down at the lyrics on the sheet. Despite the occasion, the momentum seemed to grow and by the time we all reached the end, everyone was more or less into it. We let the last note hang in the air. Walter stole an extra bow, Tiffany burst into fresh tears, Carlyle comforting her, and Lola just shook her head.

* * *

"Walter has more off-the-wall ideas," Lola said, as we took our places under the tent by the grave site.

"It was kind of sweet," I said. "Unusual, but in keeping with the spirit of Antonio's life."

The ceremony was short and to the point. The reverend was taking no chances. After we'd laid our single roses on the casket, Lola invited everyone to the church basement for coffee.

We all turned to go and in my peripheral vision I saw a young woman approach the grave, stare intently at the coffin, laugh lightly, and drop her rose flippantly on the casket. I remembered her from earlier. She'd seemed to be slightly underdressed for the occasion and came very late—just as the singing started. My little hairs were standing on end.

I tugged on Lola's jacket. "Did you see that?"

Lola was shaking hands with the reverend and thanking him for his service. She looked back at me just as the woman strolled easily out of the cemetery. "What?"

"That woman. In the jeans and green jacket. She was at the funeral parlor."

"What about her?" Lola was engaged, smiling and nodding at everyone and thanking them for coming.

"She just about threw her flower on Antonio's coffin and then laughed. Who in the world is she?"

"I'm sorry, Dodie, what did you say?" Lola asked.

"Nothing. I'll meet you inside the church."

I hurried out of the cemetery and skirted groups of people nattering on about Walter's tribute to Antonio, how brave Tiffany was to stay in the show, and what kind of pastries Georgette had provided for the repast.

In front of St. Andrew's I paused on the sidewalk. A car or two were pulling out of the parking lot adjacent to the church. None I could identify, since the Etonville crowd would probably remain for the coffee and cake. Anyone leaving was more than likely from out of town. I walked quickly along the edge of the lot, scanning the automobiles, peering into aisle after aisle to find the mystery woman.

Then I saw her, one green-sleeved arm hanging out the driver's-side window of an older yellow Honda, holding a cigarette. That alone made her conspicuous.

I debated talking to her. What was I going to say? *Why were you laughing at Antonio's grave?* She tossed her cigarette stub onto the pavement and started her engine. The car sputtered, then came to life. I lost my moment as the automobile leapt forward out of its parking space. But I had learned my lesson: When chasing a questionable vehicle, get the license plate number! I stared at her beige New Jersey plate, shut my eyes, and memorized the mix of six letters and numbers.

"Awesome. Okay so, like, everybody say cheese." Pauli aimed his digital camera at the front entrance to the Windjammer, where the staff had gathered for our photo. Henry was swathed in a white apron and chef's hat; Honey, beaming, held a short stack of boxes; Enrico and Carmen stood arm in arm; Benny had a wise-guy grin; and I posed with what I hoped wasn't a scowl.

Pauli snapped shot after shot. Had us rearrange ourselves, had Henry remove his hat, had Honey abandon her boxes, had me try to smile. After twenty minutes the staff lost its pizzazz, so I suggested Pauli call it a day and evaluate what he had. We could always do another session later, I said to him under my breath.

"Very cool," he said as he clicked through his pictures, Honey hanging over his shoulder. "I think we totally crushed it."

I butted in. "Pauli, text them to me, okay? I'll check them out."

"Dot, you look kind of tired," Honey said, scrutinizing a picture of me.

Pauli nodded in agreement.

It had been a tiring kind of day. First the funeral and Walter's sing-along, then the appearance of the woman in green, then a quick stop at the repast—just long enough to sample the pecan Danish and watch Lola mollify Carlyle, who pouted by the punch table over who-knew-what—and then lunch at the Windjammer, where the staff almost outnumbered the customers. I was expected to look chipper and perky?

"You know this one's a good shot, but, like, who's that in the background?" Honey asked.

I squinted at the tiny frame. "That's the beer delivery guy standing at the bar."

"Like I can totally photoshop him out," Pauli said.

"Great idea." I ruffled his hair. He ducked and grinned.

I left Honey and Pauli chatting outside the Windjammer, and headed in to help Henry with the prep for tomorrow's football game. In the crunch of the funeral and website work, I hadn't focused on Bill's picnic. We had to organize burgers, fries, and sodas for thirty little Etonville athletes. Ordinarily this would be an extra burden for Henry; in fact, when I'd made the commitment the Windjammer was deep into the theme-food festival. But now, with so few customers, cooking cheeseburgers and fries was a welcome diversion. I agreed to join Henry in the morning to assist while Enrico and Benny handled a modified lunch menu.

Two hours later I sat in my back booth, kicked off the heels I'd been wearing since the funeral, and inspected some inventory sheets. Dinner was a bowl of Henry's homemade cream of asparagus soup. I transferred my attention from next week's menus and a list of potential vegetable dishes to a scrap of paper that I'd been doodling on. I wrote:

Antonio's curious behavior, Brianna's and Lola's conflicting stories on Antonio's health, Imogen's neighbor's cousin's report, the note left under my windshield, the mystery woman at the funeral (and her license plate number), and no trace of Antonio on the Internet before 1998 and after 2000 until 2013.

What did it all add up to?

I finished my soup and tucked the paper into my bag. I had to talk with Bill, despite my feelings about the brunette in Creston.

10

I picked my way delicately across the grassy strip that surrounded the Etonville High School football field. Everything got drenched with the morning's downpour, and muddy patches were visible where the green was sparse. With the temperature hovering in the sixties, I opted for my leather jacket and ankle boots. I might have done better with a raincoat and sneakers.

I checked my watch. Eleven fifteen. "I hope the rain holds off until at least one o'clock. That should give the kids time to eat lunch," I said to Enrico, who was hauling four dozen cheeseburgers and servings of fries in insulated food-delivery bags, stacked up on a hand truck. "Let's set up here."

Bill had placed two folding tables by the end-zone bleachers—away from the meager but passionate crowd of parents who had gathered to brave the weather and watch their kids do battle with a Youth Football team from Clifton, New Jersey. While I arranged food and eating utensils, Enrico made several trips to Henry's van for coolers filled with sodas.

"You can head back to the Windjammer, Enrico. I'll call when the picnic is nearly over."

"Miss Dodie, you like football?" he asked.

"Some. I used to go to games in college. I liked the atmosphere, you know, yelling for your team, celebrating afterwards."

Bill looked our way and waved me over.

"Have fun," Enrico said and winked.

Did everyone in Etonville think Bill and I might be an item? I sent Enrico on his way and walked toward the other end of the field. I remembered Saturday afternoons in the rain and cold, watching my college's football team lose to weak and strong schools alike. Despite the fun, it was an embarrassing time on the gridiron.

The officials called a time-out. Bill's kids stood in a huddle near the bench. They were damp, some bored and ready to call it a morning, some sidetracked by their parents or other kids, some fiddling with their helmets and cleats.

"Listen up, offense," Bill said, holding a dry-erase whiteboard covered with X's and O's. A few players snapped to. "We're going to run E21. The option. Remember?" Three or four nodded, two boys shook their heads. One sat down on his helmet. "Okay." He scribbled with a marker. "Wishbone formation. Sweep right. Zach, hand off to Jimmy here"—he grabbed the jersey of number 32—"but if the coverage breaks down, check down to Alvin." He pointed to number 44. "Got it?"

The quarterback, Zach, gave Bill a high five.

"Jimmy, wait for your blockers. Offensive line, let's see some holes out there. Let's play!" The team ran onto the field.

The score was seventeen to three, Etonville losing with five minutes left in the game.

"Maybe that play is a little complicated for them," I said and pulled my jacket around my midsection.

Bill looked at me as if I didn't really understand the finer points of X's and O's. "They're improving every game. I like to challenge them." He pointed to the offensive line. "We practiced all week."

When the referee whistled, the players got set, the center snapped the ball, and Zach took off with the halfback running right. He pitched the football to Jimmy, who turned in the wrong direction, and it landed in the arms of a defensive end, who ran forty yards for a touchdown.

Bill grunted and pulled his cap lower on his head.

"Don't worry about it," Bill said to Zach, whose mouth was full of French fries. "We'll work on the play action and pitching drills next week."

The kid grinned, cheeks bulging. "Can we do the shotgun?"

"Sure." He tousled Zach's hair.

Bill was good with them. Leading his team onto the field after a solid drubbing to shake hands in a display of good sportsmanship, giving them a post-game pep talk about how they were like a family, one for all and all for one, reminding them about Monday's practice, and guiding them to the picnic area, where they tore into the burgers and fries.

"Nice of you to treat them to this," I said.

"They're great kids."

"It must be tough fitting football practice into your schedule," I said.

"Yeah. It is. Especially since I'm helping out with the Creston thing."

"How's that going?" I asked lightly.

"Coming along," he said.

His expression became guarded, police chief–style.

Jimmy joined us. "Mrs. O'Dell, can we have seconds on the fries?"

"I think there's enough extras." I punched in the number to the Windjammer. It was time for Enrico to return.

"Thanks, Mrs. O'Dell," he shouted, and ran to spread the good news.

"Yeah, thanks, Mrs. O'Dell," Bill said, his lip curving.

My heart melted, almost erasing the image of him kissing the brunette in Creston. I forced my attention away from his laser-like eyes in order to concentrate on Antonio's death.

I bit into my burger. "You missed the funeral yesterday."

"I heard that it was a rather sedate affair for Etonville." He laughed.

I liked his laugh. "That's right. No costumes, no bizarre eulogy, although Walter did lead us in singing 'There's No Business—'"

"'—Like Show Business.' Yeah. Edna filled me in." Bill cleaned a bit of ketchup from his mouth. "So other than that, the service was uneventful?"

"Are you asking as the police chief or just an interested citizen?"

Bill looked puzzled. "Why would I need to ask as the PC?"

I knew I should tread carefully. Everyone considered the death a closed case and Bill hadn't shown any inclination to pursue Antonio's odd behavior.

"I just thought you might want to check out a few . . . loose ends," I said, hoping to pique his curiosity.

He leaned into me. "What do you mean, 'loose ends'? Antonio's late-night wandering?" He shook his finger gently in my face. "You have to keep your imagination in check, Mrs. O'Dell," he teased.

He was kissing-close. My face was hot. "Well . . . there are a few things I didn't imagine."

He stepped back. "Such as?"

"There was a strange woman at the funeral. I didn't recognize her. She came to the cemetery, and after everyone had *laid* a flower on Antonio's coffin, she kind of *threw* hers down. And then laughed as though she was taunting Antonio. Don't you think that's weird?" Before he could answer, I snatched a piece of paper from my bag. "I followed her into the parking lot and memorized her license plate number. Do you think you might check her out?"

Bill looked at the paper, then at me. "Let me get this straight. You want me to run a plate because a woman laughed?"

I could see he was incredulous. Of course, when you put it like that . . .

"Okay, that's not all." I took a breath. "One of the shampoo girls at Snippets has a neighbor whose cousin—"

"Oh no, not the Etonville rumor mill. Didn't we have enough of all that last time?"

"Maybe, but that rumor mill helped us answer some questions that led to an arrest."

Enrico appeared with his hand truck and started to pick up leftovers and trash.

"Look, Dodie, I know Antonio's death has been hard on the Windjammer. But you just have to give people space. They'll come back."

"But that's not everything." I dug into my bag to remove the note telling me to leave Antonio alone.

A crack of lightning zigzagged in the sky off to the west of Etonville. Heavy drops of water fell. "Dodie, sorry, I have to get the kids." Bill took off and herded the team out of the stadium and into the shelter of the locker room.

Enrico had packed up the coolers and paper goods and the two of us hurried to clear the field just as the deluge hit. By the time Enrico and I had flung ourselves into the front seat of the restaurant van, we were soaked, raindrops dripping off our faces. My boots were wet through to my socks, and water trickled down the front of my blouse.

We limped back to the Windjammer, unloaded the van, and I went home to dry out. Benny had offered to take my place in the evening, with Honey waiting tables. Though restaurant customers had dwindled in number, it was a Saturday night and the bar would still be busy. I accepted his offer.

I was still slightly chilled from the afternoon's dousing, so I lay on the sofa wrapped in a blanket; a towel, turban-like, swaddled my hair. I clutched the latest Cindy Collins mystery in one hand, a glass of chardonnay in the other. I sneezed. Uh-oh, I didn't have time for a cold.

I exchanged the wine for hot tea and sucked on a zinc tablet. I tried to distract myself with television, but nothing interested me. I logged into my computer and played a few games of solitaire. But beating myself was no fun. I'd have called Lola, but I knew she was at rehearsal. Carol had mentioned a family wedding in Morristown. I was restless.

The list of questions that I had scribbled down yesterday at the Windjammer begged to be investigated. I fished the scrap of paper out of my bag and ran through them. Any activity that directly involved Lola, Brianna, Imogen's neighbor's cousin, and the mystery woman were out of the question tonight. That left the Internet.

I opened my laptop and re-Googled Antonio Digenza, then added "+New York" as before. I was hoping for some miraculous intercession, that different links with new information would materialize. But no, the same links appeared. I clicked on a few, but I knew I was spinning my wheels.

My mind meandered . . . I wondered how Lola was doing at rehearsal, who knew their lines, were Carlyle and Walter speaking, was Tiffany still in the show, what silly theater games was Walter inflicting on the cast tonight; many of them started with "what if" and went downhill from there. What if your character was an animal? What if your character lived on a deserted island? What if your character found buried treasure?

I felt my neck tingle, goose bumps rose on my arms, and a "what if" thought popped up on my mental screen. What if Antonio did not die from a heart attack? What symptoms would mimic a heart attack? I Googled Web MD and found a Heart Disease Health Center that provided descriptions of the symptoms of coronary artery disease, a heart attack, heart valve disease, and heart arrhythmias. Basic indicators might be shortness of breath; dizziness; a choking feeling; sweating; nausea; discomfort in the chest, back, throat, and jaw areas; and weakness.

As I remembered, Antonio had been short of breath, then grabbed his throat, choked, turned red. As for the rest of the symptoms, I wasn't sure. They seemed awfully generic. I could think of a number of things that might cause dizziness, sweating, nausea, and discomfort. Thinking about the future of the Windjammer for one; sitting through an ELT rehearsal for another. By the time I finished the heart-issues websites, I was ready to walk out the door and get my cholesterol tested.

Antonio's heart certainly stopped, but did he have signs of heart disease that would have triggered an attack that led to the cardiac arrest? His doctor would know, but Brianna indicated he avoided doctors; Imogen's neighbor's cousin said he'd visited one recently.

My mind was racing: What if Antonio *had* died from something he ate or drank, but not something that originated in the Windjammer's kitchen or bar? If he died of something else, surely it would be discovered by the lab running the tests. Bill was correct: My powers of invention could get out of hand.

I was worn out from what-ifs and jumping to conclusions. A hot bath was in order, so I filled the tub, poured in a generous amount of lavender bubble bath, and settled in for a nice, fragrant soak. I was drifting off when my cell jangled and I jumped. I'd left it on the vanity out of reach, and now I debated. Should I spoil my nirvana just to hear someone try to sell me a new roof or a Life Alert system? My curiosity got the better of me. I stood up, flinging suds onto the bath mat, and grasped a bath towel. By the time I picked up the phone, the caller had hung up. I checked the voicemail and tapped the number.

"Hi, Dodie. Sorry I had to run off today. I had to take care of my team." Bill took a pause. "I know you're worried about the restaurant. Believe me, I understand. But law enforcement has taught me a few things, and one of them is that sometimes it's hard to accept the obvious. Even if we think there appear to be"—I could hear him struggle to avoid the word *evidence*—"things that can't be explained." He stopped. "By the way, the kids loved the picnic and wanted to know when we're having another one. Tell Henry his cheeseburgers were a hit with the nine- to eleven-year-old crowd."

He laughed and I could hear his eyes crinkle.

"Well, hope you're having a good night. I'll stop by the Windjammer this week just to prove that the food is safe. Bye now."

That was it? He'll stop by the Windjammer? The cell rang again and my mind was so full of spring and our almost-budding romance, that I answered, "Hi. Thanks for the voicemail!"

"What voicemail?" Lola asked.

"Oh. Sorry," I said, disappointed.

"Are you okay? What are you doing?"

"Taking a bubble bath until my phone . . . never mind. What's up? Are Carlyle and Walter on speaking terms?"

There was a loud crash in the background. ". . . you'd want to know."

"What? I can't hear you."

"Rehearsal's over. Are you up for some company?"

I sat on the edge of the tub and closed my eyes. Any hope of coasting into a gentle sleep was probably over. "Sure. I've got some chardonnay in the fridge."

Lola had kicked off her shoes and was stretched out on the sofa. I was in my recliner bundled up in my terry cloth robe, a gift from my great aunt Maureen. It came with some sage advice: *Darling, after a warm body, a terry cloth robe is the next best thing to cuddle up with on a cold night.* How right she'd been.

Lola and I were polishing off the remainder of the white wine with some semi-stale crackers and a half block of cheddar. I was patiently waiting for her to get to the reason for dropping by, but first she had to wade through the evening's saga.

"I had the entire rehearsal schedule laid out for the week, and then Walter decided that we needed to have a dress parade Friday—"

"At least it won't be a speed-through," I said, remembering that disaster.

Lola giggled. Then I giggled. Soon we were both snorting and whooping. "Could you even believe that night?"

"Abby in Romeo's lap and Carlyle stealing Penny's whistle." I hooted.

Lola frowned. "The actors are good sports up to a point. But I think everyone is just fed up and ready to have the play open." She took a drink of her wine. "It's such a shame. I had high hopes for this production."

"Hey, Lola, I've seen real disasters at the ELT turn into hits."

She eyed me over the rim of her glass. "I'm thinking of resigning as artistic director once the show's up."

She threatened to resign at least once a week. "Wait and see how things end up," I said. "So what were you trying to tell me on the phone?"

Lola bolted upright. "I almost forgot! Penny had just announced a break, and Carlyle and Walter were fighting over the hinges on the window seat so that the bodies, which are not going to be real bodies, of course, but dummies—"

"Lola, focus!"

She nibbled on a cracker. "I went to the office to pay some bills because you remember the accounting problems on the last show . . ."

Which was Lola's euphemism for Walter "borrowing" from the box office till.

"Okay, and . . . ?"

"I went to open the door, but could sense someone standing behind me. I kind of jerked around and dropped my file folder with papers. There was this man." Lola paused.

"Who was he?"

"I don't know. No one I'd ever seen at the theater," she said.

"What did he look like?"

"Average height with a stubbly beard and glasses and a baseball cap. I was startled at first, but he smiled and picked up my folder."

"Then what?"

"He asked me if I knew Antonio. And I said 'yes, of course.' That it was such a shame about his death. That we were so happy to have him as a guest director. Oh, I don't know, I think I just kind of rambled on."

"And what did he do while you were talking?" I asked.

"He just stood there and listened to me politely. Then I asked him if there was something I could do for him and he just smiled again and said no, that Antonio had been a friend and had mentioned the ELT." Lola finished off her wine.

"Did he leave?"

"Not right away. He asked me if he could stick his head in the theater and look around, and without thinking I said 'sure, go ahead.' I went into the office and did some work. By the time I went back into the theater he was walking out the door and saying good-bye. What do you make of it?"

"I don't know. By the way, I meant to tell you about the woman at the grave site," I said.

Lola listened to my description of the cemetery visitor, her jaw dropping when she heard about the flower on the coffin. "She actually laughed?"

"Yep," I said. "You know, if we counted Brianna and the mystery woman at the funeral, the guy at the theater was the third stranger with a connection to Antonio to just show up."

"Brianna was his ex-wife and it sounds like they still had a good relationship."

Brianna. I'd already made up my mind to pay her a visit. I planned to give her a call in the morning and see if I could meet with her. I also decided to keep my Internet trolling on the subject of cardiac arrest to myself for the moment; no sense in alarming Lola unnecessarily if all of my digging came to nothing.

"Maybe you could nose around and see if anyone else talked with the mystery man," I said.

"Penny might have noticed him," Lola said. "I wonder how he and Antonio knew each other." She bit her lip. "I wonder what else we don't know about Antonio."

11

Sunday afternoon I backed my Metro out of my driveway and noticed the gas tank was only a quarter full. I'd need to stop at some point. I cruised down State Route 53 and entered the Garden State Parkway. All signs of yesterday's gray gloom had disappeared and left behind sunny skies and a light breeze, temps in the low seventies.

Rumson was about fifty miles away, courtesy of MapQuest. My old stomping grounds. I was happy to have any excuse to visit. I reached Brianna on her cell phone, and was deliberately cagey. "I'm planning to be in the area this afternoon and wondered if you'd mind speaking to me for a few minutes."

She was gracious, agreed to meet me at five. "Stop by my shop. I'm in the office catching up on orders today." If she was surprised by my request, it was well hidden.

My heart lifted as I crossed the Driscoll Bridge. The shore! The air was saltier, with seagulls wheeling back and forth against the blue sky. I could feel myself unwind. I left the parkway and followed my Genie's directions, driving up and down various streets in the borough. Rumson was located on a picturesque peninsula, bordered on two sides by the Navesink and Shrewsbury Rivers and a stone's throw to the ocean. Homes were worth millions in this picture-postcard of a town.

I arrived at 27 River Road and pulled into a metered space. Brianna had told me the door would be locked but to knock and she'd hear me. I glanced down the street. An outdoor café, upscale boutiques, a bookstore, and, at the end of the block, a boat dock. Downtown Rumson was hopping today.

The storefront was inscribed with Flowers by Kincaid in an art deco font. I rapped lightly. Brianna appeared at an entryway in the back of the store and briskly walked to the door. She was dressed fashionably in black trousers and a pink blouse, and wore a diamond pendant on a chain around her neck.

"Hello," she said. "Please come in."

"Thanks for seeing me." I entered and inhaled the fragrance of cut flowers and plants in containers spread throughout the shop. "It smells wonderful in here."

"Autumn flowers are just coming into their own." She pointed to a few pots. "Roses and mums. Of course, carnations and some left-over peonies."

"They're all beautiful."

She pinched a dead leaf off a mum, moved a vase of roses to the counter. "It's nice in here on Sunday. All of the beauty and none of the traffic."

"Thanks for seeing me on such short notice. I hope I'm not keeping you from your work."

"I'm due for a break. Would you like a cup of coffee?"

"Sure."

I followed her to the office in back—a bright, airy room with windows on two sides that allowed for both light and cross-ventilation. She poured two cups of coffee from a pot that was half-full, and gestured to a chair opposite her desk. "Please."

I accepted the coffee gratefully. I was feeling drowsy in the warm sunlight and needed a jolt of caffeine. "I'm sorry I didn't get a chance to speak with you at Antonio's funeral."

"I was first in and first out, I'm afraid," she said. "It was a hectic day here and one of my staff was out sick."

"I can appreciate staff issues. I manage the Windjammer restaurant."

"Where the food festival took place," she said over the rim of her cup.

"Yes. Unfortunately."

"I heard that the medical examiner's report indicated a heart attack. True?"

"Yes, well, a preliminary report. It was cardiac arrest. But I don't have any knowledge of Antonio's heart condition. I mean, what caused his heart to stop."

"I see. So you're spending the afternoon down here?"

"I'm a born and bred shore girl. It took Hurricane Sandy to drive me up north," I said ruefully. "I miss it."

"I would, too," she said.

I needed to get to the point. "Brianna, I'm wondering about a few things having to do with Antonio."

"Oh?"

I didn't know how much I could trust her, but I had little choice. She was the only link available to Antonio's past. "I happened to be checking Antonio's history. Research for the theater," I added when she frowned. "I found some East Coast reviews from 1998 to 2000 and then nothing until 2013. But I was curious about his career before 1998. And between 2000 and 2013. I couldn't find any mention of him on the Internet for those years." I smiled in what I hoped was an open, sociable manner.

"Why not just check his résumé? I'm sure the theater received one when they hired him."

Why hadn't I thought of that? "Good idea. I was just curious."

"In the nineties he was in Los Angeles doing a variety of things. As all young directors do on their way up. As I said, we were separated by the late nineties. I haven't seen him much in recent years."

This line of questioning felt like a dead end and I had the feeling I was overstaying my welcome. I stood up and hitched my bag over my shoulder. "By the way, did you notice a young woman at the funeral in jeans and a green jacket? She was the last one to place her flower on Antonio's casket."

Brianna studied me. "Are you looking into Antonio's death?"

"No. I was just struck by the woman's . . . demeanor. She was less than mournful, you might say."

Brianna shook her head. "I didn't see anyone by that description." She crossed her arms. "If the authorities are investigating what happened to Antonio, I would like to know," she said firmly.

"Of course." I backed up to the door, pivoted, and brushed against a showy evergreen plant with gorgeous pink flowers.

Brianna stepped to my side and pushed the pot into a corner. "White oleander. Mostly grows in California and out West. I have a customer who loves them." She smiled and opened the front door.

I dropped into the café two doors down from the flower shop for a bite of dinner before I got on the road. Tomato soup that could not touch Henry's and a grilled cheese that was too brown on one side and too mushy on the other. I contemplated my disappointing conversation with Brianna. Nothing new, except for the fact that she handled poisonous plants. Surprisingly, she neglected to mention how dangerous white oleander bushes could be. Several years ago I visited my younger brother Andy in San Diego. One day I reached out to pick a flower from a striking bush in his neighbor's yard. Andy slapped my hand and pulled me away. *Stay away from the oleander. Every bit of it is poisonous*, he'd said.

The sun was setting as I scanned the side streets for a gas station with reasonable prices. On the outskirts of town I found one, requested a fill-up, and rapped the steering wheel as a young man pumped my gas. He made me think of Pauli and the pictures he had taken for the website, which I had yet to see. Hmm . . . Pauli! I'd bet he could find something on Antonio's past.

I forked over thirty dollars and drove off. Being Sunday evening, traffic was light on the access road leading to the Garden State Parkway. I was a mile or so from my entrance when the car behind me seemed to speed up, then jam on its brakes. I supposed it wanted to go around me, so I slowed down to let the driver pass. The car dropped back and I focused on the road ahead, keeping one eye out for the parkway entrance. Again, the car zoomed up, nearly rear-ending me, its bright lights blinding in my rearview mirror. I couldn't see the make or model and definitely could not see anyone in the front seat. I needed to get away from this jerk, so I hit the gas. The automobile kept pace. My speedometer needle touched sixty, way too fast for a two-lane road, even in this sparsely populated area.

I kept my foot on the accelerator, praying for the sudden appearance of a flashing red light, the entrance to the parkway, or an open, well-lit store. In that order. My hands were clammy on the steering wheel; I felt a lump of anxiety sitting squarely in my chest.

I could see a road sign up ahead signaling the entrance to the GSP. I glanced in the rearview mirror again. The car had crept forward until its front bumper was practically touching my Metro. Then it grazed my car. My heart jumped into my throat and I floored the gas pedal, determined to reach the parkway before my pursuer could bump me again.

I raced onto the highway as the car dashed past me; I moved into the middle lane where the stream of traffic was thickest and where I felt safest. My hands were shaking, but I was okay. My Metro and I headed home, never straying beyond the speed limit. I checked all of the locks on my doors and windows and lay down on the bed. Was I being followed?

I was still a little disturbed from yesterday's encounter with the menacing car, but my Metro had only a minor scratch on the rear bumper. Of course, it had had a previous run-in with a fireplug on a warm summer night about five years ago when I'd lent it to my then-boyfriend Jackson. But that's another story . . .

I had a full agenda Monday: first a trip to Snippets—before the Windjammer opened—to talk to Imogen and get information on her neighbor's cousin; then a visit to the Etonville Police Department during my break; and finally, a meeting with Pauli after school.

I had just enough time to grab a caramel macchiato from Coffee Heaven before Snippets opened for business. I sat at the counter and Jocelyn brought me my regular.

She leaned into me confidentially. "I hear things are tough for the Windjammer these days. Too bad. This town can be so stubborn."

"Hey, why don't you come by for dinner? Henry's making caramel chicken. Really great. With a vinegar soy sauce to cut the sweetness—"

"Sorry, hon. I have plans tonight. Maybe next week."

I felt like I'd been dumped by a date as I watched Jocelyn make the rounds with her coffeepot, which made me think of Bill, which made me think of Antonio, which made me think of Snippets. I paid and got up.

The salon, having just opened its doors, was quiet. "Hey, Carol. Like a morgue in here," I said.

"The best part of the day for me." Carol cackled and took messages off the voicemail while she checked the day's schedule.

"When is Imogen due in?"

"Any minute. Why?"

"I'd like to ask about her neighbor's cousin who—"

"—works for the doctor? You think she might know something about Antonio? Because you know, nobody in Snippets thinks it was just a heart attack."

I knew. "They all still think it was something from the food festival, right?"

Carol nodded. "Well, yes. All except the Banger sisters."

I held my breath. "What do they think?"

"Anxiety over the show."

"If everyone who had anxiety over this show died, we'd be holding funerals every day," I said.

The chimes over the front door tinkled. It was Imogen, fully studded, one side of her head shaved, the other side sporting hair over her ear.

"New do," I murmured to Carol.

"Every week. This one's the most extreme," she whispered back. "Hi, Imogen."

Imogen dropped her bag on a seat in the waiting-area alcove. "I'm bushed."

"Already? It's not even nine and you haven't started working yet," Carol said.

"Big night last night." Imogen plopped into a chair in a cutting station.

"Imogen, you remember Dodie O'Dell? From the Windjammer?" Carol nodded to me and returned her attention to phone messages.

"Hi. I wanted to ask you a question," I said.

She squinted at me. "I washed your hair last week."

"Right. I'd like—"

"You know, everybody's wrong about that director."

Imogen caught me off guard. "They are?"

"I mean, like, I saw him drinking out of his own cup when he walked up to the bar that day. Maybe he was out bar-hopping before he showed up," she said and tossed her head, flipping her hair out of her eyes. "I mean, like, sure I think he probably died from something he ate or drank but, like I said, he had his own cup." She smiled proudly as if she'd solved the entire mystery.

"Come to think of it, I saw him with a cup in his hand, too, before Benny poured his wine from the bar." I felt a bolt of excitement run up my spine.

"Uh-huh." Imogen stuffed a piece of gum in her mouth as the front door tinkled again. The first customer of the day.

"I understand your neighbor's cousin works at a doctor's office in

Bernridge and she saw Antonio a few days before he died?" Bernridge was another, mostly working-class, community next door. Smaller than Creston but larger than Etonville.

"Sure." Imogen stood and walked to the back of the salon.

I followed her. "Did she say why he was there?"

"My neighbor?"

"The cousin," I said.

"Nuh-uh. Just that he came in to see the doctor." Imogen slipped into an apron.

"Do you know the name?" I asked calmly, trying to control my enthusiasm.

"The cousin? Tess."

"The doctor," I said patiently.

She thought for a moment. "Something Chinese. Sounded like 'shoe.'"

I considered. I didn't want to set off any gossip alarms around town so I decided to play it cool and resist asking any further questions. I'd find the doctor on my own. "Thanks."

Carol signaled to Imogen to shampoo a customer. I waved good-bye.

I unlocked the front door of the Windjammer, turned on some lights, put on the coffee. I had half an hour before Henry and Honey would show, and I agreed with Carol—having a moment to myself at the top of the day to focus my mind was a treat. A pounding on the back door interrupted my reverie. I grabbed my clipboard, admitted the delivery guy, and began to check off items: squash for Henry's soup today; zucchini for tonight's special; onions, tomatoes, and corn for a handful of other dishes. I searched through the crates.

"Where's the tilapia? And we're thirty pounds short on the beef tenderloins. Again," I said.

The kid pushed his Yankees cap farther back on his head. "Look, I only deliver. I don't decide what goes *in* the delivery."

I scrawled my name on the packing slip. "Tell your boss to expect a call," I said sternly.

The driver assumed a "yada yada yada" expression and left.

Now I had to face Henry and redo the day's menu. He hated change under the best of circumstances; since the food festival he was more inflexible than usual and cooking on autopilot. Without the customers raving over his specials, what was the point of racking his brain to create tantalizing dishes? I couldn't listen to another rant about La Famiglia. I'll bet they were swamped with customers.

I was midway through sorting the onions and potatoes into vegetable bins in the pantry when Henry and Honey strolled into the restaurant. "Hey, you two," I said.

Henry grunted, Honey flipped her sunglasses off and perched them atop her head. "Dot, I can't work late tonight. I have a date."

Poor guy. "That's nice. Carmen and I can cover."

Honey eyed me suspiciously. I ignored her. "Henry, we're all set with the zucchini pasta for dinner."

He put on an apron, poured himself a cup of coffee, and listlessly headed for the refrigerator. "Whatever."

A week ago he was keen to introduce a lower carb, gluten-free vegetable dish: zucchini noodles topped with fresh basil pesto. Etonville was ready for a counterpoint to the heavier meat-and-potatoes meals that we served. Henry agreed and we put it on the menu. But now . . .

He was rummaging around in the seafood. "Dodie? Where's the—"

"Tilapia. Delivery mistake. We'll need to substitute." Panko-crusted tilapia was now officially off the menu for tonight.

The refrigerator door slammed. Henry trudged past me out the back door to the herb garden. He must really be frustrated. No threats to shut down the Windjammer, his default position whenever he was overwhelmed.

Lunch was as slow as it had been all week. Only the Etonville Police Department was as loyal as ever. "Make that two squash soups, a spinach salad, and one tuna on rye," said Edna.

I wrote the order up and sent it back to the kitchen via Honey, who had been filing her nails and talking on her cell simultaneously. "So, the chief's into squash soup," I said, making change from Edna's twenty and a five.

"Nope. It's for me and Suki. Ralph's on his own."

"And the chief?" I asked.

"Gone. Probably on a 211 in Creston."

"Let me guess. That's a robbery, right?" I said.

"Bingo," she said. "Confidentially, I think they're closing in on the thieves."

"Yeah?" Good news for me. If Creston was off Bill's radar, not to mention the mysterious brunette, maybe Antonio—and I—could get back on. "I guess that means there's been a break in the case."

"You didn't hear it from me," Edna said and stuffed change into her wallet.

"10-4."

12

My heart sank a little as I approached the Municipal Building. The "Reserved for Police Chief" parking spot was empty. *They can't catch that cat burglar too soon for my taste.* I resolutely opened the front door, coming face-to-face with Suki Shung.

"Oh, Officer Shung."

"Suki," she said, with a mix of serenity and solemnity, no doubt the side effect of her being a Buddhist cop. "Are you looking for the chief?"

"I was." I hesitated.

She slanted her head, her blunt-cut black hair swinging to the right side of her face. "Can I help?"

"Are you on your way out?"

"I have time." She turned without another word, leading me past the dispatch window.

"Great soup today," Edna said as Suki and I disappeared around a corner.

In the outer office, Suki took a seat behind her keyboard and monitors and placed a chair opposite. I sat down.

"I'm not sure where to begin. I did speak with the chief, but he didn't think there was anything to follow up on. But now I'm sitting here with information that someone should have." I waited.

"Go on," she said as if I hadn't just rattled on without saying much of anything. I guessed that was the Zen in her.

"It's about—"

"Antonio Digenza," she finished for me.

"How did you know?"

She smiled mystically. "The chief mentioned that you had concerns."

"Oh. So I guess he told you about—"

"Antonio's disappearances."

"And his—"

"Ex-wife's claims that he had some unhealthy habits, while he told Lola Tripper that he had the heart of a twenty-something."

I slumped in my seat. Suki more or less took the starch out of my opening salvo. "Well, there's more. At Antonio's funeral there was a woman who looked as if she was happy about his death and I took down her license plate number. I gave it to the chief."

Suki nodded and continued to gaze at me.

"And last night I was coming home from Rumson . . ."

She waited while I paused.

"Visiting a friend." Brianna's name stuck in my throat for some reason. "A car followed me onto the parkway. It actually bumped my bumper."

"It was tailgating?"

"Yes. Well, no. It wasn't just driving too closely to me. I think the car was stalking me."

Her face was still a blank. "And you think it had something to do with Antonio's death?"

My information sounded flimsy at best.

I produced the note encouraging me to leave Antonio alone, in its plastic baggie. "I found it on my windshield Friday night."

Suki took the note and studied both sides. "Friday?" she asked. Her expression shifted from "om" to OMG.

"I had planned to show the note to Bi—Chief Thompson at the football game Saturday, but the rain came, the kids needed chaperoning, and Enrico and I had to clean up the picnic." I couldn't admit that I wanted to deliver it in person and prod Bill into action. "It might be a prank."

"We can have it analyzed. I'll make certain the chief sees it." Suki's eyes drifted to a clock on the wall.

There didn't seem to be any point in mentioning Antonio visiting a doctor or a strange man dropping by the theater to see where he worked. All of my evidence was circumstantial. "Thanks for your time."

"I'll tell the chief you came by."

* * *

I trekked back to the Windjammer, glad for the fifteen-minute walk to clear my head in the brisk air. I tugged my jacket collar up around my ears. Since my conversation with Suki had been so efficient—or futile, depending on one's point of view—I had a half hour of break time before Pauli arrived to work on the restaurant website. Lola might be at the theater now; it seemed as though she was there twenty-four/seven these days.

The lobby of the ELT was empty but for a stack of plywood and two-by-fours that stretched from the box office to the entrance of the theater making it difficult to navigate. I knocked on the office door. "Lola?"

I peeked in. Two desks faced each other, one piled with props and costume pieces, the other, no doubt Lola's, neatly covered with stacks of posters and programs. I picked up a program. Antonio received the directing credit on the cover, but the inside page recognized the assistance of Carlyle and Walter. I skimmed the cast list, crew, acknowledgments—including the Windjammer, bless Lola—and turned to the back page of bios. Antonio's head shot was the same one that had appeared in the *Etonville Standard*. He was young and gorgeous. I supposed this was how he'd looked when he married Brianna. I read his bio, short and to the point. It listed plays that he had directed off-off-Broadway, and a handful of regional productions at small professional theaters in upstate New York, Pennsylvania, and Connecticut. But nothing in Los Angeles or New Jersey, until now.

"Can someone get this wood out of here?" Lola yelled from the lobby.

A muffled voice responded.

"I don't care if the door falls off its hinges and the stairs collapse. I have a PR session with the *Etonville Standard* in one hour and I need the lobby emptied!"

Lola came in the door, shook her head. I'd never seen her quite so disheartened, not even when Walter was a person of interest in the murder of Jerome Angleton. Her blond hair was yanked into a frizzled ponytail and her cotton blouse looked slept-in. "I am at my wit's end." Her face crumpled.

"Can I help?"

"Can you drag a dozen two-by-fours to the stage?" she said.

"Unusual place to deliver lumber," I said.

"The loading dock is covered with drying window frames and the stage floor has furniture stacked all over it, so Penny had them dumped out here." She blew a strand of stray hair off her forehead. "JC insists the staircase needs to be reinforced and the front door is too flimsy."

"Sounds like *Romeo and Juliet*, when he wanted to go a little overboard on the balcony." JC was used to building the real thing, not simulated scenery.

"If it wasn't for this interview, I'd head next door for a drink," she said. "I'm sorry to be such a grouch."

"Hey, I get it." I placed the program on its pile.

"They look nice, yes?" Lola asked.

"They look super. I was reading Antonio's bio. Doesn't seem to be anything from his younger days. You know, where he went to school, acting gigs . . ."

Lola picked up a playbill and turned to the back page. "I didn't notice. I had one of the business crew summarize his résumé." She frowned. "You're right. These are all shows from the last fifteen years or so."

The last thing Lola needed now was to be distracted by my digging into Antonio's background. "Maybe he didn't have a career before that. A late bloomer." Of course, Brianna had said he was in Los Angeles doing the things all young directors do on their way up the ladder of artistic success.

Lola's cell jingled. I stood up to go.

"Hello? Oh, yes. Earlier? You want to come in half an hour?" There was a note of alarm in her voice. "Fine," she said. "No problem."

Lola ended the call and let out a massive scream. Penny came running in from the street, just off work at the post office, still in uniform. "What's the matter? Who's hurt? I've got it." She stood in the doorway, legs spread, hands on hips, ready for battle.

"Empty the lobby, please," Lola pleaded, pulling her hair out of its elastic band and tucking in her blouse.

"Go get pretty," I said. "I'll help Penny."

Lola nodded gratefully and ran out of the office.

"Thanks, O'Dell, but I have actors on crew today."

I followed Penny into the lobby and watched as she ordered two cast members—the policemen I identified from the food festival—to haul the lumber into the theater.

Penny checked off their names on her ever-present clipboard. "See you, O'Dell."

"Penny, I have a question . . ."

"Yeah?" She pushed a pencil behind one ear.

"You pretty much notice everything that goes on around here?"

She crowed. "Nothing gets by me, O'Dell."

"I didn't think so. You being the stage manager and all. Do you remember seeing a stranger in the theater Saturday night? Lola mentioned a guy with a scruffy beard in a ball cap."

Penny smirked. "Like I would miss seeing some guy who wasn't a member of the ELT?"

"So you did see him?" I asked.

"Duh."

"Did you happen to talk with him?"

Penny shoved her glasses up her nose. "Uh-huh."

"Who was he?" I asked eagerly.

"Friend of Antonio's. Actor from his New York days."

"Why did he come to the theater?" I asked.

"O'Dell, there's some things about theater you don't get," she said assertively.

"Like what?" I already knew about theater time versus real time from Penny's previous lectures on protocol.

"Theater people stick together. When something happens to one of them, they don't abandon ship." She nodded wisely.

Huh? "So the stranger . . ."

"Ed."

"Ed . . . he came to . . . express his sympathy for the Etonville Little Theatre 'ship' because his friend, the director, had passed away?"

"Yeah."

"Wow. Nice of Ed. Maybe he'll come to see *Arsenic and Old Lace*," I said.

Penny snickered. "O'Dell, you're funny. He's a pro. Doesn't have time for community theater."

"Probably in a show in New York."

"Yep. Gotta go."

I tucked the information about Ed into my mental file folder on Antonio's death. Maybe they were theater friends from the beginning of Antonio's career, before he met Lola and Brianna.

Carol and Pauli were sitting at the bar when I walked into the Windjammer, Pauli sucking down a soda and texting, Carol glancing at her watch.

"Hey. Sorry I'm late. Lola was in a dither next door and I . . ." I paused. "What is it?"

Carol grinned like the cat who ate the canary. "I have to get back to Snippets, but I wanted to deliver the news in person."

I looked to Pauli. He just shrugged and brought up the Windjammer website on his laptop.

"I've solved your problem, at least for one night," Carol said.

"Yeah?" Exactly which problem was she referring to? There was the Windjammer, Antonio's death, Bill—

"My shampoo girl—"

"Imogen?" I asked.

"The other one. Rita."

"With the tattoo . . . ?" I asked.

"That's right. She's getting married next weekend and, ta-da! She's having her rehearsal dinner at the Windjammer," Carol said triumphantly.

"She is?" I was flabbergasted.

Carol spoke sotto voce. "She was going to have it at La Famiglia, but I convinced her to come here."

"How did you manage that?"

"I gave her a raise." Carol laughed heartily.

"A payoff?"

"Basically. But it's for a good cause!"

I gave her a kiss and a hug. "You're a doll. Wait till I tell Henry."

"He already knows. I had her call him this afternoon. I have to run. Pauli, I'll see you at home, okay?" She eased off the stool, mussed his hair affectionately, and left.

Pauli dipped his head and began scrolling through the Windjammer links.

"So we're going to add a staff photo and blurbs on last year's theme-food events and Saturday's football picnic." I pulled a sheet of paper out of my bag. "I scribbled a few things here."

Pauli read the paper. "Awesome."

"I don't think I'm ready for a blog. But I like the gallery of pictures idea."

While Pauli went to work, I gave Benny a thumbs-up sign and headed for the kitchen. I figured Henry had to be happy about Saturday night, but I had no idea how happy. He was slicing beef for his classic Stroganoff while Enrico browned mushrooms and onions in butter. And he was humming. Henry was actually humming! I hadn't seen him in this kind of a mood since . . . well, since a while.

"Great news about the rehearsal dinner," I said. I stuck my face close to the pan. "Mmmm."

Henry nodded. Enrico grinned.

"Dottie, I can't find the carrots and celery." Honey, in charge of tonight's garden salad, held a kitchen knife and cutting board. She'd taken to lengthening my name lately from Dot to Dottie, another version I disliked. But I was too giddy about the impending rehearsal dinner to give it much attention. I crooked my index finger and led her to the vegetable bins in the refrigerator. All she had to do was look under the asparagus.

Benny stuck his head into the kitchen. "You're not going to believe who just walked in."

"I give. Who?"

He motioned for me to join him. I glanced out. The Banger sisters were seated at the table in the corner, from which vantage point they could keep an eye on the whole restaurant.

"Things are looking up." I sauntered past him into the dining room. "Evening, ladies," I said to the sisters. "It's nice to see you in here again."

"Hello, Dodie," one said.

"We are adventurous, don't you know," said the other.

"Aha. Well, I'm sure you'll find something you like on tonight's menu."

"What's safe?" one asked innocently.

"Everything," I answered politely.

"Oh, don't worry," said her sister. "We've taken precautions."

They both bobbed their heads.

I was afraid to ask. "Precautions . . . ?"

One of them pulled out a sheaf of papers. "Our last wills and testaments." They smiled and picked up their menus.

Geez.

13

It was comforting to have a few regulars back in the Windjammer. Even if they were the Banger sisters, cautiously picking through their beef Stroganoff.

Pauli was gobbling up an order of French fries, adding my new text, and editing the gallery of photos. I browsed the staff pictures, looking for the warmest, friendliest grouping. One or two fit the bill.

"I think this one is best. Everybody is sort of smiling. And the delivery guy is gone from the background. The magic of technology," I said. "How's your class going?"

"I'm into the second one. Databases and Internet searches."

My fingers beat a tattoo on the table between us. "Remember when you said everybody could be found on the Internet?"

"Yeah. We're like doing some cool things with missing persons sites and stuff."

"What if someone doesn't pop up?" I asked quietly.

He stopped typing on the keyboard and looked up at me. "Totally not possible. Now, anyway." He leaned in. "Is this, like, about that . . . other thing . . . you were kinda asking about . . . like back then?"

"Can you keep a secret?"

"The first rule of digital forensics—"

"Confidentiality. Got it. So I'm interested in finding out about the director. The one who died at the food festival."

His eyes lit up. "Awesome." Then narrowed. "What'd he do?"

"Nothing like that," I said hastily. "I'm just curious. I found some things about him from recent years but nothing much from the last decade or before the late 1990s. No mention of shows he directed, or classes or workshops or anything."

Pauli shrugged. "Maybe he wasn't working then."

"Maybe. But he would have been in his thirties and forties. Too old not to have some kind of a track record."

He thought. "Are you spelling his name right?"

"Antonio D-i-g-e-n-z-a. I found other Digenzas but they're not our Antonio."

Pauli snapped his laptop shut. "Maybe he changed his name." He jammed it into his backpack.

Of course. Writers did it. Actors did it. Why not directors?

I bent over the tabletop and kissed Pauli on the top of his hank of brown hair. "You're a genius!"

He blushed and whipped his hoodie over his head.

I planned to take my scheduled day off tomorrow. Benny wanted the extra shifts and the restaurant traffic was still sluggish. "Want to do a little Internet sleuthing at my house?" I asked. "What are you doing after school tomorrow?"

"I have my online class from three thirty to five. I could come after."

"Great. Tell your mom you'll have dinner with me, okay?"

"Sweet."

"We'll keep this just between us for now?" I said.

He swiped his hair to one side and saluted me impishly. It made me think of my old friend Jerome . . .

At nine o'clock I helped Carmen reset tables. At the bar, a couple was eating burgers, and three solos were drinking alone. It would be at least another hour before the Etonville Little Theatre crowd might stop in for a drink. Depended on how badly rehearsal had gone.

I sat down in my back booth with a seltzer and next week's menu and inventories. I reminded myself to remind Henry to call Rita from Snippets to confirm the menu for the rehearsal dinner. It was only one night, but a group reservation at this point was manna from heaven. I pulled my hair back and secured it into a ponytail. I felt sticky from the day's efforts and fantasized about a warm bubble bath. I closed my eyes and smiled.

"Hope it's a good one," Bill said.

My eyes fluttered open. He was a sight for sore eyes—out of uniform in crisp chinos, a white dress shirt, smelling great. I felt grimy and sweaty and self-conscious.

"H-hi," I stuttered.

"Looked like you were having a terrific daydream." His eyes crinkled and his mouth curved up on the left side.

"Not really." I casually eased the elastic band from my ponytail and ran several fingers through my tousled locks. "Just planning my day off tomorrow."

"Lucky you. May I?" He gestured to the bench opposite me.

"Sure."

I collected my papers and placed them in a pile on the seat.

"Is the kitchen still open?"

"Absolutely." His blue eyes had hypnotized me. I sat there paralyzed.

Fortunately, Benny had watched Bill enter and now appeared with a menu. "Hi, Chief. What can I get you?"

Bill decided on a glass of red wine and the Stroganoff. "Business picked up yet?"

"Not really. But we do have a rehearsal dinner coming up," I said.

"For the theater?"

"For a wedding party."

"Oh." He folded his hands on the table and leaned back.

"How's the case in Creston?" I asked.

"Coming along," he said. "I can't say any more, you understand."

"I guess the police department over there is happy to have you on board."

"Chief Harmon's a good guy. I'm happy to help out."

The brunette with whom he shared a PDA moment appeared before my eyes. "I guess they have a large staff?"

"Larger than Etonville. Nice guys. And women."

I'll bet.

Benny brought his wine and dinner and Bill began to eat immediately, as if it was his first meal all day. "I spoke with Suki."

Now that I finally had his attention, I wasn't sure how to respond. "She told you I dropped by?"

"Yep." He took a bite of beef. "Why didn't you show me that note earlier?"

"I intended to Saturday, but with the storm and the kids and the picnic . . . I thought it might be a joke."

"You did?" he said skeptically, his stare captivating enough to raise my heart rate.

"Well . . . maybe someone knows I have questions about Antonio's death."

"Uh-huh."

"What do you think?" I asked politely.

"Look, Dodie, I don't know if it was someone fooling around or whatever. I do know *you* don't think it was a joke. I'll have it checked out."

"That's good."

"And what's this about a car following you on the parkway?"

"On the access road. It followed me for a while, tapped me, so I speeded up. Then I got on the parkway."

He frowned, looking concerned. "You do have a way of attracting . . . trouble."

I could feel myself bristling. "It's my fault a car was stalking me?"

"Stalking? Of course not. If that's what happened."

"What would you call it?" I asked, a trifle too energetically. I saw Benny look up from his crossword puzzle.

"Did the car actually hit you or was it just travelling too fast too closely? Maybe you put on the brakes and it had no choice—"

"You don't believe me, do you? This feels like Jerome's death all over again." Last time it had taken Bill a while before he was willing to trust my instincts and my evidence.

Bill placed his fork on his plate. "What's that supposed to mean?"

I plunged in. "I think someone followed me. *And* I think Antonio's disappearing act was very weird. *And* I don't think the note was a prank."

"Look, I'm sorry, but you know you have an—"

"—overactive imagination."

We sat in silence. After a moment Bill pulled out his wallet. "Time for me to go home."

"For what it's worth, I think the woman in green at the funeral was very suspicious. And why would a complete stranger who claimed to know Antonio show up at the theater just to take a look around?" I was on a roll and probably saying too much.

"What are you talking about?" He looked genuinely perplexed.

"Never mind." I took his check and cash and stood up.

"I'll let you know about the note. If there are any useable prints, the lab guys will find them."

"Thanks." I studied his money as though I'd never seen two twenty-dollar bills before.

"Oh. I forgot this." He withdrew a pleated piece of paper from his pocket and laid it on the table. "The lady in green."

I blinked. "You traced the license plate number?"

"I do listen to what you say, you know. Contrary to what you think," he said softly.

I stared at the name on the paper: Regan Digenza. "What?"

"A sister, a cousin. Someone in the family who did not take kindly to his life or death maybe. You see, given her name, there's a logical explanation for her behavior."

I was stunned. I knew nothing about Antonio's family other than the fact that Lola had said she thought they—whoever they were—lived on the West Coast. Neither Bill nor I had any idea what was logical.

"Thanks," I mumbled and picked up the slip of paper.

"Hey, I know things are little stressful here now." He glanced around the restaurant. "Business will pick up. You'll see."

My heart sank. I think I botched it with him. Again.

I slept in and dreamed of hordes of people fighting to get into the Windjammer. If only. I awoke in a cold sweat, relieved to be in my bed. I reran my conversation with Bill last night. He was sympathetic to the whims of my creative illusions, up to a point. It was clear he didn't see any reason to pursue Antonio's death as anything out of the ordinary. I had cashed out my goodwill account with the note and the license plate; I was now on my own, at least until I had something more substantial to present to him.

I hopped out of bed and into the shower. As the warm water splashed off my face and neck, I ran through my day's agenda. I had decided that the only way to tie up loose ends was to manipulate the strings myself. With Pauli coming later, I had the day to explore a few matters—Regan Digenza and the doctor in Bernridge. I ran a brush through my hair, stepped into a fresh pair of jeans, and tugged on a warm, fleecy pullover. I made a cup of coffee and rye toast—I intended to avoid Coffee Heaven today and circumvent the risk of running into Bill.

I powered up my laptop and parked myself at the kitchen table. Who was Regan and did she have a more visible Internet presence

than Antonio? As I sipped coffee, I typed in her name and hit Enter.
I was prepared to have to dig around. Not necessary. A handful of
links with Regan Digenza in the top line came up immediately. I
clicked on the first one: LinkedIn. There was no extensive profile,
only a listing of positions and a picture. It was my lady in green, all
right. Her hair was a different color—brown instead of black—but
her expression hinted of the disdain she'd demonstrated at Antonio's
grave site. Her profile indicated she'd held a series of jobs—a casino
dealer in Las Vegas and, more recently, in Atlantic City. I scrutinized
the photo. Regan looked to be in her midthirties, posed at the entrance to a commercial building inside a revolving glass door. A
hotel or casino?

Another link referred to a newspaper article revealing that she
had been part of a group of casino workers who won a $100,000 lot-
tery in Nevada. Nice. I scrolled down a few links and stopped at one
that mentioned her work in a web series that played on YouTube. An
actress and a casino dealer. Regan was versatile!

I clicked on the last link and watched a three-minute episode of a
series called *On the Clock*, where a handful of actors, including
Regan, ran around a stage throwing cream pies at each other while a
guy timed them with a stop watch. I sat back in my chair. What to
make of her? Other than the fact that she seemed to lead a colorful
life, I had no information on her connection to Antonio.

My cell jingled. I checked the caller ID. "Hi, Lola. How's things?"

"Did you have to ask?"

"Sorry."

"Dodie, can you do me a favor? Could you come to rehearsal
tonight? It's our run-through and I need an objective opinion. I know
I can trust you."

I could hear the desperation in her voice. "I guess so. I have a few
errands to run today and then a meeting with Pauli—"

"That reminds me. I need to call Carol and make an appointment
to get my roots done before opening."

"How would sevenish be?"

"You're a good friend," Lola said gratefully.

I was. "By the way, I saw Bill yesterday and he gave me the name
of the woman in green at the funeral."

"What woman in green?"

"You remember . . . she threw a flower on top of Antonio's casket and had this look of vengeance—"

"That's right!" Her tone changed. "So, Bill, huh?" she teased.

I let Lola have a light moment since she hadn't had much to smile about lately. "He's been preoccupied with the Creston robberies. But he came by the Windjammer last night."

"So who is she?"

"Are you ready? Her name is Regan Digenza."

"She's related to Antonio?"

"I guess. But I've been on the Internet for the past hour and can't find any connection to him, although she is an interesting character." I enlightened Lola on Regan's work life. "Bill thought she could be a relative who didn't care for him. But I don't know. You said you thought his family was out West?"

"California. But I got the impression that he was estranged from his parents and had no siblings."

Which reminded me, it had been a few weeks since I'd called my own parents, who had been living in Florida since before Hurricane Sandy. They'd traded one beach for another.

"Huh. I might pay her a visit."

"Where is she?" Lola asked.

"Atlantic City maybe?"

Lola was silent for a moment. "Dodie, you think there was more to Antonio's death?"

"You know me and unanswered questions."

Lola laughed softly. "You go, girl. Let me know if there is anything I can do."

"How about drinks after rehearsal tonight?" I said.

She groaned. "If I make it that long."

14

By late morning I was ready for some fresh air. It was a balmy fall day. According to my weather app, temps would be hitting the high seventies by late afternoon. I was always happier when I was actively pursuing solutions to problems. Digging into Antonio's visit to Bernridge lifted my spirits. There were only three doctors in town with Chinese names. It wasn't difficult to connect Imogen's "shoe" with a Dr. Xiu; the others were a Dr. Wang and a Dr. Chen.

I left the parkway and followed the off-ramp to Lambert Street, where my Genie commanded me to drive two miles and turn left onto Charter Drive. Like both Etonville and Creston, Bernridge was a bedroom community of New York City, although a more blue-collar version than the other two. Its most prominent claim to fame was a box factory that dated from the 1920s and recently went out of business. I cruised slowly down Charter until I reached number seven, a modest two-story Victorian, painted maroon and white. Attached to a light pole in the front yard was a sign that read "Dr. Xiu. Traditional Chinese Medicine." What was Antonio doing with Asian medicine? I parked, two cars down from the house.

I expected miniature waterfalls and burning incense. But the waiting room was occupied by typical reception seats, stacks of magazines, and fluorescent lighting. An Asian woman and child, holding hands, sat against one wall, and against the opposite, an elderly man with headphones moved his head up and down rhythmically. The receptionist was a young African-American. Imogen's neighbor's cousin Tess? My plan was to claim I had back pain—generic enough—and ask to see the doctor.

I approached the receptionist's window. Her ID tag read Theresa. Bingo.

"Hello," I said. "I would like to see Dr. Xiu."

"What's your name?"

I didn't want this visit to reach the ears of Etonville. "Maureen." My middle name. "McDermott." My mother's maiden name. Might as well keep it in the family.

"You don't have an appointment," she said.

"I know, but I was hoping you could squeeze me in."

Tess studied me. "What's your reason for wanting to see the doctor?"

"Back pain," I said and hunched a tad, frowning.

Tess clicked a few computer keys and read a screen. "I have an opening at one o'clock."

Forty-five minutes. "Fine," I said. More time to figure out a way to approach Dr. Xiu.

She handed me an information sheet and I sat down to answer a few questions, acting as though I was deeply engaged with my medical history, of which there was very little. Ten minutes later, an assistant ushered the woman and child into the doctor's office. The man was still engaged with his iPod. I finished the form. "Excuse me, but do you have a cousin in Etonville?" I asked as I handed it in.

Tess looked up from her keyboard. "What?"

"Imogen, she works at Snippets hair salon, said her neighbor had a cousin who worked for Dr. Xiu."

"I met Imogen once." She checked the sheet I handed her. "Have a seat and I'll call you." Tess wasn't especially unfriendly, just brusque and to the point.

The assistant opened the inner door again. "James?" He removed his headphones and followed the assistant out of the waiting room.

Imogen was *not* going to be a lead-in. I had to go for broke. "I was wondering if you remembered my friend Antonio Digenza?"

Tess looked impatient. I might have been getting on her nerves. "Who?"

"He was here a week or so ago. He died of a heart attack shortly after. Imogen mentioned that *you* had mentioned—"

Tess sat up straighter, her eyes immediately sympathetic. "Oh yes. At a food fair or something."

Antonio's death might be forever linked to the Windjammer. "I was surprised to hear that he was being treated for heart disease. Antonio seemed so healthy. A vegetarian, I think." Is that what Lola had said? "I didn't know that you could heal heart issues with Chinese medicine."

Tess shook her head. "Poor man. Dr. Xiu treats everything with herbs, but Mr. Digenza wasn't a heart patient." She leaned across her desk. "He nearly collapsed," she added confidentially.

I didn't know if she was violating any HIPAA protocols but seemed suddenly eager to talk. I felt the little hairs dancing on the back of my neck.

"Antonio had been looking a little pale lately." I was amazed at my growing facility with manipulating the truth.

"Gastrointestinal issues will do that to you."

Antonio had gastro issues. "So Dr. Xiu uses herbs to treat everything?"

"Yes. Colds, cancer, infections. Even your back pain."

I remembered why I was here. "You know, I'm feeling a lot better. Maybe—" The assistant appeared at the inner door. "Maureen?"

"You might as well see Dr. Xiu," Tess said.

I sat on the examining table as Dr. Xiu, a diminutive, older woman, poked, prodded, and pressed every square inch of my back. Her face was tranquil—ageless and wrinkle-free.

"Have you ever had acupuncture?" she asked.

"Needles? No."

"It would help."

I had to think fast. No way was I going to become a pincushion for an ailment that was nonexistent. "I was hoping that I could be treated with herbs. At least for this first visit?"

Dr. Xiu scrutinized my face. "Yes. But if the pain persists you will need to consider additional therapies."

I dressed quickly and took my prescription: a brown grocery bag. I peeked inside as Tess checked me out. It was full of twigs, dried brown and red leaves, chunks of moss, and pieces of bark.

"What do I do with all of this?"

"You boil it and make an infusion and drink some as a tea. Then you pour the rest into your bath water and take a nice long soak. I guarantee your back will feel lots better."

"Uh-huh," I said. "Does this stuff really work?"

Tess smiled knowingly. "It's not called 'ancient medicine' for nothing."

On impulse I asked, "I guess Antonio had a bag like this as well?"

Tess's brow puckered. "He was scheduled to come back for his weekly prescription, but he never made it."

"So Antonio came here more than once?"

It must have finally occurred to Tess that she was violating his privacy. Her eyes became hooded, her expression guarded. "That will be seventy-five dollars."

I paid and left.

I couldn't imagine the degree of pain that would force me to drink, much less take a bath in, a tea made with clumps of my backyard. I pitched the brown bag into the backseat. So Antonio had been seeing Dr. Xiu for gastrointestinal problems. Not heart disease. Rather than answer questions, my visit to Bernridge had raised more. How long had Antonio had stomach issues? For that matter, why did he opt to see a Chinese herbalist instead of a traditional doctor? Did he drink the infusion or soak in it?

Pauli was right on time and I was ready for him. I'd brought home a pan of spaghetti and meatballs from the Windjammer last night; it wasn't his mother's recipe, but Henry made a pretty good Italian entrée, despite what La Famiglia thought. Meanwhile, there were chips and oatmeal-raisin cookies to hold him over.

"So, like, you want to go deep on the Internet?" he asked, opening his laptop on my kitchen table.

"Whatever we have to do to find out more about Antonio Digenza. Maybe there are search tools I don't know about?" I was a civilian, so of course there were Internet antics that were not on my radar.

"Beyond Google, Bing, and Yahoo! searches," Pauli volunteered.

"He wasn't on Facebook. I checked."

"No social media presence." Pauli cracked his knuckles and went to work.

He concentrated on a variety of search engines that could be used to find people: ZabaSearch, NamUs, Wink People Search, and a few others. With each one he typed in "Antonio Digenza" first, and then added "+actor", "+director", "+New York City". Nothing showed up beyond what I'd already found.

"Some of these engines are just for missing persons," he said, and finished off a can of soda.

"Remember when you suggested he might have changed his name? Could we still find him?"

"Sure. Like government search engines with his social security number." He broke out in a grin. "We found out about those in my last class."

"Great," I said. "What if I don't have his social?"

Pauli weighed options. "We could keep digging into, like, other activities."

"Such as?"

"Did he belong to, like, organizations?"

"I don't know. Maybe acting or directing unions? Lola might know if he was a member."

"IMDb," he said. "Internet Movie Database."

"Right." I had no idea if Antonio had had a movie career either in front of or behind the camera, but it was worth a try.

Pauli kept at it while I warmed up dinner; the only find was a brief mention of a short film that Antonio produced and directed in 2013. One of the cast members was a Regan Digenza! Confirmation of a theater/film connection. Pauli was ecstatic that we'd made progress.

We lobbed around other ideas as we downed the spaghetti and meatballs, and he gave me an update on his latest digital forensics assignment: examining personal electronics in criminal investigations.

"Wow. You mean you can locate someone from his tablet or cell phone?"

"Give me your cell." Pauli began with the Settings app and tapped until he reached Frequent Locations. "You were at Ames Street . . ."

"Right," I said.

"And Charter Drive in Bernridge, Main Street here, and River Road in Rumson—"

I took my phone back and gawked at the screen. "Whoa." I was dumbfounded. I knew that my smartphone asked to have access to my location from time to time, but I had no idea it was tracking me. If I had Antonio's cell, I would know where he'd been in the days before his death. I looked at my wall clock.

"I have to run, Pauli. Thanks for your help."

"No problem. I gotta bounce anyway."

I cleared the table and placed the dishes in the sink. The dishwasher was on the blink again, but my landlord had promised a repair visit. Then I dropped Pauli off at the other end of town. "Tell your Mom hi."

Pauli slung his backpack over his shoulder and bounded out of the Metro. "If you want to keep searching . . ."

"I'll call you."

The Etonville Little Theatre was, as usual, in a state of organized chaos. Technical rehearsal was less than ten days away. Walter was struggling to gather the cast onto the stage for a warm-up exercise, Carlyle was gesturing wildly at Lola about the upstage wall of the set, and Penny was scurrying around, clipboard in hand, whistle at the ready, like a sheepdog herding its flock. It was exhausting watching them.

I planted myself in the back row of the house for the run-through. Knowing Walter, I probably had a decent amount of time before the show started. The houselights had been dimmed, so I dropped my head onto the back of the seat, contemplating the events of the day.

"Bunch of amateurs."

I twisted to my right. Tiffany stood in the center aisle, shaking her head. "I guess that's community theater," I said quietly.

Tiffany glanced at me. We had not really spoken in the weeks before Antonio's death, and certainly not in the days since, if you don't count my attempts to mute her wailing at the food festival upon seeing Antonio's face in his plate. "He never should have taken this gig. He'd still be alive if it wasn't for the Etonville Little Theatre."

Technically, I guess that was true. Without the ELT directing job, he wouldn't have come to town or been at the festival. Or maybe had some sort of gastro reaction.

"It did seem strange that a man of Antonio's professionalism would agree to direct a small-town theater troupe," I said.

"It was the money. And a role for me." She caught her lower lip between her teeth. "Besides, he wanted to get out of the city for a while."

"I heard that he liked it so well he was planning on moving to this area."

Tiffany snorted. "Who told you that? He was going to beat it out of Etonville on opening night."

"And leave you in the show?" I tried to laugh companionably.

"Carlyle would still be here."

Chalk up another score for Penny and her ear-to-the-ground re-connaissance. "I'm certain the ELT is grateful that you stayed in the production."

Tiffany shrugged. "I don't have anywhere else to go." She studied me for a second. "Aren't you the Windjammer person who arranged the food thing?"

"Yes, I am. I just want to extend my sympathy again—"

"Can you get me some food? I didn't have time for dinner and I'm starving."

"Um, sure. What would you—"

"A burger's fine. Rare. And a Dr Pepper. Large." She deigned to join the rest of the cast onstage.

I texted Benny and put in Tiffany's dinner order. Hmmm. Tiffany had no concerns about Windjammer food. Did she know something?

Carlyle and Lola had reached some sort of détente because he was nodding his head and she was wearing a lopsided smile, probably the result of biting her tongue while choking back an opinion. Penny tooted one blast of her whistle and everyone quieted down. Carlyle headed out of the theater, for coffee; no doubt to escape the warm-up.

Walter gathered everyone in a circle and explained the premise of the exercise. Lola slipped into a seat next to me.

"What's Carlyle's beef?" I asked.

"He thinks the back wall isn't anchored properly." Lola rolled her eyes.

"At least the scenery looks almost finished." The doors were on their hinges, the floor was painted to resemble hardwood, and the furniture was stacked at the back of the set.

Lola crossed her fingers.

Walter demonstrated a new exercise: Arms spread out, he floated around the space until he came close to an actor. Then he held out a hand and said, "Hello." The actor was to respond in kind.

"What's this?" I asked.

"It's called Balloon Hello," Lola whispered. "First you drift around weightless like a balloon, and then you greet whomever you touch."

I slid my eyes in her direction. "And the point is . . . ?"

Lola frowned. "I think it's about communing with the space and treating the cast like friends. Or family. Walter is all about theater as a family."

Edna dove in enthusiastically, twirling until she bumped into Romeo and gave him her hand. He shook his head and slapped her fingers.

"Light as air, up on your toes. Float! Float! And greet each other with awareness," Walter shouted.

Abby reluctantly clomped around in a circle, then stuck her hand in Tiffany's face, who batted it away and "floated" off stage to the green room.

"Faster! Faster!"

The actors began to run, leap, twirl, grabbing each other's hands, yelling and hooting until they were breathless.

Walter was taking little notice, having committed himself fully to the Balloon Hello, spinning, rotating first in one direction, then another, reaching out for actors who by now were flopping on the floor in fits of laughter.

"At least they're enjoying themselves," I said.

Lola looked dubious. "I hope they have something left in their tanks for the run-through."

Walter finished the warm-up with the actors in a circle holding hands, eyes closed, visualizing themselves romping around the set. Romeo coaxed Tiffany out of the green room and stood next to her, hand in hand, while Abby and Edna moved as far away from each other as possible. Some family.

Penny signaled a ten-minute break. The actors scattered to the bathrooms and dressing rooms. Lola ran down the aisle to intercept Walter before the run started, and I had my fingers crossed that all went well.

"You better do more than cross your fingers," Penny hissed in my ear.

I jumped. How did she do that?

"Why? What's happening?"

"The guy playing the minister—"

"Mildred's husband Vernon?"

"He forgot his hearing aids. He'll miss every cue," she crowed.

For someone in charge of managing the production, Penny got a perverse pleasure out of seeing the show on the brink of ruin.

"Can someone call Mildred to drop them off?" I asked.

"Already checked. She's at choir practice."

"Do you want me to go get them?"

"Nah. I'll tell everybody to yell their lines to him." Penny hurried

off. "Hey, you two"—she shouted at the policemen who were lounging on the settee—"move your butts off that thing and help me with
the furniture."

Honey stuck her head in the theater door. She plunked Tiffany's
dinner on the seat next to me. "Here you go, Dottie."

"Thanks. Much traffic next door?"

She flicked her hair off one shoulder. "Like, no. I only made
thirty dollars in tips. I should get a real job."

As if working at the Windjammer is volunteer labor. "Customers
will come back soon."

Honey looked unconvinced. "You should forget about theme
food next time."

I clamped my mouth into a tight line to prevent a toad from es-
caping. "I'll just go and deliver this." I picked up the Styrofoam
package and brushed past Honey. "Maybe you should get back to the
restaurant."

"What for? I'm just hanging around the dining room."

I put Honey out of mind and scanned the stage, where actors were
beginning to gather in rehearsal clothes. "Edna, have you seen
Tiffany?"

"I think she's in her dressing room." Edna looked around and
lowered her voice. "Having some line difficulties, if you know what
I mean."

I knew what she meant. Lola had complained on several occasions
that Tiffany hadn't completely memorized the script yet. "Whoops.
Maybe she needs some food."

"She needs a prompter," Edna muttered.

"Well, good luck tonight," I said and moved away.

"We're going to need it."

I crossed the stage and opened the door to the green room, a cozy
hangout with a sofa, folding chairs, and a soda machine, which, in
turn, led to the dressing rooms. Two actors exited the men's dressing
room, pulling on rehearsal jackets. "Hi, Dodie," Mildred's husband
said.

"Hi," I answered.

"What did you say?" he asked, hand to his ear.

"Nothing." I turned to the women's dressing room. The door was
ajar. Through the crack I could see Walter and Tiffany.

"I have Act One down," she whined.

"But you promised you'd have the entire play memorized by tonight," Walter said, a tinge of terror seeping into his speech.

"I've had a few things on my mind lately, in case you didn't notice," she said roughly.

"I know this hasn't been easy for you but you insisted on staying in the show." I could hear him sigh. "Look, if you get into trouble, just skip to the next line you know. Whatever. Just keep the play moving."

Tiffany must have been weighing this advice in the silence. "Well, I could do that if the play was like, in my system, you know? But right now it's only up here in my frontal lobe." She pointed to her forehead.

I figured Walter was about to say *frontal lobe this*. It was my cue. I knocked on the door and entered. "Tiffany, here's your dinner."

She grabbed the bag and unwrapped the sandwich in one move. "I'll be ready to go in five minutes," she said to Walter, her mouth full, and fled the dressing room.

He watched her exit, his jaw hanging off its hinges. "This is what we get for casting the director's wife. Who can't act!"

A scream came from the stage. Walter looked stricken and hurried away, with me close behind.

The cast stood around Tiffany, who sat on the ground on top of a bentwood chair that had shattered legs, the remains of her dinner on the floor next to her. "I knew that chair was not safe. I told Penny it was too rickety."

Penny gaped, about to blow her whistle, when Edna pushed through the crowd of actors. "What have we got here? Looks like an 11-80 or 11-81. Depending on the injuries." She raised her voice as if Tiffany was hard of hearing—of course that would be Mildred's husband. "How badly are you hurt?"

Tiffany brushed Edna away. "It's my back."

Romeo and one of the cops helped Tiffany to her feet and set her on the sofa. Walter was running his fingers through his beard and pacing as Lola entered the house.

"What's the matter?" she yelled, and ran down a side aisle.

I intercepted her advance toward the stage. "A chair broke under Tiffany and she claims her back is hurt."

"Oh no."

"Why don't you let me take her to your place, get her something for her back, and if she's up to it I can run lines with her. Meanwhile, the rest of the cast can run the show."

Lola hesitated for only a moment. "That would be so . . . great." She closed her eyes and sighed.

15

It took only a minute to convince Tiffany to leave with me—and I sidestep efforts to challenge her frontal lobe—and even less time to persuade Walter that I could help Tiffany run lines and handle her back issue at the same time.

Carlyle insisted on helping Tiffany to my Metro, asking her repeatedly if she was okay. Tiffany teased him about being a mother hen and the two of them hugged briefly before he settled her in my front seat.

I drove carefully to Lola's house in the upscale, north end of town—unlike my neighborhood in the south end of town, which was middle-class and practical. I parked in her driveway, watching with amusement when Tiffany needed no assistance springing out of my car. I followed her into the living room, where she threw herself on one of Lola's pristine leather love seats and chucked her bag on an antique table. I'd dutifully rubbed my feet on Lola's entrance mat. She was particular about her wood floors and Persian area rugs.

"How is your back?" I asked.

Tiffany studied me, probably calculating what she could get away with. "It aches."

I had a sudden brainstorm. "I have the perfect cure for you. It will make your pain disappear in a second." I hoped Tess was right about the herb prescription. "Why don't you head upstairs and get undressed and I'm going to prepare a nice warm bath with a special remedy."

Immediately suspicious, Tiffany sat up. "What kind of remedy?"

"It's a prescription from an herbalist for my back pain." Or at least it would be if I had back pain.

She shrugged. At least this got her out of rehearsal and a reprieve

before she had to confront the script and Walter. Tiffany went upstairs to change and I went to work. I retrieved the brown bag from
the backseat of my Metro and deposited the contents into Lola's
largest pot. The mess of twigs and leaves soon boiled, filling Lola's
gleaming kitchen with a stench that could only be described as bad
corned beef and cabbage. For the heck of it, I ladled a bit in a mug
and sniffed the contents: cow dung seasoned with just a soupçon of
decayed tree bark. I held my nose and carefully stuck the tip of my
tongue into the liquid. There was a gritty texture to the tea and the
sensation of swallowing dirt.

I strained the pot and hauled it upstairs to the bathroom. I turned
on the spigot, emptied the contents of the pot into the warm water,
and swirled the mixture as the tub filled. My fingers felt tacky on
contact with the water and I could see a dirt ring start to appear
around the inside of the tub. My hands floated in the murky water
like buoys in a polluted lake.

Tiffany appeared at the door of the bathroom in a crimson che-
nille robe. She wrinkled her nose when she saw the color of the
water. "I'm not getting into that!"

"I really think this bath will be awesome for your back."

"No way." She stood her ground.

I pulled my cell out of my pocket. "Walter texted a few minutes
ago. Wondering if your back felt better."

Tiffany looked from me to the tub. "What do I need to do?"

"Just sit down and let the infusion soak into your back muscles."

She sidled into the bathroom a few feet and untied her robe.

"Call me if you need anything. I'll be out here." I left the bathroom and closed the door behind me. I could hear Tiffany lowering
herself into the water. I wondered if Antonio had done the same.

"Yuck," she yelled.

Oh well, maybe the herb bath *would* cure her, and if I could get
her to study her lines, it would be my contribution to the Etonville
Little Theatre. I decided to stay on the second floor in case Tiffany
needed my help.

I noticed the door to the guest room was ajar and my inner snoop
got the better of me. I peeked in. Clothes were strewn around on most
surfaces—the unmade bed, a soft armchair, one of the drawers in the
bureau. The closet spewed hangers with slacks and sweaters and a
jacket or two. I entered and approached the wardrobe. There were

men's clothes, too. A black turtleneck sweater, a leather jacket, and several dress shirts. OMG. Tiffany hadn't gone through Antonio's possessions. Maybe she couldn't bring herself to part with his things?

I backed away from the closet and saw the bedside tables. On one side of the bed there was a soda can, a paperback romance novel, and a cell phone in a bright pink case. On the other side there was another cell phone, reading glasses, and a copy of *Arsenic and Old Lace*. My heart skipped a beat. I walked to the hallway and listened at the bathroom door. Tiffany must have surrendered to the cloudy water; all was quiet.

I tiptoed back to her room and grabbed Antonio's cell phone. What had Lola said about his password? I tapped out the letters TONY. Then I closed my eyes and concentrated on my conversation with Pauli just a few hours ago: I started at Settings and worked my way to Frequent Locations of the places Antonio had visited in the days prior to his death. I recognized Charter Drive in Bernridge and various locations in Etonville, but there were also addresses Antonio had visited in Creston and Rumson. But the Rumson location was not Flowers by Kincaid, and I couldn't identify the Creston locations. Antonio had been a busy guy. I memorized the most recent Creston address.

I heard the faucet run in the bathroom and dashed to the hallway. "Are you okay, Tiffany?" I called out.

From behind the door, I heard, "Need more hot water. This herb stuff stinks and is sticking to my skin. I'm getting out."

"I'd give it ten more minutes."

There was a muffled response. I ran back to the bedside table and replaced Antonio's cell phone, which I was still holding. I examined the room. I tried dresser drawers—underwear, T-shirts, several sweaters. I spied the small drawer in the bedside table. I pulled on the little knob, but the drawer wouldn't budge. It was stuck, or locked. I looked around for something to pry it open with and found a nail file on the top of the dresser. I stooped down, inserting it into the lock and twisting first to the left and then to the right.

"What is that smell in the kitchen? What are you doing?"

"Aaaah!" Startled, I fell backward onto my bottom. "Sh—"

"Are you breaking into Tiffany's things?" Lola asked, almost a reprimand.

"Antonio's. Help me out here." I motioned to the bedside table.

Lola grasped the knob, jiggled it back and forth, and the wood gave. The drawer opened jerkily. "Why are you—?"

"See if Tiffany's still in the tub."

Bewildered, Lola walked into the hallway. "Tiffany, it's Lola. How are you?"

An envelope lay in the bottom of the drawer, empty but addressed to Tony Dickson at a New York City location on the Upper West Side. My mouth dropped open; I joined Lola.

The water began to drain from the tub. "I need to take a shower now and get this gunk off me," Tiffany said.

"What gunk?" Lola turned to me.

"I'll explain later," I whispered and flattened my face against the bathroom door. "Good idea, Tiffany. A hot shower will finish you off."

Another muffled response.

I grabbed Lola's arm and pulled her into the guest room.

"Dodie, what is going on here?" she hissed.

"I might have found out where Antonio's been disappearing to."

"What? How?"

"It's a long story." I stuck the envelope in my pocket and pushed the drawer closed.

"This herb bath didn't do anything for my back," Tiffany said, standing in the doorway to her room, wrapped in a large bath towel, hair dripping, unconcerned about our presence there.

"What herb bath?" Lola was, by now, completely baffled.

"Tiffany, how about a nice cup of tea?" I asked.

"I'll take a bourbon and Coke," she said.

I gently ushered Lola out the door ahead of me. "Come downstairs when you're ready."

"You're never gonna get that sticky mess out of the tub." She flipped her head forward and shook her hair.

"What did you cook down here?" Lola asked, peering into her best pot as I rummaged in her liquor cabinet.

"An herb prescription from a Dr. Xiu in Bernridge. For my back. Ancient Chinese medicine."

"Since when do you use ancient Chinese medicine? My God! I didn't know you hurt your back," Lola said, concerned.

"I didn't. I went there because Antonio went to see her."

"For his back?"

I finished pouring Coke into two fingers of whiskey. "For a gastrointestinal problem." Where had Antonio boiled *his* prescription? Lola would have known if he'd done it here.

"How did you find that out? And what did you do to this pot?"

"I'll tell you everything after Tiffany checks out. By the way, how is the run-through going?" I asked.

"Not so bad. Of course, Walter is thinking we may need an understudy for Tiffany. Even if the person has to be on book."

"That's probably not a bad idea."

"Walter's thinking of asking Honey," Lola said.

"Honey? She can't act."

"Well, she was sitting in the house and we needed someone to read Tiffany's lines and she volunteered. She wasn't half-bad—"

"Henry won't like it. That's two of us at the ELT. And besides, we need her in the dining room," I said.

Lola lowered her voice. "Don't say anything to Tiffany yet."

Geez. Honey was difficult enough to take, with her packaging and complaining and mispronouncing my name. I couldn't imagine how much worse she'd be if she were actually performing in an ELT production.

I poured a little more Cabernet into my wineglass while Lola kicked off her shoes and stretched out on a sofa. We'd seen Tiffany— two bourbon and Cokes later—off to bed, and relaxed in Lola's cozy den, away from the stairs to the second floor, where it would be impossible for Tiffany to hear us. I'd told Lola about Regan Digenza, Imogen's neighbor's cousin Tess, Dr. Xiu, Antonio's cell phone, the envelope with the New York address, and the use of her stainless steel pot to boil the mess of sticks and leaves and dirt.

"Dodie, I can't believe what you've been up to," Lola said when I'd finished.

"Sorry about your pot."

She shrugged off my apology. "So you think Antonio was disappearing from rehearsal to go to Rumson and Bernridge?"

"And some places in Creston. Did he ever talk about knowing anyone there?" I asked.

"No."

"How long did Antonio have stomach problems? Who is Regan Digenza?"

Lola frowned. "And what about that strange man at the theater?"

Not to mention the note on my windshield and the car that bumped me in Rumson. We were both stumped on all angles. "So Antonio Digenza is probably Tony Dickson," I added.

"I never heard him use that name," Lola said.

"It explains why he wasn't on the Internet until 1998. I'm going to do a little digging first thing in the morning." I rubbed my eyes.

"So what does all of this mean?" Lola asked, yawning.

"I'm not sure," I said slowly, "but I'll bet most of this is tied to his death."

"Are you going to talk with Bill?"

"Yes, when he returns full-time to Etonville."

"I'm so tired, I can't keep my eyes open." Lola dropped her head on the sofa's armrest.

I covered her with an afghan, washed and rinsed our glasses, and stepped out into the cool air. It was eleven thirty and most of Etonville was buttoned up for the night.

I took the long way home from Lola's, cruising past the town park, Georgette's Bakery, and Snippets. I veered left onto Main and slowed down. I saw Benny turning out the lights in the Windjammer. I was tempted to stop in and check on things, but a day off was a day off. He exited by way of the back door.

I left the restaurant in my rearview mirror and coasted by the ELT. The only light visible was a security lamp in the lobby. But then an outline moved by the old oak that stood guard over the theater's entrance. Was it just the branches of the tree swaying in the night breeze? It was late and I was sleepy. I blinked my eyes and continued down Main Street, but on impulse, unable to let it go, I turned right onto Amber and made another quick right into the alley that ran parallel to Main and behind all of the businesses on the street. I switched off my headlights. There was no sign of Benny's car by the Windjammer loading dock. Nor was there any activity by the Etonville Little Theatre. Still, I felt a chill from the hairs on my neck. Who would be prowling around the theater at this time of the night?

I came to a stop by the dumpster behind Books, Books, Books—Etonville's answer to Barnes & Noble—stuffed my cell phone into my back pocket, and got out. I shut the door carefully and took two steps. The gravel crunched under my sneakers, the only sound in the stillness of the night. Drifting clouds covered the moon for a moment and then passed, leaving a slice of light bright enough to make out the shapes of the theater and restaurant.

I moved forward, stepping to the side of the road where a sprinkling of dirt and clods of green softened the noise of my footsteps, and sprinted to a passageway three feet wide that ran along the side of the theater and opened onto Main. The ELT rarely used this path, as it only led to the alley behind the theater and the loading dock. Scenery was generally removed by way of the rear shop-door exit.

I paused at the corner of the building. My blood ran cold. Twenty yards away a hooded figure was crouching behind the oak tree, directing a pinpoint light into the office where Walter and Lola did business. Aside from a safe that was kept locked and held a minimal amount of cash since last spring, an old computer, and a copy/fax machine, there was little of value in the theater office.

The figure was of medium height and medium build, but I couldn't make out if it was a man or a woman, the hood pulled low over the intruder's face. I peeked around the corner to get a better look and my jacket scraped against the brick of the building. I froze. The individual stood and looked my way. I held my breath and leaned into the wall, making myself as flat as possible. Then the person backed away from the theater and ran down Main past the Windjammer and disappeared. I considered my options: I could get my car and try to follow, I could run after whoever was casing the theater, or I could go home and call Bill in the morning. But by the time Bill made a move on the possible attempted break-in, this person could be anywhere.

I stepped around the corner and peered down Main again. The street was empty except for a lone pickup truck that rattled past the theater. What if the person had cut down a side street and vanished into a backyard, or hopped in a getaway vehicle that had been stashed several blocks over, or had a companion waiting somewhere?

I felt vulnerable on foot, but in my Metro I could scour the streets off Main and look for any sign of the prowler. I spun on my heel to dash to my car. An explosion of light blinded me. It took a moment before I realized what it was. Someone was deliberately shining a powerful utility flashlight in my face. I raised my hands to block the light and felt a thud from behind. A heavy object connected with the back of my head and a burst of colors detonated in my brain. I saw stars. And then black. I crumpled to the ground, my last thought, *There were two of them.*

16

"Ow!" I jerked backward in response to the Emergency Medical Services technician dabbing at the back of my head with a cotton swab and alcohol. I had a minor cut but a good-sized lump. "They must have used a crowbar on me."

"Probably something blunt," the EMS guy said, then handed me an ice pack. "You sure you don't want to go to the hospital and be checked out for a concussion?"

"I'll be fine," I said, sitting on the back end of the ambulance.

I was out cold for a minute; when I came to, I had a tremendous headache but managed to call 911. Officer Ostrowski was on duty and he sent the EMS. Since Bill became police chief, Ralph was usually assigned crowd control in crisis situations. But without a crowd on Main Street at midnight in Etonville, Ralph was taking it easy, leaning against his cruiser, texting.

A second black-and-white careened around the corner of Amber and Main, did a wide U-turn, and pulled to a stop, lights flashing. Bill slammed his door shut and walked briskly to the ambulance. Ralph snapped to attention.

"What do we have here?" he asked Ralph but stared straight at me.

"Hit on the head and blacked out."

Bill knelt down, his eyes level with mine. "What happened?" His voice was businesslike, but his face was all concern.

"I was driving home from Lola's and I saw a person trying to break in to the theater."

"You actually saw someone?" he asked.

"Not at first . . ."

"What does that mean?"

"I saw a shadow by the oak tree," I said and pointed toward the theater entrance. "I thought maybe I should check it out, so I drove around the corner and came down the alley—"

"You pursued a perpetrator?"

"Not exactly pursue . . ."

Bill frowned. "By yourself." It wasn't a question.

"I just wanted to see if it was really a person I saw." I ignored the implication that I had no business investigating a possible break-in alone at that hour. "I walked down the alley—"

"You got out of your car . . ." He exhaled noisily.

"That's when I saw that the shadow was a person. I couldn't tell if it was a male or female. It was wearing a hoodie pulled down low over the face."

Bill waited for me to go on.

"He or she was shining a flashlight into the ELT office. But when I moved to get a better look, I guess whoever it was saw me and ran off. I turned down the alley to go back to my car when this huge light blinded me. And then I got hit from behind." I removed the ice from the back of my head and tentatively touched the goose egg. It was a whopper. "So there were two of them," I said, hoping that was a helpful piece of information.

"Did you get a look at either face?"

I shook my head. "The light was too bright."

Bill rose and scanned the area. "I think you should go to St. Anthony's."

St. Anthony's was the area hospital in Creston that featured a trauma center. "I'm okay."

"That's an order," he said brusquely.

"Good thing it's the middle of the night and no one's awake. Otherwise Etonville's gossip mill would be having a field day," I mused.

Bill wasn't buying my attempt to make light of my escapade. "Ralph will follow the ambulance and see you get home afterwards." He nodded at Ralph, who clapped his cap on his head and hopped into his vehicle. "And tomorrow I'd like to have a little talk if you're up to it."

His eyes had dark circles under them—long nights in Creston? But they still cut through me like a hot knife through butter. I was definitely up to it.

* * *

Bill stayed behind in Etonville to survey the crime scene, such as it was, while I was trundled off in the ambulance to Creston. By 3:00 a.m. St. Anthony's had discharged me, a neurological exam and CT scan indicating no concussion, just a good whack on my skull that would require aspirin and ice for twenty-four hours. We picked up my Metro in the alley behind the theater and Ralph followed me home, only too happy to be released from babysitting; he had more important things to attend to like an early breakfast at the Donut Hole out on the highway. I climbed into bed, yanked the covers over my still-pounding head, and swore I would not be able to sleep.

I was snoring in ten minutes.

I dreamt I was wading in a mudslide of gooey brown muck. My legs weighed a ton and each time I tried to lift one, I fell backwards, mud wrestling with myself. A muffled ringing nipped at my consciousness and tugged at my eyelids, glued shut from lack of sleep. I twisted onto my side and flinched. The pain at the back of my head reminded me of the ELT intruder, the thump on my noggin, Bill stooping in the moonlight to look gently into my eyes—

The ringing was persistent, originating from the pocket of my jeans. I covered my head with a pillow, hoping the sound would die; no such luck. I crawled to the foot of the bed and snatched my jeans off the floor where I had dropped them. "Hello?" I croaked. My alarm clock read seven thirty.

"Dodie? Thank God you're alive!"

"Hi, Lola."

"What were you doing chasing a criminal down Main Street at two a.m.?" she asked breathlessly.

The Etonville rumor machine always generously embellished whatever hint of a story it came across. "I didn't chase anyone and it was midnight, not—"

"I heard they hit you with the butt of a gun," she said.

"A gun? Who said they had a gun? It was probably just a—"

"Does it hurt much? I can come and stay with you today," she offered.

"I'm not bedridden. Just hungry. Let's meet at Coffee Heaven in an hour. I'm moving kind of slowly."

I clicked off and dragged myself into the shower, letting the hot water cascade off my head and face and back. As I became more alert, last night's events created a sharper image on my radar screen. Someone wanted something from the theater. And that twosome also wanted to discourage me. After all, why come back to assault me when they could have easily sped off and left Etonville in the dust? The attack had to be a warning of some sort.

I washed and conditioned my hair tentatively, lest I irritate the swelling, and brushed out my auburn strands. I hesitated over my wardrobe. I needed to stop by the police station to talk with Bill after breakfast. I knew he would be scrutinizing me and my every word. There was nothing wrong with taking advantage of his extreme focus; my stretchy crimson sweater and skinny black jeans might help hold his attention. I scooped up my leather jacket and sunglasses to ward off the bright glare of the morning sun. It was going to be a clear, bracing fall day in the upper fifties.

Etonville was its usual morning self. Citizens strolling up and down Main, shops opening their doors to customers, light traffic cruising the streets. It was difficult to dredge up the incident that had resulted in my trip to the emergency room.

Coffee Heaven was full of patrons when I opened the door and the welcome-bells jingled. As if on cue, every head turned and stared at me, first in amazement, then in curiosity. Before anyone could intercept me and inquire about my health, I ducked into the booth where Lola was waiting, fiddling with her camera. Customers watched me sit before setting the place atwitter with who-knew-what latest story on my demise.

"Here you go, hon," Jocelyn said and placed a caramel macchiato on the table. She leaned into me. "Etonville is becoming a hotbed of criminal activity."

"Thanks, Jocelyn. It's not that bad—"

"The Banger sisters think someone tried to rob them," she said knowingly.

"They think?"

"They can't remember where they put their jewelry. It might have been stolen." She walked away to wait on a customer.

"This town," I said, laughing, then wincing at the throbbing that started again.

Lola's eyes were wide.

"What?" I asked.

"You don't look too bad," she said. "I mean for someone attacked only hours ago."

"It was only a knock on my head."

"And a trip to St. Anthony's," she added. "What were they doing at the theater?"

I shrugged. "I only saw someone looking in the window with a flashlight."

"Walter thinks it might have something to do with the show."

"What would make anyone break in over *Arsenic and Old Lace*?" I asked.

"Sabotage. Someone trying to disrupt the opening," she said. "He doesn't trust that new theater in Creston."

"Walter actually thinks someone would knock me out because they wanted to upstage—no pun intended—the ELT?"

"It is a little far-fetched, isn't it?" She bit into a slice of whole wheat toast.

"I have a meeting with Bill today. I'm going to tell him everything, starting with the food festival."

Lola picked up her camera. "Speaking of which, I am way behind on these pictures. I've been going through them all morning." She flipped through photos of actors posing with festival-goers, pausing to shake her head. "Some of them are fine, others not so good. But I guess I need to email or text all of them. I didn't realize how many pictures I took. Over a hundred." Lola studied her work. "Here's the Banger sisters with Walter, and Mildred and her husband Vernon with Edna, and two cute young girls with Romeo."

I held out my hand and she turned over the camera. I swiped picture after picture. They were nice shots and everyone looked to be having a fun time, at least before Antonio's death. "You might need to photoshop some of these."

"Why?"

"Look here." I showed her a snapshot. "Abby's boyfriend walked into the frame and made a face behind her shot with Jocelyn."

"Oh, that Jim. He's such a big kid. I've never done photoshopping."

"Pauli can show you. He eliminated a delivery guy out of a shot he took for the Windjammer website."

"Are there many like that?" Lola asked.

I swiped a few more pictures. "Not really. Just some people wandering in the background." I stopped swiping. "Can you enlarge this photo?" I showed Lola a picture of the two policemen characters with Honey. She was supposed to be manning the cookie and pretzel booth, but obviously had taken a break.

"Sure." Lola zoomed in on the shot and handed it back.

"I think that's Regan Digenza in the background."

"Regan Digenza?"

"The woman in green from the funeral. But I don't remember seeing her at the festival."

Lola studied the photo. "I remember taking this. Honey said she had to hurry up and get back to her booth, so I was working fast. It was middle of the afternoon just as the crowd was peaking."

"Can you text it to me?" I asked.

Lola struck the screen a few times. "Done."

When I'd dug my cell phone out of my jeans this morning, I came across the envelope addressed to Anthony Dickson that I'd stuffed in my pocket earlier in the evening. I needed to surf the Internet on my break to get some answers on Antonio's identity, so I'd stowed my laptop in my bag; but first I had an hour before I had to get to the Windjammer, time enough to meet with Bill as requested.

I said good-bye to Lola and strolled to the Etonville Municipal Building, musing over the latest development: Why *was* Regan at the food festival and what *exactly* was her relationship to Antonio?

I was happy to see the chief's parking space occupied. Despite the off-and-on headache, I was feeling pretty perky. I might be close to discovering Antonio's backstory and I had a meeting with Bill. I opened the door to the building, imagining his blue eyes and crooked smile as he hovered over me, anxious about any lingering consequences from last evening. I would reassure him that I was fine, only a little tired, and maybe—

"Hey, Dodie! You had quite a night! A 240."

I assumed that was the code for an assault. "Hi, Edna. Is the chief in?" I was eager to bypass small talk.

"In a meeting." She checked the wall clock. "It should be over soon. He has an event to attend in Creston."

"Oh." I tried to hide my disappointment.

"Haven't you seen the paper?" She whipped a copy of this morning's *Etonville Standard* out of her bag and placed it on the counter.

The front page headline was a splash of large type: CRESTON THIEV-
ERY THWARTED. Under the heading was a set of photographs—no
doubt the perps. I glanced at the story about the recent thefts and the
Special Crimes Unit established with the help of Etonville's own Police Chief Bill Thompson.

"Wow. They caught them!"

"Yep, 487."

"That would be . . . ?"

"Grand theft." She lowered her voice. "They couldn't have done
it without the chief."

"So it seems." Beneath the fold on the front page was a small story
on my assault last night. RESTAURANT MANAGER HAS RUN-IN WITH
BURGLAR. There was a brief description of someone "attempting a
break-in" at the Etonville Little Theatre, followed by several lines on
my attack and removal by ambulance. At least there were no exaggerated theories on the identity of the burglar.

I heard laughter floating down the corridor and turned to see Bill
and the brunette from Creston, still elegant, still in a business suit to
die for, and still sporting three-inch heels. Instinctively, I stood up
straighter, flipped my hair off my neck, and whipped on my sunglasses. As if he could sense my attempt to compete with his companion, Bill rotated away from the brunette and looked at me, his
mouth still in that lopsided smile.

"Dodie, hi. I'll be right with you."

I'll be right with you? How personal was that? Where was that
look of concern that he'd flashed at me early this morning?

"I'll be in touch, Pia," Bill was saying, grinning like a fool at the
brunette.

My heart thunked and my shoulders sagged. What chance did I
have with that kind of competition? As she did on the prior occasion
in Creston, Pia lifted her face to receive Bill's kiss on her cheek.
TMI. I almost turned on my heel and strode away. Instead, I smiled
at Pia as she clip-clopped her way out the door.

"Come on in," Bill said.

I followed him to his office. "A lot for you to celebrate today."

"Yeah." He laughed ruefully. "The *Standard* likes to make a big
deal out of everything." It must have occurred to him that I was part
of the front page as well. "How are you feeling?" he asked quickly.

"I'll live," I said.

"Good." He knocked a pencil against his desk blotter.

Was he distracted thinking about the Creston achievement? Or the brunette?

"If this isn't a good time . . ."

"No. No. I just need to be in Creston in forty-five minutes for a press conference." He opened a file. "But I want to be sure I have everything on the record from last night."

"Okay."

I waited while he appeared to be studying the police report. Then he confirmed the time of my arrival on the scene, parking in the alley behind the theater, observing the person from my location on the pathway, and finally being blinded by a light and getting conked on the head.

"I guess that's about it," he said.

"Any chance of finding them?" I asked.

"Not unless we get lucky. There wasn't any evidence to go on at the scene, and you didn't notice anything particular about the pair . . ." Bill raised his hands in surrender.

"Why would someone want to break in to a place and then hit me on the head when there's nothing much to steal?"

"It's hard to know what motivates perpetrators to commit crimes. Even petty theft."

"Unlike the major thefts in Creston," I said lightly.

Bill checked his watch again.

"Did you find anything on the note?"

He looked perplexed.

"The one from my car? 'Leave Antonio alone'?"

"Oh that. No usable prints." He stood up and pulled on his uniform jacket.

"Uh-huh. Well, I did a little Internet browsing on Regan Digenza," I said quickly.

Bill stopped with his second arm halfway into its sleeve. "Oh?"

"Regan has quite a background. She was a casino dealer in Vegas and then in Atlantic City. Might still be. And she's an actor. Part of a web series," I said in a rush, aware that Bill was easing his way out of the office.

"How did you—?"

"LinkedIn. The Internet Movie Database." I left out Pauli's name to protect the innocent. "She was in a short film Antonio directed in 2013, but otherwise no specific mention of a connection to him."

"You've been active." He raised an eyebrow and buttoned his jacket.

"You know me and unfinished business . . ."

He wagged a finger in my face. "I *do* know you. I also know how that mind of yours works overtime."

With Bill on his way out the door, I had no other option but to postpone disclosing Antonio's visit to Dr. Xiu and my snooping on his cell phone. It would have to wait—

"Look, I know I've been a little tied up with the Creston business . . ."

More like AWOL.

"But with the thieves arrested, I'll be back in Etonville full-time," he said, and the left side of his mouth crept upward. "Maybe we can sit down and hash through all of your concerns about Antonio's death."

That almost sounded like a date. I felt a warm sphere in the center of my chest; something inside was melting.

"I have football practice Thursday night after school. How about stopping by and we can get a bite afterwards? If you can get a break from the Windjammer."

I would make it work. "Sure."

He opened the door and I stepped through.

"By the way, did it occur to you that Regan could have been another ex-wife?" he asked.

I halted in my tracks. "He had three wives?"

Bill shrugged. "It's been known to happen. Some people just need to be married."

Now what did that mean?

17

Henry had an appointment with Rita, Carol's shampoo girl, to finalize menu ideas for the rehearsal dinner. I opened the door to the Windjammer, put on coffee, and laid out menu sheets before either of them appeared.

Rita arrived first and I set her up in my back booth with a cappuccino and a piece of apple pie left over from yesterday's dessert menu. Her fiancé couldn't leave his post at a construction site in Jersey City, so she was on her own in choosing the food. I'd seen Rita in Snippets dozens of times over the past two years, but I'd never really studied the most memorable aspect of her appearance: an intricate tattoo of a leafy vine that began somewhere on her back and coiled over her shoulder and upper arm onto her chest, where it culminated in a bright red rose against a background of two entwined hearts. I was fascinated watching the flower and hearts jiggle whenever Rita bent to dig something out of her bag.

"Can I get you anything else?" I asked.

"Sorry?" She removed an earbud that was connected to her iPod.

A little louder. "Another cappuccino?"

"No way. Too much caffeine makes me jumpy." She waggled her head to the sounds in her earphones. "I have to run to work after this. Carol's promoted me to assistant manager." Rita pushed a few loose strands of highlighted hair behind her ears.

"Congratulations." Henry and Honey walked in the door. "We can get started now."

Henry joined me in the booth while Honey trudged off—somewhat sulkily—to the kitchen to join Enrico chopping vegetables for today's soup, and Rita went to the ladies' room.

He eyed me warily and dropped a copy of today's *Etonville Stan-*

dard on the table. "This is how you spend your day off? It might be safer coming to work."

"I see we have a sense of humor this morning," I said.

"Hunh," he answered.

Henry described some selections for Rita, stressing several of the Windjammer's signature dishes, such as French onion or cream of asparagus soup, or baby greens with walnuts, pears, and goat cheese; parmesan chicken cutlets with a choice of pastas, or panko-covered tilapia with saffron rice, or herb-crusted pork loin and rosemary potatoes; desserts were courtesy of Georgette's Bakery.

Rita and Henry noodled over this choice or that, with Henry emphasizing which entrées would complement which starters, while Rita emphasized that she and her groom were on a budget. It was only a party of a dozen; still, it was a big enough group to hold Henry's attention.

By eleven thirty, Honey and Carmen had set up the dining room, Benny had cleaned the bar and restocked beer and liquor, while Henry and Rita had agreed on a menu: baby greens, pork loin, rosemary potatoes, and assorted pastries.

My mind wandered from time to time and I felt fidgety. I couldn't wait until my break and the opportunity to research Tony Dickson. A few customers ambled in for lunch, along with a couple who were passing through on their way to Pennsylvania to see the leaves changing colors.

Benny and Carmen had the dining room well in hand, so I took the opportunity to eat an early lunch and do a little Internet mining. I typed Tony Dickson into the search bar and watched as a list of links appeared. There were Tony Dickson profiles on LinkedIn, several Facebook Dicksons, and a Wikipedia page for an actor with that name. I scrolled down and viewed the page of links. None were promising; all were recent. I was into the third page of Dickson entries when my cell rang. I checked the caller ID. "Hi, Lola."

"Did you see the paper? I was so distracted this morning I put it aside and only looked at it just now." Lola sounded as though she was choking on her words.

"Yeah. Why?" I asked.

"The article on the Creston burglaries? Dodie, I recognized one of the men," she whispered.

From the kitchen there was the dull clatter of objects hitting a tile floor. Benny looked over and winced.

"Can you speak up? I'm having trouble hearing—"

"One of the robbers. I met him."

"You met . . . Where?"

"Remember that guy who came to the theater and said he was a friend of Antonio's and just wanted to look around?" she said.

I also remembered that he bonded with Penny and claimed to be an actor in New York.

"Well, he was one of the men breaking into houses in Creston and robbing people," she added.

"Are you sure?"

"His face was inches from mine when he stooped down to pick up my papers."

I paused to organize my thoughts. Notions were flying randomly hither and yon. Why would a friend of Antonio's stop by the theater for a visit during the same period he must have been lying low to avoid capture for a series of thefts in a neighboring town? "It makes no sense," I said aloud, and found Henry's copy of the *Standard* on the bar where Benny was doing the crossword puzzle. Despite his silent protest, I eased the front page away from him with a smile. "You need to tell Bill."

"I called the station. He was away. Maybe I should speak with Officer Shung?"

"Good idea."

Lola sounded agitated. "Walter is calling me. He and Carlyle are fighting over some costume choices. I should go."

I scrutinized the two pictures of the Creston culprits. "Which one was he? The one on the left or—"

"The one on the right. I'll check in with you later." She clicked off.

I sat down in the booth. I had skimmed the article in Bill's office but hadn't given much thought to the two offenders. The one on the left had a gaunt face, a shaved head, and a grim expression. I wouldn't want to meet up with him in a dark alley. The other man had kindly, attractive features, a half smile that was mysterious, yet reassuring. Wow. The two couldn't have seemed more different. I reread the story until I reached their names. Johnny Bilboe, the bad boy, would probably be released on bail; and Lola's acquaintance, Kenneth Amberlin, was in the hospital recovering from an injury he'd received during the arrest.

The lunch crowd had exited, Henry and Enrico were busy with dinner preparation—it was a comfort-food menu featuring shepherd's pie and mac-and-cheese. I needed to clear my head, so I grabbed my jacket and waved to Benny. "I'll be back in an hour."

"Maybe you should go home and rest. After all, you had a traumatic night."

"Thanks, Benny. That's sweet of you. I just might do that."

There was no way I was resting. There were now *many* questions, and all of them led back to Antonio and the theater. If this case were a Venn diagram, he and/or the ELT would be the two things all of these people had in common: Kenneth Amberlin, Regan Digenza, Tony Dickson, Dr. Xiu, and my attackers.

I climbed into my Metro and cranked the engine. I drove through Etonville, past Snippets, Georgette's, and the frame shop. I toyed with dropping by the Etonville Public Library just to find some quiet space; but all of Etonville was a vast pool of innuendo and I didn't feel up to having last night's incident being the subject of conversation.

I found myself on the outskirts of town, heading onto Route 53, as if my reliable Chevy Metro had a mind of its own and knew what was best for me. Four miles down the road I took the turn-off to Creston. *So this is where I intended to go!* I threaded my way through the town center and debated about taking a breather at my favorite Creston café. I decided against stopping and allowed my instincts full rein. I turned left and slowed down as I passed the Creston PD—Bill's cruiser was still out front. But I didn't have time today to fret over Bill's relationship with a beautiful brunette in Armani.

I'd memorized the Creston address Antonio had visited shortly before his death. I had no idea whether it was near the town center or the soup kitchen or the police department. I punched 112 Terrace Road into my GPS and listened as Genie led me to another part of Creston. I turned left, then right, then left again, past a strip mall and a cemetery, and noticed that small, boxy houses built in the forties and fifties gave way to stately homes on a half acre or so of land. Farther down the road, the street climbed upward, cresting at the top of a hill that overlooked the New York City skyline. The stately homes had become mansions that backed up to a wooded area, with tree-shaded verandas and circular driveways.

"Destination is ahead on the right," Genie said.

I pulled over to the curb, threw the Metro into Park, and leaned back in my seat. I turned off the engine and stared at the house. Or rather the mansion. Probably dating from the 1920s, it was an elegant gray stone Tudor nestled among mature trees that partially hid the driveway. It was set well back from the street on several acres. I could just make out the heavy wooden front door; the slate roof and turrets gave it an English country feel. There had to be over a dozen rooms—probably worth a million or more. I looked across the road. The view of the city was spectacular.

I put my Metro in Drive and inched up the driveway until I could see the entire façade of the house. No lights were visible, though the sun was sinking lower in the sky and casting shade that covered the oval turnaround at the top of the driveway. I pulled up in front, then it occurred to me: This neighborhood could have been a target for the high-end burglaries. I turned off the engine and smoothed my crimson sweater under my leather jacket. While I might pass muster, my Metro wouldn't, I thought ruefully.

I tried for confidence as I approached the door, but had to settle for brave; after all, the future of the Windjammer was at stake. I pushed the bell and waited. From deep within the recesses of the house I heard a chime reverberate, followed by the soft barking of a dog. Possibly a watchdog. Footsteps padded to the door, one set light and quick, the other slow and labored. The barking grew louder. I held my breath as an outdoor light blinked on.

A maid, in a traditional black dress with white collar and cuffs, opened the door. "Yes?"

Behind her, a tiny woman with thinning silver hair and a heavily lined face had both of her hands on the collar of a German shepherd. Her eyes were bright, though rheumy.

"Hello. I'm sorry to bother you. I was looking for 120 Terrace Road. I'm not familiar with this neighborhood . . ." I let my explanation dangle and slid my eyes in the direction of the dog. He must have noticed and gave out a shrill yowl.

"Quiet, Rex. You have to forgive him. He's not very gracious with people he doesn't know. He likes to bark but really is gentle as a lamb," the older woman said.

I glanced at Rex. A lamb? Really?

"He's blind in one eye and as old as me." She let out a tinkle of a laugh. "It's fine, Maria."

The maid nodded, stepped aside, and disappeared into the interior of the house.

"Oh. Well, it's good he barks at strangers. I read about the thefts in Creston." I backed away a step. My quick movement must have startled Rex. He jerked at the woman's hands and I involuntarily yelped.

"Rex!" she said crossly and tapped him on the top of his head. He collapsed on all fours and whimpered.

"Would you like to come in?" she asked, almost wistfully. "My name is Adele."

I guessed she was lonely. But I was a stranger and no matter how old he was, Rex didn't like strangers.

"Maria made an apple strudel," she offered with enthusiasm.

"I guess I could stop in for a minute." I skirted Rex, following her into a grand foyer that led to a winding staircase on one side and opened into a living area on the other.

"Let's sit in here," she said, as though we were two old chums having afternoon tea, and gestured toward the parlor.

"Thank you."

"Maria will serve us." She pushed a discreet button on the outside wall of the room and proceeded to perch on the edge of a green velvet armchair. I sat opposite her on a matching settee. "It was so nice of you to call," she said affectionately.

Since she had no idea who I was, I now guessed she was a tad senile as well as lonely. Rex stretched, bored.

"My name's . . . Dorothy and, well, I was in the neighborhood looking for 120 Terrace Road," I reminded her. Only my mother used my baptismal name. Mostly back when I was a teenager caught in flagrante delicto. But this setting seemed to require formality.

"Oh yes."

What were the odds she'd heard about Antonio's death? I decided to take a chance. "A friend of mine is staying in this area. Antonio Digenza." I scanned her face for any sign of recognition.

She frowned. "That name is not familiar."

"Maybe I have the wrong street. Or number."

"You might want to ask at the house two doors down. They're new to the neighborhood. Maybe your friend is staying there," she said helpfully.

"I'll do that."

Rex had lowered his head onto his paws and was now snoring at Adele's feet while Maria served us tea and strudel. It was delicious, and when Adele forced a second piece on me, I didn't protest.

"I hope you weren't one of the victims of those break-ins," I said with sympathy.

"Goodness no! Rex is as good as a security system."

Rex must have been chasing squirrels in his sleep. His back paws quivered and I swore he was grinning.

"Several of my neighbors had substantial losses," Adele confided.

"Is that so? It's such a relief the police caught them."

"Did they?" She seemed honestly surprised.

"It was in the *Eton*"—I stopped myself—"the Creston paper today. Maybe you don't read the paper?"

"Only the *New York Times*," she said. "Where did you say you were from?"

"South Jersey. The shore area."

"Oh, I love the Jersey Shore," she said.

"Me too." Fall was a perfect time at the beach—the tourists were gone, the ocean had finally warmed up, and the nights were cool. I could feel damp sand on the soles of my feet.

"More strudel?"

It would have been my third slice. I shook my head. "Thanks for the lovely afternoon." I stood and Adele accompanied me to the door. Rex couldn't have cared less. "Maybe you should look into a security system anyway."

"Oh, we have one. At least we did before it broke."

"Maybe Maria could call someone and have it repaired?"

"No need. That nice man is going to take care of it. He should be back any day now," she said.

For some reason my little hairs were acting like Mexican jumping beans. "Nice man?"

"The one who sold security systems. He went all through the house and explained what I'd need for the windows and doors.

"But the system was never installed?"

"Oh, I expect he'll be here in the next day or so. He was such a gentleman, so charming." She smiled. "And so handsome." She twittered girlishly.

"Is that right?"

"My yes. And that beret? So French, you know."

I had a knot the size of Newark in the pit of my stomach. I knew only one person who wore a beret. And was charming. And handsome. And had Adele's address in his cell phone. Could it be that Antonio was participating in the oldest scam in the book? Prey on lonely senior citizens, convince them to relinquish money for services that are never delivered. Was he connected to the robberies? But Adele hadn't been one of the Creston robbery victims. I was dizzy from bouncing one theory against another and so preoccupied I found myself back in Etonville by five o'clock.

Benny was on his cell phone with his wife. "I'll get her. I'm on my way out now." He clicked off. "Got to get the princess. She has a cold," he said. "I'll be back."

Talk about someone who needed a nap. "Go," I said. "See you tomorrow."

He nodded gratefully. "Thanks. I can cover for you tomorrow night if you want."

"We'll see."

Carmen took over as bartender when Benny was out, and Honey picked up tables in the dining room. That meant I would also be serving. But business was not back to pre-Antonio levels, so it would be an easy night.

Honey sat at the bar, concentrating furiously on a sheet of paper. From time to time she scribbled something on a pad. She raised her head, frowning. "Oh hi, Dot." She returned to her task.

Honey had been less snarky lately. I decided to reciprocate. "What's that?" I asked and poured myself a seltzer.

"I'm doing my schedule of classes for next semester."

"You're going back to school this spring?" I hoped I didn't sound too excited. Poor Honey. Learning the restaurant business had not been all she thought it would be.

"Of course. I mean working with Uncle Henry is, like, you know, okay, but I can't miss the Student Packaging Jamboree."

I coughed on a mouthful of seltzer.

"Last year I was part of the Innovation in Design and Sustainability Competition. We won second place," she said with satisfaction. She tapped several times on her cell phone and a one-minute video appeared courtesy of YouTube. "We're, like, receiving our award here. It was insane."

Honey shoved her phone up close to my face. "Wow. Impressive." I started to fold napkins.

Honey took a cue from me and set tables. "If it hadn't been for my Tamper Evidence and Legibility class . . ."

"Rough one, huh?" I asked.

"Dot, you have no idea." Then she beamed. "But I killed Shelf Life."

18

I had to work hard to keep my mind on customers. What was I to do with the information I had gathered this afternoon? Henry's mac-and-cheese was a particular favorite tonight, even though the Windjammer was only a quarter full. Mildred, from the library, came in with her nephew Zach, the Etonville quarterback, and Abby stopped in with her boyfriend Jim before rehearsal.

"Getting close to opening, Abby," I said, just to make small talk.

"Huh." She scowled. "This show has been one calamity after another."

Jim scooped up a last forkful of shepherd's pie. "I told her bad rehearsals mean a good production."

"Jim, that only refers to a dress rehearsal and an opening. Not weeks of disasters."

"Uh-huh. Well, good luck tonight." I cleared Abby's plate and left the check.

I fervently hoped the ELT could withstand *Arsenic and Old Lace*. It was supposed to be a fun evening of theater, not a misfortune plagued by the death of the director, infighting among actors and staff, and costume issues—

"Just give me one of everything on the menu," Lola said and slid onto a stool at the bar.

"Whoa. How about a drink to fortify yourself for the evening?" I said.

"I'm on the wagon tonight. I need to stay sober for this costume parade. Carlyle and Walter have been squaring off all day. And Chrystal is ready to turn her hot glue gun on both of them."

Chrystal's favorite method of hemming costumes in a hurry: hot glue.

I lowered my voice. "I need to tell you something. Let's go."

Carmen delivered Lola's shrimp salad and coffee to my back booth. "Remember when we found those addresses on Antonio's cell phone? One was in Creston. I went there this afternoon."

Her eyes widened. "You did? Dodie, you are some investigator. What did you find?"

I told Lola about Adele and the house and Rex. Then I finished with the charming man who wore a beret and sold her a security system.

"Oh no! You think Antonio was scamming old ladies?"

"I'm not sure how all of this fits together, but what if he was involved in the Creston burglaries?"

Lola held her head in her hands. "I can't believe this. It's just a nightmare that gets worse and worse. If I had suspected any of this about Antonio, I never would have brought him in to direct."

"This might explain his bizarre behavior. And also his friend who came to the theater. Did you tell Suki about Antonio's friend being one of the thieves?"

"She wasn't available. I left a message."

"I have the feeling that Antonio was deep into something illegal, even if it wasn't the Creston break-ins. And it might have gotten him killed."

Lola checked her watch.

"Just wondering . . . did you contact Antonio about directing at the ELT?" I asked.

Lola thought. "No, he emailed me first. Is that important?"

"Not sure. Go to rehearsal. I'll talk with you later."

"I'm fed up with the show. I don't care if the whole set falls in and every actor's naked." She groaned. "That can't happen, can it?"

Physical labor had a tendency to help me think. I sent Henry, Honey, and the rest of the staff home. Then I went to work mopping the dining room floor, wiping down the tables for the second time, and scrubbing the bar. Finding out what had made Antonio's heart stop might unmask a killer and, hopefully, a motivation. I wondered if the arrest and interrogation of Antonio's friend had revealed anything about Antonio. It was difficult to tell what Bill knew. He'd been pretty tight-lipped about the Creston case, skeptical about my questions on Antonio's death, and generally unavailable to really hear what I had to say. I wrung out a cloth. It was exasperating.

My cell rang. Lola probably had had a horrendous night. "Hi. How did it—?"

"Dodie O'Dell?"

It was a female voice that I didn't recognize immediately. The caller ID was no help: Private. "Yes?"

"This is Brianna Kincaid. I'm sorry to be calling this late." She paused.

My mind shifted gears and I replaced images of ELT turmoil with one of Antonio's classy first wife. "No problem. I'm just closing the Windjammer. What can I do for you?"

Brianna took a breath, her voice wavering. "I'd like to speak with you. Can we meet?"

"Sure."

"I have to be in New York tomorrow morning for a meeting and I pass Etonville on my way home. Would lunch be convenient? We could meet at the Windjammer," she said.

So she wasn't afraid of the food here either!

"That's fine. I might have to keep one eye on the dining room," I said.

Her laugh was soft and heartfelt. "I understand. I manage a business and often find myself multitasking. I'll be there around one."

She clicked off. I caught a glimpse of the wall clock. It was almost midnight. I locked up, checked out Main Street for errant night wanderers, and hopped into my Metro.

I ransacked the laundry basket I'd left in the living room and changed into flannel pajamas and my terry cloth robe. I brewed a cup of coffee and sat down at the kitchen table with my laptop to continue hunting for a Tony Dickson who would turn out to be Antonio Digenza. I picked up where I'd left off earlier in the day and returned to the third page of links and began scrolling.

For another forty-five minutes I read about Tony Dicksons: a software executive in Seattle, a real estate agent in Texas, a retired naval officer in San Diego, and a dentist in Kentucky. I stretched and yawned. What would Antonio, or Tony, gain by adopting another name? Using a pseudonym was not a crime, lots of artists did it. Of course, they were not all hiding questionable pasts.

I debated whether to continue my digging on the Internet or give up and sleep, to search another day. I was exhausted but due to the caffeine still bug-eyed. I decided I could survive another half hour. I skimmed the links on page ten, bypassing an article on a Tony Dickson who was a building contractor in Queensland, Australia, and marveling at the breadth of the online world, when I saw it: a story on the frequency of senior-citizen cons. It linked to a brief mention of the 2004 Las Vegas arrest of Tony Dickson and K. T. Amberlin for a telemarketing scam that sold bogus health-care products to the elderly. They were sentenced to three-to-five years each. The last line of the article added that Dickson had previously been convicted of misdemeanor check fraud and given probation.

I collapsed against the kitchen chair, my brain whirling. Despite the warmth of my flannel pajamas and robe, I felt a chill in the room and shivered involuntarily. Antonio had a criminal record as Tony Dickson, and had experience scamming senior citizens. Selling phony security systems to wealthy, lonely folks like Adele would have come easy; his looks and acting skills would have been a bonus. Antonio had evolved from theater artist to con artist. Suddenly my eyelids felt like bricks. I shut down my laptop and tucked myself into bed. As I dozed off, I felt a tickle at the back of my brain. Something that I had read . . .

19

K. T. Amberlin! I bolted upright in bed. My alarm clock said seven, which meant that I'd been asleep for less than five hours. Never mind. I didn't have any time to waste today. Something in the foggy depths of my consciousness had remembered *Las Vegas arrest of Tony Dickson and K. T. Amberlin* . . . Kenneth Amberlin. Lola's stranger who was arrested for the Creston burglaries. The first concrete link between Antonio and the break-ins.

Usually I luxuriated in a morning shower, but today I rushed into and out of the water, dressed in dark slacks and a black sweater, stared longingly for a brief moment at my Keurig before deciding I didn't have time to sit and drink coffee. My morning java would have to wait.

I grabbed my windbreaker and dashed to my car just as the first drops of rain hit the windshield, the sky an ashen blanket of gray that threatened a deluge at any minute. The *slap-slap* of my wipers sounded like a drumbeat: get-going-get-going. I stepped on the accelerator and my Metro lurched forward. I coasted across Etonville; at this hour the town had not yet completely awakened and many people would wait until the storm had passed before venturing outside.

I hoped I wasn't waking Lola up too early, but while I shampooed my hair in the shower, I'd made up my mind to confront Tiffany. What did she know about Antonio's past? Regan Digenza? The Creston capers? Even in the worst of marriages—and I wasn't assuming theirs was—a husband and wife probably shared information. Antonio had to have let some things slip. I also intended to pressure her into asking Bill to speed up the lab analysis of Antonio's blood and tissue samples, maybe have them run additional tests to check for toxins.

I reached the light at Main and Anderson and flipped on my left turn signal. I glanced at my cell and tapped on Lola's name. I wanted to talk before the light changed and I put myself in danger of breaking the law.

"Hello?" Lola said, sounding groggy.

"It's me. I'm on my way to your place. Be there in a minute."

"What time is it?"

"Almost eight. I have to speak with Tiffany. I have a few questions for her and you're not going to believe what I found out about Antonio's past," I blurted out.

"Are you okay? You sound like you're on speed. How much caffeine have you had this morning?"

"I'm fine, but I think we can crack this case wide open. I surfed the Internet for hours and—"

"Did you say you wanted to see Tiffany?"

"Right. Anyway, I'm going through all of these Tony Dickson links and—"

The light changed and I hung a left off of Main Street just as a white Mercedes sailed past me turning right onto Main. The car was somewhat familiar; the driver more so.

"But Tiffany's—" Lola said.

"—not at your house. She just passed me on the road."

"She received a call a little bit ago and said she had to meet someone in Creston. I think it's Carlyle."

I slowed down and pulled over to the curb. "Doesn't he live in Queens with his mother?"

"Carlyle's been staying at the Daytime Inn in Creston."

"Do you know where it is?" I asked.

"You're going there now? You could catch her later at rehearsal—"

"I can't wait until rehearsal," I said.

"Come by and pick me up. I'll go with you," Lola said.

"I don't have much time—"

"I'll be ready in five."

True to her word, Lola was ready to go five minutes after I pulled into her driveway. Blond hair meticulous, brown tweed slacks and brown blazer making her look as though she'd just stepped off the cover of a fashion magazine. How did she do it?

"Let's take my Lexus."

It was fine by me. I knew Lola preferred to glide along in her sleek, luxury vehicle instead of bouncing around in my old Metro.

"But first we need to pick up Carol at Coffee Heaven," she said as she cruised down Main.

"Carol? Why?"

"We were supposed to have breakfast this morning. We've been trying to get together for over a week and I—"

"Okay fine. I just want to find Tiffany as soon as possible." Of course picking up Carol also gave me the opportunity to grab a caramel macchiato.

"Oooh this will be fun," Carol said, and slammed the back door of the Lexus. "Tailing a suspect. I'm glad Rita's opening the shop today."

I savored my coffee. The hot liquid trickled down my throat and warmed up my insides. The temperature had dropped ten degrees since last night; a streak of lightning and clap of thunder off to the east of Etonville made us all recoil. "Tiffany's not a suspect and we're not really tailing her. We're just going to pay her a visit at Carlyle's motel room. You do have their cell numbers, right?"

"The contact sheet for the production is in my purse. Look in the outside pocket."

I rummaged through Lola's bag and found a sheaf of papers. "This looks like a rehearsal schedule."

"On the bottom of the pile."

"The girls at Snippets were right all along. Tiffany and Carlyle are a 'thing.'" Carol laughed and took a bite of her bagel.

"*You* said the *girls* said it was Tiffany and Romeo." I found the contact sheet. "Got it."

"Well, it was Romeo at the beginning, but then after Antonio died, Tiffany went to Carlyle for comfort."

Did Antonio know about Tiffany's romances with his assistant and her leading man? Of course, he was a probable serial groom with three wives. Lola shot onto State Route 53, zigzagging in and out of traffic. I clutched the passenger-side armrest until my knuckles were white.

"The Creston exit is right up here," I said.

"You don't want to get off there," Carol said. "The Daytime Inn is closer to the following exit. It's at the other end of town."

"Are you sure?" Lola asked.

"Positive. My in-laws stayed there last Christmas." Carol spoke with confidence and ate the last of her bagel.

"What should I do?" Lola glanced sideways at me.

"Keep going, I guess."

The GPS had a different opinion. "Recalculating."

We took Carol's exit and came to a stop sign at the end of the access road. "Turn right here," she said.

"But the GPS says straight ahead," I countered.

"You turn right here and then about a mile down the road you turn left. The Daytime Inn is on the corner."

I shrugged. "Okay." Lola eased into the stream of cars heading down the street.

"Recalculating," the GPS announced.

"What's the point of having a GPS system if we ignore it?" Lola asked.

"They always take you the longest way around," Carol offered.

I didn't agree, but there was no point in arguing as long as we arrived at the Daytime Inn soon. I felt an urgency to speak with Tiffany that was driven by my upcoming meeting with Bill.

Carol leaned forward between the two front seats. "Turn here. The Daytime Inn is just beyond the post office."

Lola followed orders, but instead of "Your destination is on the left" we got "Recalculating."

"Carol, are you sure you remember where the inn is?" Lola was getting a little impatient.

Carol hesitated. "It was right here last Christmas."

I cut in. "Never mind. Let's just see where the GPS takes us."

Three minutes later Lola steered her Lexus into a full parking lot between a van and a pickup truck. The Daytime Inn was a typical motel strip of rooms—about a dozen on this side of the building. I assumed there was another parallel set of rooms in the back. The complex was whitewashed, with a bright red roof; the packed parking lot suggested it was doing a brisk business.

"Now what?" Lola asked.

"Isn't that Tiffany's car?" I pointed to a white Mercedes an aisle ahead of us.

Lola craned her neck. "Yes, I believe it is. Should we call her? Or Carlyle?"

I didn't want to startle them; on the other hand, the three of us showing up at his motel room at 9:00 a.m. was going to be a surprise any way you looked at it. But calling either of them gave Tiffany an opportunity to refuse to chat with us. "Let me try to get his room number from the clerk on duty. If that fails, we can always call. You two stay here. I'll be right back."

The steady torrent of rain that had fallen since we'd left Etonville had reduced to a drizzle. I walked quickly to the inn's office, opened the door. The man on duty was in his late forties, had an overnight growth of stubble on his face, drooping eyelids, and wore a wrinkled, pale pink shirt. As I entered he stubbed out a cigarette.

I smiled at him through a hazy wash of blue smoke. "Good morning."

His eyes travelled from my head to my feet. "You need a room?"

"Not really. I'm trying to locate one of your guests. Carlyle . . ." It dawned on me that I had no idea what his last name was. "Carlyle," I said firmly.

"Sorry, but we don't give out room numbers." He withdrew another cigarette from a pack he'd stashed underneath the counter. He rolled it between his thumb and forefinger, no doubt eager to see me leave.

"I understand. But Carlyle is a relative of mine . . . and there's been a bit of a family emergency." I tried for sad, but only got as far as forlorn. "He's medium height, brown hair . . . maybe if I took a look at the register—"

"Why don't you call him. You gotta have his phone number. If you're his relative." He dismissed me as though he'd seen and heard it all, and my lame explanation didn't even rise to a level worthy of his attention.

"Of course I have his number—"

A horn honked in the parking lot. Several short beeps, then a long one.

"What the . . . ?" he said, and walked to the door.

I looked over his shoulder to see Carol standing outside the Lexus waving at me furiously to come back.

"Do you know her?" he asked.

"Uh . . . thanks for your help," I said and hurried out.

Lola had the engine running as I vaulted into the front seat. "What's going on?"

"Tiffany and Carlyle just left." She backed out of her parking space, swung a wide arc around an aisle of automobiles and floored the gas pedal.

"They turned left at the light." Carol searched the roadway ahead.

"Quick thinking, you two," I said. They both grinned.

We barely beat it through the intersection before the light turned red. The drizzle became a deluge and Lola flipped on the windshield wipers. Four cars away, Tiffany crawled to a stop behind a dump truck. A battered Volvo hung a right and a delivery van turned left. It was as though both cars knew we needed a clear path to the Mercedes. There was only one car between us now.

"Do you think they know we're following them?" Carol asked.

"No idea. But unless they spotted you two in the parking lot, they'd have no reason to suspect we'd be here," I said.

Tiffany meandered down the street for several blocks before reaching the town center. They were certainly taking their time.

"Where are they going?" Lola asked, inching along.

I checked my watch. "Breakfast?"

Carol mused. "So this low-speed chase might end up in a coffee shop?"

Sure enough, Tiffany edged her Mercedes into a metered space in front of my favorite café, after Coffee Heaven. "I know this place. Great food."

Tiffany and Carlyle got out and sauntered into the café, not a care in the world. We found a space farther down the street.

"Now what?" Lola asked and switched off the ignition.

"I'm in the mood for an espresso and a Danish. What about you two? Follow my lead," I said as we entered the café. "We don't want to spook them."

Tiffany and Carlyle were seated at a table in the far corner. I requested a booth near the door for us. Lola and Carol slipped onto one bench; I sat opposite, leaning slightly to my right. I could see through the restaurant to the back, where Tiffany and Carlyle had their heads bent over menus. "I have a good view. Let's order something, give them a chance to eat, and then—"

"Pounce?" Carol asked excitedly.

"More like slink."

We ordered coffee and food and talked quietly among ourselves. I wasn't sure what I was waiting for; I figured I'd know it when the time was right.

I was halfway through my strawberry pastry when Carlyle rose and proceeded to walk toward us. Too late I realized we'd put ourselves directly in the path to the restrooms.

He glanced our way, then looked back again. "Lola?"

Lola had a forkful of omelet on the edge of her tongue. "Carlyle. Oh! Nice to see you."

He gazed from one to the other of us. "What are you doing here?"

Lola swallowed the omelet, Carol fiddled with her napkin, and I was left to speak. "Actually we're here to speak with Tiffany."

"Tiffany?" He looked over his shoulder as if to check that she was still at their table. "Why? Is this something about the show?" he asked suspiciously. "I don't care what Walter says, that kid from the restaurant is not replacing Tiffany."

Good news for the Windjammer, not so good for Honey. "It's not about the show. It's about Antonio."

Carlyle's back straightened. "What about him?"

"I suggest we join you at your table," I said coolly.

Carlyle forgot about the restroom and Carol and Lola forgot about their meals. We made our way to the back of the café. Tiffany was, as expected, shocked to see us, especially Lola.

"Did you follow me?" she asked with a touch of belligerence.

"Well . . ." Lola stalled.

"Yes," I said, fastening my eyes on hers and refusing to let go. "There are some things I need to ask you. About Antonio." At the mention of his name, her face crumpled.

"Leave Antonio alone!" Carlyle demanded. "It upsets Tiffany."

Those words are familiar. "So it was you who put the note on my windshield."

Carlyle looked dumbfounded, Tiffany mystified.

"You threatened Dodie?" Lola asked.

"I just wanted her to back off," he said.

I pressed my advantage and dove gently, but resolutely, into Antonio's past: his name change, his scams, his time in prison. I concluded with the pièce de résistance: Kenneth Amberlin—one of the two crooks arrested for the Creston thefts—was, most likely, an acquaintance of Antonio's and his former partner. I left out the Creston security scam, and the implication that Antonio might have been involved in the break-ins himself.

Tiffany and Carlyle swung from suspicious to dazed to flabbergasted. If I had any doubts that they were blameless with regard to Antonio's death, their responses dispelled all reservations. Especially Tiffany. She was not that good an actor.

Needless to say, Lola and Carol were equally stunned. Carol shook her head in disbelief from time to time and Lola commented under her breath.

"He never mentioned any of this to you?" I asked.

"Of course not. Do you think I'd marry an ex-con?" Tiffany said defensively.

"But didn't you ever ask him about his past?"

She shrugged. "Not really. I wasn't interested in what he did before he met me. But he's dead. So what do I do with all of this now?" she whined.

Carlyle took her hand. He'd been in the dark about his mentor, too.

"I don't think he died of simple cardiac arrest. I think he was murdered." There. I'd said it out loud.

Carol and Lola traded uneasy glances.

"Antonio murdered? Now wait a minute," Carlyle said. "The police never said anything like that." He slid his eyes to Tiffany, just to be sure.

"I'll be delivering this evidence to Chief Thompson this afternoon."

"But this will ruin his reputation," Tiffany wailed.

"It was bound to come out sooner or later. Look, you're his widow. There is one last thing you can do for him," I said, hoping to play on her guilt.

"What?" all four of them asked in unison.

"Call the chief and pressure him to get the lab results. Maybe insist that the lab test his blood for toxins."

"Toxins . . . ?" Tiffany looked truly bewildered now.

"As in something poisonous?" Carlyle asked, his face pale.

"Possibly. As his widow you could get it done."

She and Carlyle eased a couple of inches away from each other, their faces studying the table.

Tiffany hesitated. "I don't know . . ."

"Tiffany," I said softly, "don't you want to know the truth about Antonio's death?"

She studied me a moment, then took a peek at Carlyle. "Yes."

I scribbled the Etonville Police Department number on a napkin and nudged it across the table. "Do it today, okay?"

"Uh-huh," she said.

I stood up and Carol and Lola, looking wrung out from the morning's adventure, followed suit. "By the way, I know you've met Brianna."

Tiffany sniffed. "Oh, her."

I crossed my fingers on this one. "Is it possible that Antonio might have had another wife? A Regan Digenza?"

Any trace of empathy for Antonio's untimely death disappeared in an instant. Tiffany's face turned red, her expression apoplectic. "What?"

We paid our check and lit out.

20

After swearing Lola and Carol to secrecy, I picked up my Metro at Lola's and drove to the Windjammer. Benny was doing a liquor and soda inventory and Carmen was prepping the dining room.

"Hey, Benny. How's the little princess?"

"Great. A kids' aspirin and a good night's sleep."

"I wish that's all it took for me," I said wistfully. "Life was way less complicated when I was five."

"No kidding. Did I show you pictures of her birthday party?"

He had, but I pretended he hadn't, and watched as Benny scrolled through his cell phone—pictures of his daughter posing and making faces in a frilly pink dress, playing outside with a bunch of other five- and six-year-olds, eating cake and ice cream. And a last one with the princess on Benny's knee. "Really cute. She's getting so big."

"Yeah. Pretty soon she'll be in college and then getting married." He unpacked a carton of white wine.

"Slow down, papa. You've got at least a dozen years before she leaves home."

"Speaking of college, did you hear Honey is going back next semester?" he asked.

Honey burst out of the kitchen door. "Dot, Uncle Henry can't find the cream cheese."

Henry was cooking his shrimp chowder for lunch. Cream cheese was his secret ingredient to create a smooth, rich texture. "Third shelf of the refrigerator."

Honey tilted her head and proceeded to text. "Like, that Walter guy at the theater? He asked me if I ever acted." She stuck one hand on her hip. "I think he might want me to take Tiffany's place. I read her lines that one night and I think I really impressed him."

I remembered Carlyle's tirade just hours ago about Honey not substituting for Tiffany. "Oh?" I was noncommittal.

Benny grinned at me. "Did you tell him you'd do the role?"

Honey flipped her hair off her shoulders breezily. "I hate to say no, but, like, I have to catch up on my reading." She held up a paperback book. *Structural Packaging: Designing Outside the Box*. "I don't have time for silly things like plays and acting." She walked off.

Benny hooted quietly. I shook my head and followed Honey back into the kitchen. "Smells good in here," I called out.

Enrico looked up from the stove, where he was stirring green onions in butter. "Good morning, Miss Dodie." He smiled, his eyes sparkling.

"Back at ya, Enrico."

Henry peeled shrimp and tutored Honey through the blending of the rest of the chowder ingredients. It was almost endearing to watch Henry's patience with his niece. Almost.

"Dodie, you better call Gillian and see if she's available. Honey's going back to school," he said, a little woefully.

"So I heard." Gillian was our on-again, off-again server who'd quit this summer due to romantic predicaments. Her then-boyfriend moved to New York State and she'd joined him. But things must not have worked out, because she'd texted her availability just last week. "Henry will miss you, Honey."

Honey shrugged and stirred the pot of soup. "I have my career to consider."

Don't we all. My career had been the Windjammer for the past two years; but with the murder investigation of Jerome Angleton and now the death of Antonio, I was spending more time outside the restaurant. A fact that did not go unnoticed by Henry.

I did a quick check of the meat freezer and the vegetable bins and joined Benny and Carmen in the dining room. A few customers began to straggle in. The numbers were still less than before the food festival, but business was increasing. Probably due to the reality that eating establishments in Etonville were limited. Nonetheless, I was determined to see a resolution to the Antonio affair.

I sat in my back booth and answered text messages. Lola asked whether she should share Antonio's past with Walter—no. My undergraduate college asked for a donation—maybe later. And then there was a text from Bill reminding me that we had a meeting today after football practice, which was being held on the town's soccer field. My heart did a little flip-flop just seeing his name attached to the message. I texted back that I remembered.

Then I came down to earth and realized I'd have to reckon with Bill's reaction to the nosing around I'd been doing for the past ten days. In April he'd been less than enthusiastic about my investigative activity, even though he was appreciative when the murder was solved. But now?

I scrolled through some texts and found the picture that Lola had sent me of Regan Digenza at the food festival. I still felt she was one of the keys to Antonio's death. Bill had been a good guy to give me her name; how would he feel about sharing her address?

The door opened and Brianna entered, scanning the room. I waved from my booth and she smiled.

We both binged on Henry's shrimp chowder. She asked about my leaving the Jersey Shore after Hurricane Sandy. I asked about the floral business. When Brianna paused to blot her mouth on the napkin, I checked her out: tan slacks with a sharp crease, a matching tan sweater, her hair perfectly styled. She could have been on her way to an afternoon of bridge.

"So the florist shop was a family business?" I asked.

"For many years. I took over when I moved back from California. It was supposed to be a temporary job." She shrugged. "But I enjoy management."

"So do I. I found out how much I was into it when I did an internship at a Philadelphia restaurant."

"Which one? I'm down there quite a bit," she said.

"Patricia's Grill."

Brianna arched an eyebrow. "Very nice. By the way, how's the play coming along?"

I smiled. "The ELT is always on the brink of disaster. Of course, with Antonio gone . . . they've had to scramble."

"I remember Antonio pulling lots of late nights back in the day."

"This is community theater. Everybody takes off by ten, ten thirty. Many of them end up in here to drown their rehearsal sorrows."

We laughed. Carmen brought us coffee and Georgette's double-fudge chocolate cake. "You wanted to talk?" I said carefully.

Brianna ducked her head. "I think I might have given you the wrong impression about Antonio and me."

I set my fork on the dessert plate.

"I implied I hadn't seen him in a while. That wasn't true. Antonio visited me several times in the last month."

I leaned back against the seat. Of course. The other Rumson address in Antonio's cell phone. How else would Brianna have heard of the Etonville Little Theatre?

"You see, Antonio and Tiffany . . . were going through a rough patch and he needed to talk."

With an ex-wife? "I heard that they might have been headed for a divorce," I said.

She nodded. "I didn't want you to think I wasn't being completely honest about our friendship." She twisted her napkin. "Antonio and I'd been together almost fifteen years. I guess old habits die hard."

"True." I rubbed at a smudge of coffee smeared on the table. "You must have known about Antonio's background."

"What do you mean?"

"Tony Dickson. I'm guessing Antonio was his stage name?"

"So you discovered his secret." Brianna smiled, guarded. "He was such a romantic, with a touch of flamboyance. 'Antonio' was way more theatrical than 'Tony.' He thought people might be attracted by a foreign-sounding name."

"And less likely to discover his criminal record." My words landed with a thud.

Brianna paused, then spoke in measured sentences. "That was after my time. Antonio had been running a scam with a friend of his for a number of years. It started out legitimately enough, but when the two of them saw the potential profit in pretending to sell a product instead of actually selling it . . ." She shrugged. "Obviously he regretted his past and wanted to reestablish his directing career." She examined my face. "You're a smart woman. I knew that the first time we met. I have the feeling you're investigating Antonio's death."

"I'm not a private investigator. I've just been asking a few questions," I said.

"You don't believe it was a simple heart attack, do you?"

Once again I could see that Brianna was nobody's fool. She eyed me calmly. How much to tell her? I squirmed in my seat. Like the time I got sent to the principal's office for bringing a lizard to show-and-tell. It escaped and caused a mad stampede of seven-year-olds to the playground. "I'd like a definitive explanation for his death."

She frowned. "Antonio had complained of chest pain recently. I begged him to see a doctor."

"I think he had been seeing a Dr. Xiu in Bernridge. She uses traditional Chinese medicine."

"For his heart?" she asked carefully.

"For his stomach."

Brianna looked at me quizzically.

My cell rang. "Excuse me." I tapped Answer. "Uh, hey. It's me."

"Hi, Pauli. Are the website changes finished? Send me an invoice and I'll have Henry pay you."

"Okay. Uh, thanks." He hesitated.

"Something up?" I asked.

"Well . . . uh . . . remember, like, when you said you wanted to find that other person who knew Antonio? Regan Digenza . . . ?"

"Hang on, okay?"

I buried my cell in my lap and turned to Brianna. "I'm sorry, but I should take this call."

She nodded. "No problem. I have to get back to the shop. But I'd like to know what you find out," Brianna said. "I cared about Antonio, you know. And like I said, old habits . . ."

I stood when she did and, on a whim, I gave her a hug. "I'll keep you posted."

I watched her walk out the door. "So Pauli, what were you saying?"

"Well, uh, in class last night we worked on facial recognition software." His tempo picked up. "And, uh, like I ran that picture of Regan Digenza from LinkedIn and found out some stuff."

I stacked our dessert plates and smiled my thanks to Carmen as she wiped the table and cleared the dishes. "What kind of stuff?"

"Her name was, like, Regan Rottinger before she married that director. Like, she was a nurse and worked in a hospital and then she, like, worked for this doctor and then there was this problem and she got fired—"

My cell buzzed. "Great work, Pauli. I have another call coming in. I'll get back to you, okay?"

Pauli clicked off.

I didn't recognize the number. "Hello?"

"Dodie?"

It was Tiffany. She sounded upset; of course given past, present, and future events, there were many good reasons for her to be distressed. "Did you call Chief Thompson?"

"I left him a message with the other officer. And I'll tell Edna at rehearsal tonight."

"You're doing the right thing," I said.

"Yeah. Well." She paused.

I could hear I needed to coax her into revealing her motivation for phoning me. "Is there something else?"

"You know, after our meeting this morning I got to thinking. About Antonio and other things, and you mentioned a Regan Digenza."

"Uh-huh."

"How do you know her?" she asked.

"She was at the funeral service and I got her license plate number. Chief Thompson got her name." I fervently hoped I wasn't violating Bill's trust by divulging his role in this. "You didn't know her, right?"

"Not exactly. I mean I didn't know someone named Regan."

"But . . . ?"

"There was this woman Antonio met with this year. I saw them together a few times and when I asked him about her, he said she was an actress that he'd worked with in the past."

That part wasn't a lie. "Would you recognize her if you saw her picture?"

"Yeah, I think so," she said.

"I have to run now, but I'll text it. Let me know if it's Regan," I said.

"Okay."

"Tiffany, did Antonio ever complain of gastrointestinal problems?"

"Gastro what?" she asked.

"Stomach issues. Was he seeing a doctor?"

Tiffany barked a laugh. "He hated doctors."

Etonville's Youth Football Tigers were relegated to the town's soccer field since the high school was holding its own practice on the football field. It didn't matter that it wasn't a real gridiron and there were no goalposts; Bill's players were running drills and getting their confidence up for Saturday's game against a youth league in Bernridge. At least the rain had stopped and the sun was tussling with the clouds to make an appearance.

Bill schooled his quarterback and receiver to get on the same page—Zach backpedaling and throwing between defenders to a boy I didn't know. "Extend your arms," Bill yelled to the receiver. "Keep your feet moving."

Zach heaved the ball and it went wildly off course. Bill clapped his hands. "Okay, let's try this again."

Across the field, one of the dads was running defensive drills, as in tackling techniques and wrapping up ball carriers on contact. Mostly the players just fell on top of each other and rolled around on the wet turf.

The temperature was dropping gently and a light wind had picked up. I wrapped my windbreaker more tightly around my midsection and tucked my legs up on the metal bleacher bench.

"Almost finished here," Bill shouted.

"No problem. I have Benny covering. So no hurry," I shouted back.

He smiled. "Good."

My cell binged. A text from Tiffany: IT'S HER.

The message was cryptic but clear: Antonio had been seen with Regan in the year before he died. I felt thrilled at the information but more confused than ever. That made two ex-wives he was seeing. No wonder the marriage was on shaky ground . . . Chalk up another loose end.

I watched Bill motion for the team to gather. He gave me a quick wave. "Let me finish up with the kids and then we can talk."

"Sure."

Bill summarized the afternoon's practice drills, first with the offense and then the defense, scrawling on his whiteboard for clarity, while the kids, with mud-streaked uniforms, flushed faces, and a few runny noses, watched him in awe. It was fun to see their reverence for him.

He clapped his hands. "Let's do two laps and call it a day."

"Okay, Coach," they said in unison and took off.

Bill had a brief conference with his assistant dad, took off his ball cap, and rubbed the back of his hand across his forehead. "Jimmy's father is closing up. Let's go talk."

"Fine. Where?"

He squinted as he watched the kids trudge around the perimeter of the soccer field. "How about dinner at my place?"

My pulse quickened. His place . . . I instinctively glanced down at my wardrobe. My top and pants were functional if not striking. They would have to do. "Well, okay."

"I have to drop off some equipment at the high school first. Let me have your phone."

Immediately I was vigilant: Was he looking for something? "Uh . . ." I withdrew my cell from my bag.

He held out his hand. "Here's my address." He opened up my Notes app and typed in *74 Gracie Ave.* "I should be there in about forty minutes."

I didn't let on that I already knew his address. Not far from Carol's house. Not really time enough for me to go home and change, but long enough to buy a bottle of wine.

"By the way, Suki said I had a message to call Tiffany Digenza. Know what it's about?"

"Coach?" Zach tugged on Bill's arm. "Are we still going to do the shotgun on Saturday?"

Bill nodded. "We sure are!"

Zach grinned and jogged away.

"Now where were we?" Bill asked.

"I'll see you in a few." I backed away, car keys jingling.

He turned his attention to the team.

Bill's place was on the other end of town from mine. I drove my Metro to the wine shop next door to Georgette's Bakery and wandered the aisles, examining the shelf that held the expensive Cabernets. I recalled from our last meal that he was partial to reds. Of course that dinner was a disaster, and anyway, was he cooking or ordering in? I chose a bottle generally out of my price range, pulled out a credit card and paid. Once back in my car, I had a few minutes to kill, so I brushed my hair, swiped a lipstick across my lips, and called Lola.

"Hey, it's me."

"Dodie, where are you? Want to come by for a bite before I have to go off to rehearsal?" Lola asked.

"Can't. I'm having dinner with Bill."

I could hear Lola's eyes open wider. "Well, well . . ."

"Nothing like that. At least I don't think it is. This is more a business meeting."

"Call me after, okay? No matter how late," she said.

"FYI, Tiffany told me Antonio met with Regan last year. And Brianna stopped by and said Antonio had been in touch with her."

Lola gasped. "No! This plot really does thicken."

I parked in front of 74 Gracie and checked out Bill's residence: a redbrick, center-hall Colonial with white pillars and black shutters. Low shrubs outlined the front of the house and a lone weeping willow, whose leaves had already begun to turn yellow, swayed gently on the front lawn. Bill's BMW was parked in the driveway. The neighborhood was authentic early American, with the types of homes that gave Etonville its historical bona fides.

I grabbed my wine and purse and walked to the front door. I used the brass knocker to beat out a short, staccato rhythm against the plate. Bill appeared—he'd changed into a tan cashmere sweater that clung to his biceps, and khakis. His sandy brush cut was neatly arranged, his musky aftershave intoxicating. I felt a little shiver. How had he found the time to do this Superman act?

"Come on in," he said and stepped back from the door.

"Thanks. Lovely house."

"I've been doing some work on it. Got a ways to go yet."

"Really?" I gazed around the front hallway. It was all polished hardwood floors, a gleaming handrail that ran up the staircase, and fresh flowers in a vase on a small table. House beautiful! Bill's home made mine seem like a shanty.

"Let's go into the kitchen. I'm just finishing up."

I handed him the bottle of wine. "I hope this works."

Bill glanced at the label and let out a low whistle. "Nice."

"Something smells terrific." I followed him through the hallway and into a modern, fully loaded kitchen with stainless steel appliances and a center island. I had caught him chopping veggies for a salad. "Can I help?"

He gave me a corkscrew, two glasses, and an aerator. "Have at it," he said and smiled.

My heart melted. I nodded at the Crock-Pot on the counter. "What's cooking?"

"White chicken chili." He sprayed a handful of red peppers into the salad bowl. "Ever have it?"

"Years ago," I said. "My mom gave me a slow cooker as a setting-up-my-own-household gift when I graduated from college. I tried just about every recipe in the cookbook."

"It's easy to prepare dinner ahead of time."

Maybe he'd been planning our "date" as early as this morning? The thought made me a little giddy.

"I like to have a hot meal ready when I get home from work."

Nope. "Cheers." I tasted the wine.

"Let's sit in the living room. I have about forty-five minutes to go on the chili."

Bill led the way through a dining room scene right out of an American Revolution museum, from Windsor chairs around an oak table and a Chippendale block chest, to a comfy living room where a fire was ready. He lit the logs and a pungent, smoky aroma filled the room.

"I love the smell of wood burning," I said.

"I promised myself the first house I owned would have a working fireplace."

"Oh. Is this the . . . ?" I hoped I wasn't prying.

"First house? Yep. I've always been a renter."

I wanted to ask if he rented alone. "I guess you like early American."

He laughed. "I got a good deal on the house and thought I should furnish it accordingly."

"You should be on the historical landmarks tour." I relaxed into one of his cushiony loungers.

We chatted amiably about his football team and its limited prospects, the upcoming opening of *Arsenic and Old Lace* and its potential perils, and Rita's rehearsal dinner at the Windjammer. We avoided any mention of Antonio.

The timer in the kitchen rang and Bill excused himself to get dinner on the table. He declined my help, so I took it easy and inhaled the comforting, autumn fragrance of the fire. I glanced at the mantel.

Wineglass in hand, I moved to the fireplace and faced a series of photographs: an elderly couple, probably his parents, flanking a younger Bill in uniform; a large family grouping of several generations; and a more recent shot of Bill and an attractive woman. I picked up the picture and stared. It was the brunette from Creston. My heart sank.

"Soup's on!" Bill called from the dining room.

I hurriedly replaced the photo. "Coming."

"This is delicious." I scooped up another mouthful of the white chicken chili. "I can taste the chili powder and paprika. But something else . . . ?"

"Cumin. And a bottle of beer." He chuckled.

"I like the avocado garnish," I said. "You're quite the cook!"

"Well, it's not like a meal at La Famiglia."

Four-star La Famiglia. Home of our last formal dinner date, when Bill and I clashed over investigative techniques—basically my illegal email hacking—and I ended up apologizing to Henry for cheating on the Windjammer. It was the evening from hell.

"Might be good to put on the Windjammer menu," I said lightly.

"Not a bad idea." He paused to spear a plum tomato. "Is business picking up?"

"A little," I said. "But once Antonio's death is finally sorted out, I think everyone will come around."

Bill's tomato had just reached his lips. "Sorted out?"

I took a drink of wine and watched him over the rim of my glass. "Well, you know how I feel about unfinished business."

He put his fork down. "I know how you feel about digging into crime scenes. Which his death is not. At least as far as the medical examiner is concerned."

The alcohol was going to my head and sending my thought process into slow motion. I was struggling both for a comeback and to remember which pieces of evidence I had already shared with Bill, which ones I wanted to lay on him now, and which ones I should keep to myself for the present.

His cell phone rang. "Excuse me. I need to get that," he said politely and crossed into the kitchen.

I heard him answer the phone, then pause and listen. "She did?" he said. His voice grew louder and I could feel his eyes on the back of my head. "That's fine. Can you stop by my office tomorrow morning?" Pause. "Sure. I'll see you then."

He clicked off, laid his cell on the sideboard, and sat down. "That was Tiffany."

There was no point in playing dumb. "I figured as much."

"She is requesting that I expedite the lab tests on Antonio. To rule out toxic substances."

"Uh-huh."

"She said you told her to call me?" Bill said.

I placed my napkin on the table. "I couldn't ignore the mounting evidence anymore."

"Are you suggesting I am?"

It was déjà vu all over again: this night was dangerously close to resembling last spring's dinner fiasco. "Of course not. You've been in Creston and I just happened to . . . notice a few things. Come across some facts that can't be . . ."

"Ignored."

"Right.

"Such as?" he asked.

"Regan Digenza was at the food festival, even though I didn't see her there at the time. What was she doing creeping around Etonville?"

"Creeping? Just because she attended a local—"

"And why did Antonio visit a Chinese doctor for gastrointestinal problems?"

"He what? With whom?" Bill looked completely lost.

Once I started, things tripped off my tongue. "And why did he change his name from Tony Dickson to Antonio Digenza?"

"Change his name?" he asked sternly.

"It probably had something to do with his criminal background that was connected to at least one of the burglars arrested for the Creston robberies—"

"Wait a minute," he said louder than he needed to.

"And the fact that Kenneth Amberlin was a friend of Antonio's and actually visited the theater a week ago. I'll bet he was looking around for something."

He leaned forward. "How do you know all that?"

"Lola met Amberlin at the ELT and spoke with him. Penny, too. Although her account might be a little skewed," I added, remembering how impressed she was with his being a New York actor. "Lola recognized his picture in the paper. Maybe he was connected with the two people who mugged me outside the theater."

"And Antonio was a friend of his?" he asked sharply, more police chief and less dinner host.

"They had a history together." I revealed Antonio's check fraud misdemeanor and his more significant arrest in Las Vegas. I thought that was enough "evidence" for the moment, and certainly enough to complement Tiffany's request to see a tox screen of Antonio's blood.

Bill settled back in his chair and crossed his arms. "Anything more?"

"I do have a question. There wasn't a lot about the robberies in the *Etonville Standard*. I was wondering if they involved a scam selling security systems to senior citizens?"

Bill's naturally ruddy complexion deepened to red. "Where did you hear that?" he choked out. "That information wasn't made public."

"It's a long story."

"Start talking."

"Okay, but first . . . what's for dessert?"

21

We'd spent the better part of an hour munching on Bill's home-made chocolate chip cookies while I revealed the information I had accumulated: my finding Regan Digenza's image in Lola's food festival photographs, then my visit to Dr. Xiu based on Imogen's conversation with her neighbor, which allowed me to help Tiffany with her back pain, which gave me access to her bedroom nightstand and a letter addressed to Tony Dickson.

"Let me get this straight." I could see Bill trying to maintain both his patience and his equilibrium. "You lied about back pain to get access to Antonio's medical record?"

"I was curious about his health. I thought maybe the doctor appointment was related to his heart attack. But then I found out he wasn't in the office because of his heart. He was there because of his stomach. Like maybe he'd been ingesting something that was making him sick. Something that could have killed him eventually."

"Why visit a Chinese herbalist? Why not an emergency room?"

I shrugged. "Maybe he didn't want to have his background checked? A doctor's office seems a little less invasive than a hospital. Especially a traditional Chinese one."

"A lot of supposition on your part," he said grumpily.

"It's possible that Antonio did die of poisoning. As most of Eton-ville insisted. But not because of bacteria in the Windjammer's food or drinks. Someone could have put something in whatever he ate."

"Someone? Like a murderer," he said carefully.

"Right."

"For what reason?"

"I'm not sure," I admitted.

"And then you illegally searched his belongings to find a letter—"

"The house and the bedroom belong to Lola. She was there with me and gave me permission to open the nightstand drawer." Sort of. I knew I was beginning to sound a tad huffy.

"What did you intend to do with that information?"

"Dig into his past with his correct name and see if anything I found shed light on his death. And I think it did. Knowing he had a criminal past and was connected with Kenneth Amberlin is—"

"Which brings me to your hearing about the security-system scam. We deliberately left it out of the news report because this is still an ongoing investigation."

"You think there might be more burglaries?" I asked.

"You know I can't answer that," he said firmly. "Who did you speak to? We need to know if there's an internal leak in this case."

"No leak."

"So . . . ?"

I was determined not to mention Pauli's name, just as I had not given away his email hacking skills during the investigation of Jerome Angleton's murder. "I discovered that a cell phone has internal location tracking on the Settings app and if you follow a few prompts, you can actually find out where someone has travelled to in recent days. Or weeks. I guess it's part of the GPS system?"

Bill's mouth dropped an inch. "You tampered with Antonio's cell phone?"

"Tiffany was there," I said hastily. Technically, Tiffany was still in the tub.

"And you tracked his locations?"

"Uh, yes."

"That's illegal. Even the authorities have to get a warrant to search a cell phone," he said, by now annoyed.

"Really? I didn't know—"

"So far that's lying, illegal searching, and tampering. And you haven't even gotten to the Creston burglaries."

When he put it like that, my investigation did sound borderline unlawful. "Don't you want to know what I found in his phone?"

Bill hesitated. I knew from past events that he was a strictly-by-the-book officer, with a fanatical abhorrence of shady deals and anything that hinted of police misconduct. "Go ahead." He must have held his nose to say that.

"I noticed that Antonio had travelled to two Bernridge addresses—one was Dr. Xiu's—and made a couple of trips to Rumson, which I also assumed was to Brianna Kincaid. For an ex-wife she's really torn up about his death—"

"Dodie!"

"Right. Then I saw that Antonio had been in Creston on a variety of occasions the week before his death. Even the day before his death. So I just happened to be in Creston . . ."

Bill rolled his eyes.

"And I went to this one location, 112 Terrace Road, and spoke with an elderly woman—"

"You interrogated a potential witness?" His eyes bulged.

"I didn't interrogate anyone. In fact, Adele and I had afternoon tea. With her watchdog, Rex."

"This Adele implicated Antonio?"

"Well, she referred to a charming man in a beret who sold her a security system. It sounded an awful lot like Antonio to me."

We sat in silence for a moment, the only sound the snap and crackle of the dying fire. Suddenly, I felt exhausted. Wine had made me relaxed, then coffee had made me hyper, then Bill's sharp questioning had made me defensive, and finally admitting the truth had made me relieved and ready for sleep. But Bill wasn't through with me yet. His face was still creased with the same grimace he'd assumed half an hour ago, his muscled forearms tense, his fingers drumming on the pad he'd been writing on.

"I still don't understand why you felt you needed to play lone wolf here. We've been through this before. You're not the police department."

My face reddened at his rebuke. "I'm a concerned citizen and you were in Creston—"

He raised a hand to halt my justification. "Suki was in the department, covering when I was out."

I couldn't tell him that delivering a message to his assistant with her calm demeanor and om-like personality was not the same as watching the crooked smile appear on his face as he flexed his pecs and ran a hand through his bristly hair—

"Is that right?" He tapped a pen against his pad.

I'd lost the thread of his cross-examination. "Sorry?"

"I said, Lola recognized Kenneth Amberlin's photo in the paper?"

"Yes. And when he showed up at the theater he'd identified himself as Antonio's friend."

I felt a chill in the room and it was only partly because the fire had completely died out. The warm, social ambiance of earlier in the evening had vanished. In its place was a stony frustration. Bill's, because I had overstepped about a hundred bounds; mine, because he still didn't trust my instincts.

"After-dinner drink?" he asked, more out of courtesy than enthusiasm, I guessed.

From inside my purse, my cell produced a muted ring. "Guess I should . . ." I scanned the caller ID. Lola.

Almost immediately, Bill's cell buzzed.

"Hi, Lola," I said. "I can't talk now—"

"Dodie, can you come down here? Walter called the police because—"

"What?"

"Suki, what's up?" Bill said abruptly, then listened.

I watched him exhale, his face turning grave. "Call Ralph. Yeah."

"Lola, what's going on?" I said quietly.

"There's been an accident at the ELT. Not an accident, really. Penny was in the lobby and we heard her whistle—"

"I'll be there in a few minutes," Bill and I said simultaneously and clicked off.

"What is it? Lola wasn't very specific."

He strode into the kitchen, took his weapon from a drawer, and slipped into a shoulder holster. "Another assault. I guess your instincts about Antonio's death might be right."

Was there a trace of irony? "I don't want to be right. I want to find Antonio's killer."

He thrust his arms into the sleeves of his jacket. "Yeah? Well, be careful what you wish for."

Ralph's black-and-white cruiser and an EMS ambulance were already in front of the theater when Bill and I pulled up. Ralph was once more keeping the curious Etonville public from crowding near the entrance. I glanced next door at the Windjammer, where a handful of patrons craned their necks to get a look and Benny stood in the doorway. I summoned him over.

"What's going on?" he asked.

"Another attack at the theater."

"Not again. This close to the Windjammer? It's not good for business," he said.

"Did you hear or see anything?" I asked.

"Nada. Just the squad car and ambulance." He ducked back into the restaurant.

I headed into the theater, where the drama had moved off the stage and into the lobby. Two EMS personnel were attending to Penny, who sat propped up against the box office door, looking even more dazed than she had been during rehearsal recently. It was an unfamiliar position for her, accustomed as she was to running the show. At the open door of the theater office, Bill spoke with Walter and Lola. Too far away to hear anything, I could still see Lola shake her head and Walter run his hands through his beard. Both of them were frazzled.

I crossed the distance between Penny and myself. I didn't want to get in the way, but couldn't help wondering if the same two perpetrators had attacked both of us. Unconsciously, I rubbed the back of my head where there was still a slight bump. "Penny, are you okay?"

She raised her head.

"What happened?" I asked.

"O'Dell, somebody whacked me," she said, totally flummoxed, as if it was impossible to take down the stage manager of the ELT. She moaned as the medical technician slipped an oxygen mask on her face.

"Did you get a look? Were there two of them?"

She cocked her head to one side. "We made it to the beginning of Act Two and then Walter stopped to fix the window seat." She mumbled something.

I bent down to hear her. "What?"

"The show's got to open. Never cancelled a show on my watch . . ."

I was nudged aside. "Let us do our job, okay?" The EMS guys loaded Penny onto a gurney.

Bill appeared at my side. "Hey! What are you doing? Questioning victims is my responsibility. Remember?"

"I just wanted to find out what happened."

Bill stuffed his hands in the pockets of his khakis. "It appears Penny came into the lobby to use the women's room and when she didn't return one of the actors came looking and found her down here." He pointed to the space the EMS personnel had just left. "He blew her whistle and alerted everyone else."

"She was knocked out, right?" I asked.

"Lola wasn't sure at first. She thought Penny fell and banged her head. But Penny told her the box office door was open and when she tried to close it, someone hit her and she was out for a few minutes. When she came to, people were standing over her."

"Just like me," I murmured. I looked around. "Was anything taken?"

"Penny's keys. I'm going to follow the ambulance. Ralph will check the exterior perimeter and loading dock doors. Suki will stay here and wait for the state CSI guys. Try not to bother anybody." He walked away. "And I want to see you in my office first thing tomorrow morning," he called out over his shoulder.

So much for an agreeable end to the evening. I slipped into the house and hunkered down in a seat to wait for Lola. I flung my bag onto the chair next to mine as Suki corralled cast members, who were over-the-top agitated and demanding answers to questions.

"Why would anyone assault Penny?"

"What is Etonville coming to?"

"Who will take over as stage manager?"

"Is Walter going to cancel the show?"

"All right, all right," Suki said, and tried to work her calming magic. "Walter will be able to answer your questions soon."

"I'll bet it was a 417," Edna announced, and shook her wig, which sat askew. "Person with a gun. It would have taken a firearm to get a drop on Penny."

"Maybe they sneaked in through the green room," one of the actor-cops suggested.

"Too bad we don't have real weapons," the other cop said and snickered.

Abby grumped and yanked off her cape. "I don't care how they did it or how they got in here. I just want to know if rehearsal is over for the night."

"I'm outta here," Romeo said and stripped off a suit jacket.

Suki left to join the CSI team. Several other actors began to remove costume pieces and Chrystal was scurrying from person to person to retrieve accessories. "Careful with the clothing!" she cried and snatched hats and gloves and coats before they could be dumped unceremoniously on theater seats.

"Is this about Antonio?" Tiffany stood in the aisle. "I overheard Lola tell Walter that you thought your attackers were looking for something in the theater and that it probably was related to him."

Now that most of my theories and undercover work were out in the open, I knew I had to tread lightly. "Well, it makes sense that both assaults are connected. And of course they both happened after Antonio's death." Whatever that meant.

"I talked with the chief," Tiffany said.

"Good," I said noncommittally. "The test results will tell us a lot."

"Like if he was murdered?" she asked.

"Uh-huh."

Tiffany crossed her arms, staring at me defiantly. "'Course, if I had found out he'd been married a second time and didn't tell me, I'd have murdered him myself." She trounced off.

Carlyle appeared and announced that, despite the commotion with Penny, he was giving notes in the green room. *Where had he been during all of the excitement?* The actors—some of whom were halfway out the door—dragged themselves back onstage.

"Leave your costumes in the dressing rooms!" Chrystal shouted above the hubbub. She had an armful of fabric and a handful of hats.

"Need any help?" I asked.

"Thank you, Dodie. I've got to get these to wardrobe."

"Where's your crew?" I asked and took half her load.

She narrowed her eyes. "Community theater! One had to babysit her grandkids, one had to study for a test, and one had a hot date."

We walked through the green room to the wardrobe closet behind the stage. Carlyle was holding forth while the cast looked tired and bored and barely paid attention. Without Penny blowing her whistle, ELT discipline was in a sorry state.

I watched as Chrystal hung up clothes on racks and stacked accessories on shelves.

"Were you in the house tonight when Penny got attacked?"

Chrystal shook her head. "I was downstairs hot-gluing Walter's pants. He keeps ripping the inseam." She put one of Abby's dresses on a hanger. "But I told Lola we should start locking the front door during rehearsals. Anybody can just walk in, you know."

Especially now that someone had Penny's keys.

Chrystal grimaced. "The theater is getting to be an unsafe place. I hope this doesn't delay the opening. I have a four-week rental agreement on these." She gestured toward the racks of period clothing. "I don't have the budget to keep them any longer."

I patted her back. "I'm sure the show will go on. On time."

"I'm not staying in the costume shop by myself again tonight. I'm too freaked out," she said.

Chrystal walked off. I peered down the hallway that led away from the wardrobe storage and past the dressing rooms. To my right was the door to the green room, where I could still hear Carlyle drone on about "cheating out" and "upstaging your scene partner" while actors gathered their belongings and prepared to leave. Aside from Tiffany there was no reason for Carlyle to hang around anymore. Or was there? He had been Antonio's confidant and close friend. He seemed genuinely surprised by my big reveal at the café in Creston. But what if he knew more than he was letting on? He had placed the warning note on my windshield.

Chrystal was right. Anyone could walk into the theater off the street. Like Antonio's friend Kenneth Amberlin and Penny's attacker. And whoever came after me had been looking to get into the theater. What was in the ELT that connected all three incidents? I decided to check out the back entrance to the theater to make sure it was secure. I knew Bill had assigned that task to Ralph, but still . . .

At the end of the hallway was a large set of double doors that allowed access from the stage to the scene shop, which in turn provided an exit to the loading dock. There was a bit of light from the green room that spilled into the hallway, as well as a security light on the wall by the wardrobe storage. But the shop doors were open; the last person out had neglected to close them. Next to the doors was the wall switch for the overhead fluorescents. I flipped it on and light flooded the inside of the scene shop, where the scents of drying paint and sawdust filled my nostrils.

I eased past the workbench in the middle of the room, careful to avoid bumping into several flats leaning against the tool cage. There were two exits from the shop to the loading dock: a roll-up steel contraption, large enough to permit the removal of scenery, and a secondary standard door. The padlock on the roll-up door was secure and the dead bolt on the second door was thrown. I opened the door and cool night air wafted in. I stepped onto the loading dock. There was no padlock; the hasp and metal loop were empty. I came inside and had just chucked the dead bolt back into place when the fluorescents went dark. A soft click by the hallway door sounded like a deafening boom in the stillness of the scene shop.

"Walter? Carlyle?" I yelled.

Goose bumps rose on my arms. As my eyes adjusted to the darkness, I could make out the shapes of various machines. I'd been in the scene shop enough to know the drill press was to my right, the large circular table saw to my left, and straight ahead was the tool cage where Walter and JC stored the hammers and screwdrivers at the end of each work session. A bank of windows on the far wall permitted enough moonlight to throw each construction device into spectral relief. Ghosts inhabiting a metal graveyard.

I stepped slowly across the scene-shop floor. When I reached the doors that opened into the hallway, I grabbed the doorknob and twisted. It wouldn't open. Someone had just padlocked them. I swallowed to keep the fear from rising into my throat and sucked in air through my mouth—my great aunt Maureen's remedy for car sickness. I reminded myself that the exit to the loading dock was open. There was no padlock on the outside of that door. My mind knew this, but my stomach was doing a trampoline act and didn't care.

I threaded my way again around the shop machines back to the dock exit, where a faint whoosh of air rattled the steel door. I reached down and my hand grazed the padlock. Still there. I stood and grasped the knob of the wooden door. It turned but wouldn't open. My heart thudded so loudly my ears rang. In the last few minutes, someone had padlocked the outside of this door, too. A chill ran down my back. I shivered. *I'm locked in the scene shop and no one knows I'm here.* I forced myself to calm down, breathing in to the count of four, exhaling to the count of four. No problem. I would simply call Lola and have her rescue me. I shoved my hand into my front pants pocket. She might still be in the theater office with Walter or Carlyle and—

Palpitations kicked in: the pocket was empty. I groaned. My cell was sitting in my purse on a seat in the theater!

22

I pounded on the hallway door, accompanied by loud shouting, for a good ten minutes. Everyone must have left, including Walter, Carlyle, Chrystal, the cast, the CSI techs, and Lola, who probably assumed I went home. But someone else was still in the theater and had gotten me out of the way. To search every nook and cranny? To find what?

I sat on the floor, my knees pulled up to my chest, my back against the tool cage. Which was, of course, padlocked. I found a garbage can full of lumber odds and ends and grasped a foot-long two-by-four. It wasn't much of a weapon, but at least holding it firmly made me feel safer. I considered possibilities. Of which there were few. Eventually, someone would have to open the scene shop tomorrow—JC was still touching up the mock woodwork. But I was doomed to spend the night here. I lifted the face of my watch to catch a little of the moonlight: eleven thirty. The cement floor was hard and cold; I buttoned my leather jacket.

My mind raced. I ticked off a list of the people linked to Antonio who might have been responsible for the attack on Penny and my being held captive in the scene shop. Admittedly, it was a short list: Kenneth Amberlin, Kenneth's fellow crook, and Regan. As per the *Etonville Standard*, Kenneth Amberlin was in the hospital, but his accomplice was out on bail. I kept returning to Regan Digenza. I hadn't had the opportunity tonight to push Bill into giving me her address or checking her out himself. Despite the cold and my fear, I could feel my eyelids getting heavy. I scooted farther into a corner near the cage. It had been a crazy day.

* * *

"Dodie! Are you in there?"

Pounding and banging. The overhead fluorescents suddenly washed the shop in a flare of intense light.

I dreamt I was trapped inside a vending machine and a little girl kept pressing her face against the glass case, pushing B5: Raisinets. "I'm not eating candy, little girl. I'm just trying to escape." She kept pummeling the machine, yelling, "Dodie! Are you in there?"

I forced my eyes open, relieved that I wouldn't have to spend the rest of my life wedged between the peanut butter crackers and the Snickers bars.

"Dodie!"

But I wasn't in my bed, either. I was lying on the floor of the Etonville Little Theatre scene shop. The left side of my face was numb from the icy floor, my damp hair the result of drool that had escaped my mouth. All in all, not a pretty picture. "I'm in here!" I croaked.

Voices rose and fell and cut each other off.

"Is this the right key—"

"No. It's not even the right padlock—"

"Try the bolt cutters."

"Here. Let me—"

More jingling and crunching and a loud snap. The doors banged open.

"Dodie! What are you doing in here? It's one a.m.!" Lola looked as if she hadn't been to bed yet—wrinkled jeans and a sweatshirt under her rain jacket. Walter's beard was a straggle of hairs, pointing every which way. Only Bill had it together, frustration mixed with worry. I was amazed at how hot he could look at this hour.

"How did you lock yourself in?" Walter asked. "We never put the padlock on these doors."

Walter and Bill approached and each of them grabbed an arm and hauled me to my feet. "I *didn't* lock myself in here. *Someone else* locked me in here," I said, and shuddered. The cold had permeated my bones. "And they padlocked the loading dock door."

"We don't even have a padlock for that door."

"Well, I guess it was BYOP." I hadn't lost my sense of humor.

"The crew never lock up after themselves," Walter said.

"For all we know, someone could still be in the theater," I practically yelled.

"We'll do a thorough check," Bill said. Then he smiled sympathetically, but I was too tired and cold to care. "And get the padlock off the other door."

Lola rubbed my back. "It's freezing in here. You need something hot to drink. Come on. I'll take you home."

Bill stopped us. "I'll need a statement."

"In the morning, okay?"

He nodded. Then studied the padlock and door. "This padlock is brand-new."

"Like I said, we lost the old one and never replaced it." Walter struggled to stifle a yawn.

"Same with the loading-dock door?" Bill asked.

"Yes." Walter scratched his beard. "I just never thought we needed to put the theater in lockdown."

"Well, I guess it *was* BYOP tonight," Bill said, and glanced at me.

I sat on my sofa wrapped in my robe and a blanket while Lola bustled around making tea and toast, even though I wasn't hungry. Bill's scrumptious dinner had been plenty filling. But Lola thought she should treat me as though I was under the weather, so I let her. I felt warm and cozy and drowsy. "I'm still amazed that you found me."

"I tried calling your cell just after the CSI unit left, and of course no one answered. I just figured you had turned it off. Or left it somewhere. So I decided to drive by your house." She handed me chamomile tea. "Drink this."

"You must have been pretty desperate to get Walter out of his pajamas." I laughed.

"He just said you probably were staying overnight with a friend. What 'friend'? I said. I'm your best friend. I'd know."

I smiled. "Yes, you would."

"He suggested I call Chrystal, who said she'd last seen you in the back hallway by the wardrobe. So I forced Walter to meet me at the theater and then I called the chief." Lola watched me slyly. "How was dinner?"

"I'll tell you later."

"We searched backstage and the wardrobe areas and the costume shop and then Walter noticed the padlock on the shop door."

"The attackers probably assumed the theater was empty until they saw the shop lights on. They had to get me out of the way," I said, and sipped the tea.

"But who are they?" Lola asked.

"Not sure. Bill and I were sorting through the evidence when you called me, and Suki called him."

"What do they want?"

I shrugged. "To search various places in the theater?"

Lola sat quietly for a moment. "And somehow this is all related to Antonio."

"I think so."

"What could someone possibly be looking for now that Antonio is dead?"

"Well, actually, the hunt started after he died. Kenneth Amberlin, my getting knocked out, and now Penny. Whatever they're looking for must be worth the risk of detection. And since it looks like Antonio might have been involved in the Creston break-ins, I'd bet that whatever they want to find has a connection to the break-ins, too."

"What does the chief think about all this?"

"I didn't have time to lay out my theory completely. But it makes sense, right?" I asked hopefully.

"I guess." Lola shook her head. "I'm just so over this production and Antonio and these terrible . . ."

I put an arm around her shoulder. "It'll all be over soon."

"That's what I'm afraid of," she said.

I slept like a baby—like a baby who didn't turn in until 3:00 a.m., with a crick in her neck from snoozing in an awkward position on a cement floor. I awoke at eight, my muscles sore, but my brain whirring. I hopped out of bed and stepped into the shower. The hot water streamed off my back and soothed the stiffness in my shoulders and torso.

First off today, I'd visit Bill, try to keep things civil, but urge him to pull Regan Digenza into the station for questioning. I'd also suggest he interrogate Kenneth Amberlin about his connection to Antonio, which might help us determine the attacker's motivation. Then I'd spend quality time at the Windjammer. Even though Benny had been good about covering for me these last weeks, I wanted to raise Henry's spirits.

Given the events of last evening, I absolutely deserved a caramel macchiato and a hot cinnamon bun with icing oozing over its edges. Besides, Coffee Heaven was on my way to the Municipal Building.

I parked two blocks from the Windjammer, midway between the restaurant and the police station. Walking briskly in the morning sun felt good—my body needed the exercise. I swung my bag over my shoulder and sauntered into Coffee Heaven. The place was only half-full and I had no trouble getting a booth near the door.

Jocelyn appeared in an instant. "Dodie, you look good after spending the night locked in the scene shop."

"Well, it wasn't the whole night—"

"I heard they had to break the door down! Good thing Walter keeps a hatchet in his office," she said.

"A hatchet? Where did you hear that?" The gossip mill was on overdrive this morning.

"Edna was here earlier and said they had a possible 207. That's kidnapping."

"Kidnapping? They locked me in the scene shop. Nobody tried to kidnap me."

"Poor Penny. Who's going to be the stage manager now?" Jocelyn asked.

"I'm sure she'll be back by tomorrow. Maybe even tonight. You know Penny. I'll have my regular with—"

Jocelyn angled her head and frowned. "Do you think it was connected to the play? After all, there are some tempers running hot these days, and I wouldn't put it past someone to take it out on an innocent victim. Like you."

"—a cinnamon bun," I ordered as Jocelyn walked away.

She was correct about one thing: There *were* hot tempers flaring in the Etonville Little Theatre and last night's events would not lower the heat.

"Well, it's Dodie, don't you know."

I cringed inwardly. "Hi, ladies," I said to the Banger sisters.

"We're so happy to see you're alive and well," one said.

"Me too." I broke down and smiled.

"You know the story of the Etonville sea captain who was locked in the refrigerator and never made it out," said the other sister.

"You mean the one who owned the Windjammer?" I laughed.

"That's an old wives' tale. Anyway, he was only locked in a pantry for a few hours."

The first Banger sister nodded wisely. "Being locked away can make you insane."

I guess.

"It's a good thing you were only in the costume shop for a day."

"It was the scene shop and it was only for . . . never mind." Jocelyn approached with my coffee and bun. "You ladies have a good day."

They didn't take the hint.

"Dodie," one said, "did you notice that since your arrival, the Etonville Little Theatre has had its share of criminal activity?"

They both stared at me, waiting for an answer. They had a point.

Jocelyn gently, but firmly, escorted them away from my booth. "Now you-all shoo and let Dodie enjoy her breakfast."

"I'd watch my back if I were you," the other sister said as they waddled away arm in arm.

"Those two are always getting the story wrong," Jocelyn said, and waltzed off with her coffeepot.

Right.

I entered the Municipal Building just as Edna bustled out.

"Dodie! I'm so glad you're okay! The scene shop can be a risky place," Edna said as she backed out the door. "Too bad about Penny and I hope she can make it to rehearsal tonight, of course her health is more important than the show." She paused to take a breath.

"Edna, please add a black coffee to the order!" Suki called out from the dispatch window.

Edna lowered her voice. "Gotta make a run to Coffee Heaven. The chief's in a snit."

"Oh?"

"Seems like some confidential information got leaked to the press."

So what was new about that? The *Etonville Standard* was constantly jumping the gun on a story or printing rumors as facts; anything to get a leg up on the Creston paper. They thought they were Woodward and Bernstein. "Well, Edna, you know the *Standard*—"

Edna leaned in. "Not the *Standard*. It was the *Creston Enquirer*. Somebody released a list of stolen goods." She shook her head. "They ought to get the paper on a 594."

"Edna!" Bill turned the corner at the end of the hallway.

"Malicious mischief." She turned to him. "Just going, Chief."

I took a no-nonsense approach as I hurried down the corridor to meet him. Suki looked up from her console. "I have an appointment," I said and breezed right past her. Bill grunted and motioned for me to follow him. Despite the probable chaos surrounding both the Etonville and Creston cases, Bill's office was an oasis of orderliness and symmetry: stacks of files formed parallel rows on his desk. One manila folder sat directly in front of him.

"What?" he asked, suspiciously.

"I was just thinking how neat everything is in here. Especially given all of the commotion you have to deal with in Creston and Etonville."

"You spoke with Edna," he said, resigned.

"I was also thinking about last night and Antonio."

"Have a seat." He made a tent with his fingers laced together in front of his face. "So let's start with last night."

"Did the CSI guys get any fingerprints on the padlocks?"

He shook his head. "Not that I expected them to."

"And Penny . . . ?"

"She saw the box office door open and went to close it. Standing in the lobby one moment and lying on the floor the next."

"Probably two attackers. Just like my assault.

And they're determined to find something in the theater. I don't know what it is, but they want it badly. I guess I got in the way."

Bill rocked back in his seat and ran a hand through his hair. "Something connected to Antonio."

"Yes. I was locked in the shop for nearly two hours. Plenty of time for them to dig around in the theater's nooks and crannies."

He hesitated. "Kenneth Amberlin's still in the hospital. The Creston PD interrogated him again this morning, but he claims he's still groggy from the meds."

"Huh."

"If he knew Antonio Digenza, he's not admitting it. Very tight-lipped."

"So you're going to push the lab for the autopsy test results?" I asked.

"Thanks to your manipulation of Tiffany Digenza."

"I only suggested that—"

Bill raised a hand. "You didn't need to go through her."

I felt myself getting a little hot under the collar. "When I suggested another cause for Antonio's death, you stuck with the medical examiner's finding of a simple heart attack." Heat moved from my neck onto my face.

He tapped a pencil on his blotter. "We'll see what the lab has to say. I should have preliminary results by tomorrow." Bill glanced at the wall clock. "I'll have to take my coffee on the road to Creston. Some of the stolen property has been found. A fence in New York."

"That's good."

"Yeah, and some property in their possession when we arrested them. That still leaves missing jewelry and cash."

"The cash is probably gone, but maybe you'll get a lead on the jewelry."

"Maybe. But not a word to anyone outside this office. Got it?" He waggled his finger in my face.

"Right."

A knock on his door. "Enter."

Edna stood there with a cardboard tray of takeout cups. "Coffee black, Chief."

Bill stood, grabbed his jacket and the coffee. "Thanks. I'll be in touch."

As I rose to follow him out the door, my eye caught the lettering on a Post-it note on the file on his desk: aznegiD nageR. I'd learned to read proficiently upside down in grammar school, when I was called to the principal's office and scolded for some minor infraction. I entertained myself by studying the jumble of letters on memos and papers.

I blinked several times. "I have something in my eye," I said and pulled a Kleenex out of my bag.

"Turn out the light and pull the door shut when you leave, okay?"

"Sure," I said and pretended to fish around the rim of my eyelid.

Bill disappeared. I disposed of the Kleenex and leafed rapidly through the file. It was a collection of reports and notes on Antonio's death. A piece of paper on top had Regan's license plate number and address. I studied it for five seconds; my memorization of significant evidence was improving.

23

There was still a good hour before the Windjammer opened, but the restaurant was bustling. You'd have thought we were expecting a full house for lunch instead of the new normal: half a dozen tables. Still, it was nice to see everyone's energy. Benny was at his part-time UPS job until five, so I would be helping in the dining room. Carmen was setting tables and restocking the bar. Gillian had started working half days. But where was Honey?

I scribbled my name on the inventory clipboard for the Cheney Brothers delivery guy. For once, the vegetable and seafood requisitions were complete. "And don't forget we have a special order coming tomorrow." That would be for Rita's rehearsal dinner Saturday night.

The kid cracked his chewing gum and tucked his pen behind one ear. He couldn't have cared less.

"Miss Dodie," Enrico said, up to his elbows in eggs, spinach, ham, sundried tomatoes, and cheese for Henry's spinach frittata.

"Hi, Enrico."

He gestured across the kitchen at Henry, who was studying a recipe and making notes. "He is experimenting again. It's a good sign?" the *sous chef* said hopefully.

"Yep. I just hope his experiment isn't too ambitious for Etonville . . . or the Windjammer."

Out of the blue, Henry had announced yesterday that he was changing today's menu. We had planned on meat loaf and mashed potatoes, a reliable, cool weather plate. Instead he decided to go all out with rack of lamb, roasted cauliflower with capers and hazelnuts, and grilled romaine. Who was going to eat all of that food? But if it made Henry happy, well, I guessed the leftovers were worth it. So little made him happy these days.

"Dottie, I need some shelf space to store these." Honey waltzed into the kitchen, her hands full of little white boxes.

I reached for one and she backed away as though my touch might contaminate poster board.

"They're, like, very fragile."

"So what are they for?" Apparently, Honey had been assembling miniature cartons instead of prepping the dining room.

She smiled smugly. "Favors for the rehearsal dinner. I designed them myself."

As far as I could tell, they were just two-by-two-inch cardboard containers. "Kind of small for takeout." I laughed.

Honey was not amused. "I'm filling them with little bundles of rice. For the wedding."

"Okay."

"To throw at the bride and groom," she explained.

"Isn't it customary to hand out the rice after the ceremony?" I asked.

"Dot, in my business you have to think ahead. It's all about packaging. Uncle Henry agrees."

We both swung our heads and watched Henry stir his homemade vegetable soup in a stupor. His mind was not on tonight's experimental menu, or packaging, or even the dinner Saturday night.

Enough of this. Neither Henry nor the Windjammer would recover unless Antonio's murder was solved and Etonville once again embraced his culinary services.

"Honey, you can store your boxes on the bottom shelf in the pantry. Next to the packaged rice. They'll feel right at home."

Honey turned away.

"And then I need you in the dining room."

"Sorry, but I have to—"

"Pronto," I said firmly.

She blinked. "Well, okay, if you put it like that."

I assembled my staff and provided directions: Carmen was behind the bar, Gillian and Honey were waiting tables.

"What are you going to do?" Honey asked, hand on hip, mouth in a pout.

"I am going to save this restaurant," I said, pointing at her. "And when I leave, you're in charge. You are responsible for making sure lunch comes off without any glitches."

Honey's eyes widened, she straightened up, and lifted her chin an inch or two. "Like, I can do that."

Carmen and Gillian exchanged glances. They'd get over it. Besides, there wasn't much danger of Honey screwing up; I intended to wait until the lunch hour was well under way. And putting Honey in charge guaranteed that she would remain in the dining room.

I exaggerated slightly. Saving the Windjammer would require more than one afternoon escape; but Bill was preoccupied with Creston today and I had Regan's address. A match made in heaven.

At one o'clock I gave Honey a last-minute warning to stay on top of the customers, all dozen of them. I picked up my bag from the back booth. The early sun had disappeared behind a bank of clouds to the southwest, leaving a gray expanse in the sky. I fired up the Metro and backed out of my parking space. There was another reason I felt relatively comfortable paying a call on Regan Digenza during the middle of the workday. I had assumed that she was dealing in a casino in Atlantic City, a drive of about two hours from Etonville. But the address that I'd committed to memory was much closer and way more familiar: Bernridge. I could easily make it there, look her up, and return in an hour or so. There was a good chance she wasn't home, but I was antsy, my little hairs were dancing, and the trip was worth a shot.

I punched the address into my cell phone GPS and waited for Genie to begin. Just as I had done when visiting Dr. Xiu, I took the off-ramp to Lambert Street, but instead of turning onto Charter Drive, where Dr. Xiu's office was located, I entered a roundabout and continued on to Willington Avenue. Where the town was milling the road in preparation for paving. I avoided the raised manhole covers and drove past the now-closed box factory. Though it had a historical district as well as traditional residential neighborhoods, Bernridge was also home to industrial areas. Willington Avenue was one of them.

On my left were a series of windowless redbrick warehouses. A rusted No Parking sign warned people away from an active driveway. On the right were apartment buildings, boxlike, dirty beige, worn-out. Two women in old-fashioned housedresses sat on the steps leading into one of the buildings. They turned their heads in unison to watch me crawl down the street, as if traffic were new to this part of the city.

"Destination is ahead on the right," Genie said. I pulled over to the curb. The number of the building matched the address I had memorized. Unfortunately, I had no apartment number. I looked up and down Willington. The street was deserted.

I locked my car doors and approached the building. Through the glass entrance I could see rows of mailboxes along one wall and stacks of packages on another. Honey would have a field day here. Measuring, sorting—

"Yo. Going in?"

I spun around and gazed into the belt buckle of an extremely tall, well-built young African-American man. I tilted my head up. "Hello."

He slid his eyes in the direction of my Metro. "You looking for someone?"

Spilling the beans about Regan to a potential neighbor might alert her to my spying. Still, the truth seemed to be the best bet here. "Yes, I am. Regan Digenza. Do you know her?" I smiled in what I hoped was a harmless, nonthreatening manner.

"Why? What do you want?" He transferred his considerable weight from one oversized shoe to the other.

"Uh, she's . . . my second cousin. I haven't seen her in years. I just thought I'd drop by and visit."

He wasn't buying it. "She's not home."

I glanced at the row upon row of mailboxes. There had to be seventy or eighty apartments. Either he really did know her or he was busting my chops for some reason. "Lot of residents. You know most of them?"

He smiled slyly. "I'm the building manager. I make it my business to know them."

"Right. I'll stop back later. Thanks." I could feel him watching me as I returned to the car and drove down the street. In my rearview mirror I saw him enter the apartment building.

I felt like I'd been stonewalled. I could hang around the area and wait to see if Regan's yellow Honda showed up, or head back to Etonville and see what state the restaurant was in with Honey in charge. I drummed my fingers on the steering wheel. One more turn around the neighborhood wouldn't be such a bad idea. I put the Metro in Drive and with a series of right-hand turns found myself on Willington Avenue again, hoping that the building manager was nowhere to be seen. I leaned forward into my windshield to get a better angle on the street when a car whizzed past me going in the opposite direction. I jerked upright. What were the odds that there were two yellow Hondas belonging to residents of this community? I made a quick U-turn.

Regan must have had her pedal to the floor because her car zipped ahead of me, weaving in and out of traffic. Even the manhole covers didn't slow her down. I did my best to keep up and when she darted onto the highway, I was only four car lengths behind her. By the time I caught up, she accelerated and zoomed onto the Garden State Parkway, heading south. I followed her out of sheer grit, but I knew when I was beat. I couldn't afford to tail her to who-knew-where when I was due at the Windjammer.

I took the first exit and headed back to Etonville.

To my surprise Honey had managed to keep the restaurant in line, and neither Carmen nor Gillian were complaining too much. The place was empty, so I gave them all a break, cleaned a few tables, and sat down in my booth with a bowl of vegetable soup. I scooped up a spoonful of zucchini and tomatoes and savored the tangy liquid. No one made soup like Henry.

"So, Dot, like, maybe I can manage the Windjammer every lunch hour?" Honey had her apron slung over a shoulder. "Until I go back to school?"

There was a ton of hope in her eyes, a look I hadn't seen since she started working at the restaurant. "Maybe. Let's see." I was feeling positive about our working arrangement.

"Because, like, you need someone with my organizational skills." She looked around the dining room. "This place could use a makeover."

Sort of positive. "Be sure to get the dinner-special inserts into the menus before you leave."

Honey nodded, gave the room a once-over, and shook her head. "Uncle Henry had to be crazy buying this place."

I was about to offer a retort, but my cell rang. "Hi, Lola. What's up?"

"What are you doing tonight?"

"Besides working?"

"Can you slip away for a bit?" she asked.

"Probably. Benny is due in at five. I might be able to skip out for a while after dinner." I waited. "Something up?"

"Penny's back," Lola said.

"How is she feeling?" I asked.

"Well . . . you know how some people receive a head wound and then their personality changes?"

Uh-oh. "I don't think I've really ever heard that. Is something the matter with Penny?"

A torrent of words poured out of Lola. Penny had returned to the theater that afternoon and seemed fine. Then when Walter asked her to do a job, she refused. She insisted that she wasn't going to be pushed around anymore. That the ELT could get along without her if Walter didn't like it.

"Penny said that?" She'd always considered herself the pillar of the theater, its mainstay. Not that the rest of the members actually thought that.

"Can you believe it? With the opening so close, we can't afford to lose her. I knew she could be temperamental sometimes, but this is over the top." Lola paused.

"Maybe she's on some meds," I said.

"I don't think so. You've always managed to get along with her. And now you have something in common," Lola said.

"We do?"

"You both got hit on the head at the theater. Maybe you could talk with her?"

"I guess I could give it a try. I wanted to stop by and talk with you about something else, anyway."

I could feel Lola checking her watch. "We're starting later tonight so the crew can finish painting. Can you come by around eight?"

Henry's special, though delicious, received a mixed response. Mildred and Vernon, who were regularly eating entrées now after several years on a diet, announced that the lamb was magnificent and the cauliflower perfection. They passed on the grilled romaine. The Banger sisters, however, disagreed.

"I just hate to eat a little lamb. It's like eating Bambi," said one.

"Uh, Bambi was a deer," I said.

"All of those baby animals are just too cute to eat, don't you know," said the other.

They nibbled on the romaine and questioned aloud why Henry had to "cook" the salad since "greens were perfectly fine right out of the ground."

I bit my lip and moved to another table.

By eight o'clock, the dining room was winding down and I felt comfortable leaving it in Benny's capable hands. "Have a good night," I said.

"Sure. By the way, did you know that Honey is making little boxes and stacking them up in the pantry?"

I shrugged. "Yeah. Favors for the rehearsal dinner."

"She's putting bags of rice inside."

"Right."

Benny dunked glasses in soapy water. "Did you also know that she's creating a centerpiece for the rehearsal dinner, out of boxes?"

"What?" I shook my head.

He chuckled. "Helps to be related to the boss."

The early evening air was fresh. I forced oxygen into my lungs, forcing thoughts of Honey out of my head. Outside the theater, a handful of actors were killing time, chatting it up and texting.

"Hi, Dodie!" Edna called out.

"Hey, Edna."

"You coming to rehearsal?"

Suddenly the group became quiet, all ears alert for my answer.

"For the first half. I need to speak with Lola about a few things."

"Wish I could leave after the first half," one of the actor cops said.

His sidekick guffawed and Edna punched him lightly on the arm. "You boys cut it out. And don't let Walter hear you saying such things."

"He wouldn't even notice," said one cop.

"Too busy prompting Tiffany," said the second.

They high-fived each other and entered the theater.

"Still having line problems?" I asked.

Edna nodded. "She doesn't have theater chops like the rest of us."

Of course, that was exactly what Abby had said about Edna.

Abby stuck her head out the door. "Let's get this thing going. Walter's blowing Penny's whistle."

The remaining actors trudged inside. "Morale's a little low," I whispered to Edna.

"That's show biz!" Edna, ever the optimist.

Inside the theater, Carlyle was corralling actors and periodically checking in with Tiffany, who was lounging in the front row. Walter was yanking his beard—not a good sign—and waving his arms at anyone who paid him attention. I scanned the house and stage for Penny.

"Dodie, thank God you're here," Lola said. "Penny's taking a break in the green room. Taking a nap is more like it."

"Maybe she has a concussion."

"She said no. Look, could you . . . ?" She extended Penny's clipboard.

"On my way."

I grabbed the clipboard and strode onstage, cutting through the maze of furniture that Walter was rearranging. I entered the green room and saw Romeo checking his reflection in a mirror while adjusting his hair. He rotated 180 degrees and confronted me. "So you had to spend the night curled up with the band saw." He smirked.

"Only half the night," I said coolly.

"Next time you lock yourself in the scene shop, let me know. If I'm around . . ." He sauntered off.

Jerk.

"He's a jerk all right," Penny said from the depths of the sofa on the far wall.

"You're still reading my mind?" I crossed the room and sat down in a chair opposite her.

Penny shrugged. "Some things you never lose. Like riding a bike."

"So why aren't you out there?"

"I've had a dramatic trauma. They took my keys. I need to avoid stress," she said.

"Penny, this is the theater. You thrive on stress. It's what you're good at. You can get another set of keys. Besides, Walter needs you. And Carlyle," I added.

Penny raised herself on one elbow and stared upward. "Let me check my give-a-hoot meter." She paused for effect. "Nope. Nothing there." She lay back down.

Wow. It's worse than Lola thought. "Look, Penny, I know how you feel. I was attacked, too. And blacked out. And had a pretty good-sized bump on my head for several days. But you have to snap out of it."

"I'm resigning from the ELT."

"They can't get along without you!"

Penny grunted.

"The actors need discipline."

Penny snorted.

"Walter would be in over his head."

Penny barked. "Yeah."

I hesitated. "I heard that Walter might hire a stage manager from New York. A real pro."

She sat up. "I'm a pro."

"Of course you are."

"I know just as much as anybody from the City," she said.

"Of course you do."

She sized me up. "You're not making this up just to take advantage of me?"

"Penny, the ELT is your home. It's your family. Theater people stick together. They don't abandon the ship," I said, dredging up theater clichés. "And right now we're on theater time, not real time." *Huh?*

Penny bounded to her feet, pushed her glasses up a notch on her nose, and stuck a pencil behind one ear.

"You better rescue your whistle." I handed her the clipboard. "Remember that friend of Antonio's who came by the theater last week?" If Penny didn't mention that he was one of the Creston burglars, I decided not to either. Simpler that way.

"The pro from New York," she said wryly.

"Right. I know he came to offer his sympathy. But did you show him around? Give him a tour of the theater?"

"O'Dell, it's like a squid quo pro. Tit for tat. Somebody from one theater is welcome in every theater."

I wasn't sure that was always true. "So you did make him feel at home?"

"Like I said, squid—"

"Where did you take him?"

She shrugged. "He wanted to see the fly space and the scene shop and dressing rooms. The basics."

"Did he wander off by himself?"

Penny stood her full five-foot-two-inches. "O'Dell, what kind of a fool do you think I am?"

I didn't think I should answer that.

"People running around loose in the theater can get themselves in trouble. Just look at you." She turned on her heel. "I got a show to run."

I stayed in the green room for a couple of minutes, during which time I heard half a dozen sharp blasts of Penny's whistle. *She's baaaack.* I let my gaze meander around the room. If I wanted to find something in the theater, where would I begin?

I slipped into row five next to Lola. Her eyes popped as she watched Penny once again dictating orders, and actors holding their ears whenever her whistle detonated. "How did you do it? You're a miracle worker!"

"Just took a little ego massaging and some downright lying."

"Well, bravo to you."

I dropped my voice. "What are they doing up there?"

"Walter always saves this exercise for a few days before opening. To get the cast working like an ensemble. It's called counting. They're supposed to really listen to each other and sense when to speak."

The actors began in a circle—as most of Walter's exercises did—shoulder to shoulder, eyes closed, and counted. One, two, three . . . The only hitch was if more than two people said the same number at the same time, the group had to start over with "one." There was a good deal of poking and giggling and eye rolling. Which was hard to do with your eyes shut.

"Focus! Focus!" Walter yelled. "Start again."

"Okay, people, let's knock it off." Penny made some notes on her clipboard.

They started again. Silence, then a tentative "one" from Edna, followed by a competitive "two" from Abby. Romeo sneered a "three," and I thought, *Hey, not bad.* Then Tiffany lost count and jumped to "five," the two cops cackled, and Mildred's husband Vernon asked, "Should I go back to four or ahead to six?"

Carlyle exhaled heavily, Walter slapped his forehead, and Penny's whistle erupted.

"Do they ever get to ten?" I said.

"Oh brother," said Lola. "Let's go."

In the office, Lola plopped into the leather executive chair that

Walter insisted he required for his back, and I perched on the edge of the desk. "I have a theory. I haven't run it by Bill yet, but I hinted at it."

"About Antonio?"

She grasped at my notion like a drowning man clenching a life preserver. Anything to take her mind off rehearsal.

"I think that Kenneth Amberlin and whoever knocked out Penny and me, as well as whoever locked me in the scene shop, were all trying to search the theater. Now, some of the stolen property from the Creston robberies has been recovered, but some hasn't."

"I saw the story in the *Enquirer*."

"Right. We know Kenneth Amberlin and Antonio were acquaintances, so what if Antonio had some of the property at the time of his death and hid it somewhere he thought was safe?"

"Like where?" Then it dawned on Lola. "You mean there might be stolen goods hidden in the theater?"

"It's a possibility."

"Do you think Antonio told . . . whoever . . . where he hid it?"

"Probably not. If they knew where it was, they would have found it by now. They're still hunting."

"But if Antonio was in on the burglaries, why wouldn't he just tell them where to look?"

"I can think of two reasons. Either he died before he could let them know. Or . . ."

"Or what?"

"He was double-crossing someone and it got him killed." I filled her in on my trip to Bernridge. "Regan is still very much a loose end."

Lola slumped in her seat. "I'm really impressed, Dodie. I thought your finding Jerome's murderer might have been a fluke, but now . . ."

A fluke? Really?

"Thanks." I lowered my voice. "So where might Antonio have hidden the stash?"

24

L ola and I brainstormed on potential hiding places: the scene shop, the costume shop, the upstairs prop shop, wardrobe storage, dressing rooms, even the fly space. Of course, as per Bill's directive, I did not let the word "jewelry" slip out of my mouth. I simply suggested that whatever Antonio had concealed was probably smaller than the proverbial breadbox, as my great aunt Maureen would say. Since the intruders had Penny's keys they could make themselves at home.

"The ELT needs to change the locks around here," I said.

"Walter has a locksmith coming this weekend," Lola said, and headed back into the theater.

Might be too late by then. I decided to go home and think through the day's events. A light mist had begun to fall, just enough dampness to blur the windshield and require intermittent attention from the wipers. I crawled down Main and stopped for the light at Amber. Was Bill in the Municipal Building burning the midnight oil? Of course he could also be home, stretched out in front of the fireplace in his early American living room with classical music, a good bottle of wine, and the brunette from Creston—

A horn honked and jolted me out of my reverie. Someone was in a hurry. I stepped on the gas and zipped down a block before turning onto Fairfield. I pulled into my driveway and turned off the ignition. The neighborhood was quiet, except for the occasional barking of the Shetland sheepdog up the street and the revving of an engine somewhere.

Unexpectedly my neck hairs stood at attention and demanded notice. What was I doing at home, envisioning a relaxing night, when I was so close to solving this mystery? If the stolen property—maybe jewelry—was hidden in the theater and someone was desperate to find it, what was I doing fantasizing in my driveway? I hadn't pulled an all-nighter since college, but I was ready to do it now.

I drove back to the theater just in time to catch the last twenty minutes of stage mayhem as the old ladies are found out, the love interests reconcile, and the bad guys are put away. Not a bad ending.

When the houselights came on after the cast took a practice bow and the main drape fell, I spotted Lola seated next to Carlyle. Their heads together, I gave them time to confer on the night's performance before I intruded.

"Dodie? Didn't you go home?" Lola said.

"I did, but I forgot something. Don't let me interrupt you." I backed away.

Lola shook her head. "We're finished. Carlyle and Walter are doing notes."

I signaled to Lola that I would be in the rear of the house. She nodded, puzzled.

The curtain rose on standard theater bedlam: actors half in, half out of costume, Chrystal flying from person to person rescuing clothing, JC testing a door apparently missing a hinge, Walter debating with Romeo about something, and Penny slapping her clipboard against her leg. All was well.

"What's up?" Lola asked.

"I got all the way home and then decided, why go home? Why not search the theater and see if we can find whatever the bad guys are looking for?"

"We? You mean you and me?"

"We can't tell anyone else. Too many cooks . . ." I said.

"Walter sometimes stays late and does I-don't-know-what in the office."

"Can't you get rid of him? Tell him he looks exhausted and needs sleep?" I asked.

Lola was skeptical. "Where would we start? There's so much space . . ."

She was right. "I think we have to do something. Bill might know in the morning how Antonio's heart stopped. The word will get out and the perps will make a last ditch effort to search the theater. We have to beat them to it."

"Perps!" Lola said.

"You talk to Walter and I'll organize a plan." I rummaged around in my bag for a pen and piece of paper.

I'd always thought Lola was a great actress, but the scene she played with Walter was award-winning: concerned friend and colleague who just wanted him to go home and rest up and feel fresh for the weekend's technical rehearsal. She even threw in "I'm worried about you" and "You need to save your creative spirit." Walter was hooked. He kissed Lola's hand in gratitude and left her to lock up.

"Yuk," Lola said.

"I guess the bloom is completely off that rose." I stifled a laugh.

Lola winced. "I don't know what I saw in him."

We went to work, first in the scene shop, where we checked the saws, drill press, tool cage, paint storage, and worktables. Nothing. Next we went downstairs and peeked in the costume shop.

"How do we search all of this?" Lola said.

"You start with the sewing machines and cutting table. Check out those bolts of muslin. I'll look into the storage."

I began at the bottom and worked my way up a series of drawers that held costume paraphernalia—shoes and boots, hair accessories, undergarments, hats, and odds and ends of ribbons and sewing supplies. After forty-five minutes, we'd come up empty.

"Nothing in here, either," Lola said.

"We can't give up yet. Let's check the dressing rooms and the fly space."

"I can't believe Antonio would go up on the fly rail."

"You never know."

Lola yawned. "It's almost one a.m."

"I'm getting used to spending late nights here," I joked. "Seriously, I appreciate you helping me. I think we're close to cracking this thing wide open." If only.

The dressing rooms were a bust as well, if you didn't count candy wrappers, soda cans, someone's half-eaten Cobb salad, and a pair of socks. "Actors can be such slobs," Lola complained.

"It would be pretty difficult to hide anything in here." I scanned the makeup tables and chairs. "Let's take a last look in the fly space before we call it a night."

"I hate it up there. And it's hard to get to."

"Which makes it a great hiding place."

With reluctance, Lola followed me up a steep, winding stairway to the rail above the stage. The fly system was run manually. Ten or twelve steel pipes were held in place by lift lines that were connected to counterweights. The lighting for the show occupied six battens and the main drape was attached to the batten farthest downstage.

"It's so dark up here, I can't really see anything," Lola said.

I switched on my cell phone flashlight and moved it over the ground and around the fly rail. Nothing seemed out of place. Anything squirrelled away up here would have to be small and compact.

"Let's get out of here," Lola said. "It's giving me the creeps."

I flicked off the flashlight and stepped forward toward the circular set of stairs. A loud thump stopped us.

"What was that?" Lola whispered.

"I don't know. Everyone was gone when we started searching."

"Unless Walter or Carlyle came back."

Or someone else did.

I crouched and peered between the line sets where I had a decent view of the security light that lit up the front third of the stage. I tugged on Lola's sleeve. "Stoop down."

To be tucked away in the fly system would normally have seemed safe to me. But knowing someone was determined to search the entire theater made us vulnerable. I looked around the floor for a weapon of some kind. *I have to start carrying pepper spray.*

"What do we do?" Lola asked, worried.

"Sit tight until whoever it is leaves." Or finds us.

A ghostlike figure passed in front of the security scoop light and darted backstage.

"The green room," I mouthed to Lola.

A few minutes later a door slammed and then all was quiet. "I think he's gone downstairs to the costume shop. That could occupy him for a while. Let's make a break for it."

"Leave here?" Lola's voice squeaked.

"Shh! We don't want to stay here for hours, do we?" Been there, done that.

Lola nodded, then shook her head.

I held my finger to my lips and edged closer to the top step of the stairs. All was still quiet below. "Wait until I get to the stage and then come down. If someone shows up, stay put and call 911." I handed her my cell.

Before Lola could argue I slipped down the stairs, tripping on the last step and falling forward on my knees. I squatted, immobilized for a second.

"Dodie! Are you okay?"

"Shh!"

Lola hurried down the staircase. I grabbed her hand as she hit the stage floor. We sprinted through the house and dashed from the lobby to our cars. I hesitated.

"What are you stopping for? That guy could come after us at any moment." Lola thrust my cell at me and unlocked the Lexus's front door.

"You go on. I'm going to wait and see who turns up."

"Dodie, if you're right, this person might have killed Antonio. We could be in real danger. I'll call 911."

"No! The Etonville police will only scare him off. We've got to find out his identity. I'll move my car down the block where I can still see anyone entering or leaving the theater. If I feel threatened, *I'll* call the police. Go."

"Are you sure you don't want me to stay?" Lola didn't want to leave me alone, but clearly longed to beat a hasty retreat.

"I'll be fine. I'll call you in the morning."

"Or before if something happens. Promise?"

"Scout's honor. I'm probably going to sit for an hour, see nothing, and then go home."

Lola took off. I cranked my engine, locked the doors, and proceeded to drive past the theater, down Amber, and into the alley to get a clear view of the loading dock door. Was it only days ago that I sneaked around the walkway and got knocked out for my efforts? I would be wiser this time; surveillance from inside my Metro. Once again, I pulled behind the dumpster in back of the bookstore and scrunched down in my seat. Though I implied to Lola that I would be sitting safely in the car on Main Street, I knew that my chances of seeing a break-in artist come out the front door of the ELT were zero to none. That ship had sailed the last time I got caught spying. No, if someone wanted a quick, quiet getaway this time, it had to be through the shop door.

The moon glided behind fast-moving clouds. The alley darkened, killing visibility. I strained to see through the blackness: the edge of a dumpster, the theater dock with its large trash cans, and beyond all of it, Henry's herb garden behind the Windjammer. Which reminded me, I needed to create my mental to-do list for the weekend. I fervently hoped that Rita's rehearsal dinner would go smoothly, that Henry's menu would generate enough enthusiasm to trigger renewed customer traffic, and that Honey's favors wouldn't be mocked right out of the restaurant.

I adjusted my head to release a cramp in my neck. I checked my watch—1:45 a.m. The car was getting stuffy, so I cracked open the window and inhaled—just enough chill in the air to cool the inside of the Metro and set my skin quivering. I burrowed into my jacket and checked my watch again. Only ten minutes had passed.

My cell rang and I jumped. "Lola? What are you doing up?"

"My insomnia kicked in. What's going on?"

"Nothing. I have my eagle eye on the ELT but no action. Did you try chamomile tea?"

"I tried everything. Counting sheep, my white noise machine, tea. I think you should just give up for the night," Lola said.

"In a little bit. Is Tiffany in tonight?"

"She was gone when I got home." Lola tsked. "Probably in Creston with Carlyle. I must say, that doesn't seem to be an ideal match. I understand she needs someone and he's certainly sympathetic. But what would he see in her? I don't care for Carlyle all that much, but he is a really smart, capable guy. And Tiffany is . . . well . . . Tiffany."

Lola thought the same thing about Antonio, I remembered. Tiffany was a redhead with a fantastic figure. 'Nuff said. "Opposites attract, I guess."

"Or else he's got another agenda."

"Like what? Like maybe Tiffany's going to come into an inheritance?" I joked.

"You know, I asked Tiffany about Antonio's finances before his funeral and she said he'd taken care of things, money-wise."

"A bank account?"

"Some kind of insurance, she said. Antonio had told her he didn't believe in banks."

Given his history, I could see why.

"Antonio liked to spend money. Fancy cars, expensive clothes . . . maybe that's why he got into the scams in the first place," Lola said.

The moon scooted out of its hiding place in the clouds. The alley looked peaceful, the backs of the buildings dark, no sign of life. "Guess I'll head out," I said.

"I think that's a good idea."

Lola clicked off and I sat for moment. Antonio had insurance, all right. But had he sold the jewelry already? Or simply hoarded it for a rainy day?

Back on Main Street I parked a block away from the entrance to the theater. The lobby night light was undisturbed and no other illumination was visible from the office. It was now 3:00 a.m. and I couldn't keep my eyes open. I headed home. The intruder had won this round.

25

I tossed and turned for an hour, flipping my pillow back and forth to rest my head on the cool side. The last thing I remembered was 4:00 a.m. on my clock. I dreamed I was at a theater party and all of the usual suspects were present: Lola, Carol, Walter, Bill, Tiffany, even Abby and Edna. Everyone was having a grand time onstage, drinking champagne and toasting. I was grateful that the show had been a triumph. Music was pouring out of loudspeakers. Then everyone fell silent and stared offstage into the house. Antonio walked down the aisle in Walter's gangster costume, laughing, not joyfully but sadistically, at all of us. He pointed at me and nodded. I asked him where he'd been, that he'd missed the opening. He laughed harder and said it would never open. Carlyle and Regan and a third shadowy figure surrounded Antonio and draped a cape over his head. Then they all disappeared. The only sounds were Antonio's harsh, terrifying laugh and Penny's whistle. I screamed, "No!"

My eyes flew open, my face damp, the whistle still ringing in my ears. Except it wasn't the whistle but my cell. I forced myself to reach for the phone. It was eight thirty.

"Hello," I managed to sputter out.

"Dodie? What's wrong?" It was Bill's calm, reassuring voice, urging me back to reality.

I took deep breaths. "Just waking up," I said.

"Sorry to disturb you, but I have the results of the tox screen."

I went from zero to sixty. "Yeah?"

"Can you come here?"

"How's three? I can take my break—"

"Now," he said, his speech clipped.

I took a beat to let the implications sink in. "Give me thirty minutes."

I deliberately kept the shower on the cool side to coerce me into complete wakefulness. Bill's demand sounded ominous. My hands shook as I stepped into jeans and a brown sweater, my wet hair swishing around my face. I still couldn't shake the image of Antonio in my dream, the laughter, the warning. And the weird third figure.

I threw my bag onto the passenger seat and didn't even think about a Coffee Heaven pit stop. I pulled into a parking space next to Bill's, probably reserved for one of his officers. I didn't care; I was on an emergency mission. The dispatch window was being staffed by Suki, who nodded formally and hit a button to alert Bill that I was here. Before I could even knock on his door, it flew open.

"Have a seat." His face was ashy, grim, his uniform rumpled.

"Have you been up all night, too?"

He stopped in mid-sit. "Too?" he asked, suspicious.

"Never mind. What did they find?"

He slipped his thumbnail under the edge of a manila folder, maybe the same one that I had rifled through earlier, and exposed a sheet of paper. "It's just preliminary, but you were on to something."

My heart banged in my chest. "Don't tell me—"

"Poison."

I leaned forward. "But not bacteria in the food?"

Bill shook his head. "No. But it might have been in something he ate or drank. Antonio was probably killed by a fatal dose of a toxic element. Possibly two."

My head spun. "What exactly are you saying?"

"I'd like to keep this information from getting out immediately." He frowned. "Until I can sift through all of the evidence, the restaurant is a crime scene."

OMG. This was going from bad to worse. "But you said bacteria was not the cause of his death?"

Bill studied the sheet of paper. "There were traces of arsenic in his blood."

"Arsenic?"

Uh-oh. It was life imitating art. I'd read enough mysteries to know that poison could be a murderer's friend. But this was real life, not a thriller.

"Arsenic is easily available and difficult to detect in certain foods and drinks. It even occurs naturally in groundwater and soil. It might have been given in a number of doses, with the fatal dose delivered during the food festival. The medical examiner said arsenic poisoning increases the risk of cardiac arrest. Depending on the size of the doses, Antonio could have experienced symptoms days or weeks before his death."

Thoughts were tumbling helter-skelter. "Would some symptoms be gastro issues? Abdominal pain?"

"Could be."

"Dr. Xiu," I said.

He nodded.

"But why is the restaurant a crime scene? Any evidence of someone lacing Antonio's knish or elderberry wine is long gone."

"Because it was the scene of his death."

I started to stammer out my opposition, but Bill raised a hand to halt my spewing. "It's not like we're going to be closing the Windjammer. We just need to do a little poking around."

"As in showing up with CSI techs?" I asked, knowing what his answer would be.

"It won't take long. The guys are in and out quickly. They should be there within the hour."

Henry will go ballistic. "What will they be looking for? Antonio died outside."

"Traces of arsenic. The restaurant was open that day, and someone could have slipped in and doctored his food. Or his wine."

I doubted it. The Windjammer staff were the only ones handling food or drinks. But then I remembered both Imogen and myself seeing Antonio with a cup in his hand from someplace outside the festival. "Antonio brought his own cup with him. Maybe the arsenic was placed in it somewhere else."

"His own cup? What are you talking about?"

I recounted my memory of that afternoon—with Imogen's recollection as backup—as Bill's expression swung from surprise to skepticism.

"You didn't mention this before," he said darkly.

"And you were certain it was a heart attack."

Edna knocked on the door and delivered two black coffees. "Here you go, Chief."

"Thanks," I said.

She winked and left.

I waited until the door closed before I blurted out last night's story: the search of the theater, the spooky figure running across the stage. I left out sitting in the alley waiting for the guilty party to appear. I wasn't sure his system could take it. "I think Regan is mixed up in this."

I could see Bill's patience wearing thin. "There you go again with your assumptions. Why didn't you call me? Never mind."

I tiptoed into my next idea. "I know you might not want to hear this, but Antonio must have hidden stolen property in the theater." There, I'd said it. "And person or persons are pretty desperate to find it. One of your burglars is out on bail. Maybe he has something to do with it."

Bill shook his head, then surrendered. "I'll bring in Regan Digenza for questioning."

Yes! "Maybe Johnny Bilboe?"

"But I want you to stay out of trouble, and no going off on your own anymore and endangering yourself. I want to be informed."

My heart fluttered. He cared!

"I don't want any lawsuits," he grumbled.

Back down to earth. Oh well . . . "By the way, you said there were possibly two toxic elements."

"The medical examiner found another, more obscure substance. He hasn't identified it yet."

On my way to the Windjammer, I rehearsed my spiel to Henry. How the state forensic team would be in and out, how knowing that arsenic was the cause of death ruled out food poisoning, how—I hit the brakes. The Crime Scene Investigation van was already on the premises, prominently displayed in two spaces in front of the restaurant. We opened in an hour and a half.

I hurried from my Metro to the Windjammer, arriving just in time to see Henry standing, astonished, in the middle of the kitchen. He was holding a box of broccoli—for the broccoli Florentine bisque on today's menu—and looked completely befuddled as the techs moved through the kitchen, pantry, behind the bar, in the corners of the dining room.

"It's okay, Henry. It won't take long," I said and directed him to the center island, where he could chop the veggies. Enrico, sautéing onions and garlic, watched the CSI guys wide-eyed, fearful.

"Dodie, what are they looking for?" Henry asked, tight-lipped.

"Didn't they tell you?"

He shook his head. "They just barged in, waved badges and forms, and went to work."

"Arsenic," I whispered.

"*Arsen*—"

"Not so loud! Bill . . . the chief . . . will be here soon to explain it all. Meanwhile, let's get lunch going."

Enrico nodded and added vegetable broth for the soup base.

"But why are they looking for arsenic in my restaurant?" Henry demanded, attacking the broccoli.

"Because it might have been the substance that killed Antonio. They don't really think there's any arsenic in the Windjammer, but they have to go by the book, because technically this is the 'scene of the crime,' even though Antonio died outside." I hoped my air quotes would lighten the atmosphere or at least reduce the tension level. No luck there.

Henry manhandled a large blade as though he were butchering a side of beef rather than mincing broccoli florets. I left him to his own devices and stepped into the dining room. Benny still had his jacket on. He nodded toward the front entrance. "It's attracting attention."

A collection of Etonville citizens had begun to form on the sidewalk, peering in the window and exchanging whatever gossip they could invent.

Bill's black-and-white squad car pulled up next to the CSI van. I could see him gesturing to the crowd, as if asking them to be patient. It would be a few minutes before we opened. But his attempt to appease them was pointless. And when the arsenic rumor hit the mill, people would be running for the hills, in this case Creston or Bernridge, or, heaven forbid, La Famiglia. I wanted to bury my head in a hoodie, crawl into my back booth, and drown my sorrows in broccoli bisque.

Bill walked in, absorbed the scene in the dining room, and glanced my way. There might have been one sympathetic, slightly upturned corner of his mouth. He headed to the kitchen.

* * *

"Hey, Dot!"

As if things couldn't get more irritating. "Hi, Honey."

"Like, I'm doing the reservations," Honey said. She had a notebook computer open on the bar near the cash register. One of her daily tasks was to take reservations from the online service. We'd only had half a dozen since it was activated late spring, and none since the food festival. But it was Honey's responsibility, so she dutifully checked and generally made a snarky comment. "This is like... wow."

Benny stood behind her. "Yowza!"

I walked to the bar and Honey flipped the notebook to face me. There were five reservations for tonight, tomorrow, and Saturday. "What the...?"

The phone rang and Benny picked up. "Windjammer." He did a double take, shrugged at me, and picked up a pen and pad. A takeout order. What in the world was going on?

By noon the CSI techs were gone—having found no traces of arsenic in the restaurant—and the lunch rush really was a rush. Go figure. No one was bothered by the notion that there might have been a fatal dose of arsenic deliberately delivered on the premises. As long as there were no errant bacteria floating around in Henry's food, the town was good to go.

It took all hands on deck to keep the horde of customers content. Benny was pouring and delivering drinks, Carmen and Honey ran nonstop from kitchen to dining room, Gillian bussed tables, and I pitched in wherever needed, including managing the waiting line. A waiting line!

"Dodie, we're regulars, don't you know. Maybe we could cut ahead in line?" one of the Banger sisters said. The man ahead of them turned and glared.

"Uh, sorry. It shouldn't take long."

"We even came when Antonio died of food poisoning. But now that it's only arsenic, well..." the other one huffed.

"We appreciate your loyalty," I said, as I had been saying for the last hour.

"I still think one of the actors used the arsenic from the play and tampered with Antonio's wine," the first sister said.

I laughed. "It's a play. Nothing's real. There's no arsenic."

They both eyed me as if they knew something I didn't.

Honey raised her hand and motioned for the next party in line. I escorted them to a table, handed out menus, and slipped behind the bar. "Whew," I said to Benny, and drew myself a seltzer. "Be careful what you wish for." Bill had said those same words to me only days ago.

"Who knew? All it took was a dose of arsenic," Benny cracked.

"I'm just glad the monkey is off Henry's back."

Edna stopped in for a takeout order for the police department. "Business is booming!" she said with a grin. "Hope you didn't run out of burgers. The chief loves them."

"Never." I put the order in. "Guess you'll be happy when the show is over?"

Edna blinked. "Happy? Oh no, Dodie. I'm going to miss it terribly."

"You must be the only one. Seems like the rest of the cast is eager to have it done with." I poured her an iced tea.

Her brow puckered. "Lately Walter says, 'The course of true theater never does run smooth.'"

OMG. Walter's mashup of *A Midsummer Night's Dream* and his own philosophy.

"Edna's cell rang. "Yes, Chief? Uh-huh. 11-84. Got it. 10-4." She ended the call. "He's looking for Ralph. Officer Ostrowski's supposed to be on duty near the highway where they're repaving the road."

"Oops. Guess he's MIA?"

"More like 11-99. Officer in trouble," she said knowingly.

Secret burgers and the grilled cheese special were big hits, and the broccoli bisque ran out by two thirty. I slipped into the back booth and grunted in delight. A corner had been turned and the Windjammer was bouncing back.

"Here you go," Benny said and set a tuna salad platter and coffee in front of me. "Sure this is all you want?"

"This and a week off."

"Good one," he said. "Especially since it looks like we're going to be swamped from now on."

"Guess Etonville got tired of cooking for itself."

My cell rang. "Hi, Lola."

"You've been trying to reach me?" she asked. "I saw a voicemail and two texts. By the way, I heard about the arsenic. Good news for the Windjammer."

"Right. Can you talk?" I asked.

"Sure. I'm on my way to the theater. I was running lines with Tiffany—"

"How's she doing?"

Lola hesitated. "A little better. Any news from last night?"

"I talked with Bill this morning. He's going to question Regan Digenza. But meanwhile, I've had a thought. What's happening in the theater tomorrow morning?"

26

I slipped onto the bench across from Lola—who was checking email on her phone and nibbling on a meat loaf sandwich—in my back booth.

"Sorry I missed the broccoli bisque," she said.

"Had a run on it." I accepted a refill of coffee. "Thanks, Benny." I needed all the caffeine I could swallow if dinner was going to be anything like lunch.

Lola dropped her voice. "Good news that the chief's meeting with Regan Digenza."

"Right. The sooner we know who's been searching the theater, the sooner we'll find out who killed Antonio."

I knew I had put two and two together and come up with fifty. I was hoping my arithmetic wasn't too far off base. "One of these times someone is going to tear the theater apart looking for the jewelry. And expose himself as the killer."

"Jewelry?" Lola gawked at me.

Ooops. "You have to keep that piece of information to yourself," I said quickly.

Lola looked over her shoulder. "So Antonio had jewelry from the robberies that he hid in the theater?"

"Possibly," I said carefully. "So here's what I'm thinking. We rummaged through all of the theater spaces and found nothing."

"True."

"But we didn't check the stage. That's the one place we didn't search. And I'll bet no one else has either."

Lola's voice rose shrilly. "You think Antonio hid the jewelry—?"

"Shhh!"

Lola made a locking motion on the surface of her lips. ". . . somewhere in the scenery onstage?"

"I'd like to find out. We could meet tomorrow morning and go over the set with a fine-tooth comb."

Lola's brow wrinkled. "I have a color and cut in the morning. For opening night. Carol is squeezing me in at eight. Then Carol and I have a hair and makeup meeting with Chrystal at eleven thirty."

I had to be at the Windjammer by eleven o'clock. It was the day of the rehearsal dinner and I was determined that everything would run smoothly. "Lola, can I borrow your keys and search by myself? You could join me between the Snippets appointment and the meeting with Chrystal if you have time. The theater will be empty, right?"

"Absolutely. JC is finishing up the painting tonight, Chrystal's not coming in until eleven, Carlyle is busy . . . with Tiffany, and Walter . . . well, the less said the better. He's moodier than usual lately. Carlyle wanted to rearrange some props onstage and he had a fit."

"Uh-huh." If I got to the ELT by 8:00 a.m., that would give me a good two hours alone.

Lola wiped her mouth on a napkin, studying me. "This is important to you, isn't it?"

"At first I wanted to know *how* Antonio died, to get the Windjammer off the hook. But the deeper I dig, the more I need to know *why* he died."

Lola patted my hand. "You're doing a good thing, Dodie, even if certain people don't acknowledge it."

Who? Walter? Tiffany? Bill . . . ?

Lola glanced at her watch. "I have to get next door. Final runthrough tonight before the tech rehearsal tomorrow." She took a key off her key ring. "Here's a master. Just keep it for now." It unlocked the front door as well as most interior doors. "We're keeping track of these ever since Penny's assault."

"Thanks." Of course, someone *else* had a master key and was using it to scour the theater.

In the kitchen, Henry had already prepped for the evening's special—chicken and dumplings—and was up to his elbows in flour and seasonings, shaping dumplings into medium-sized balls, his face covered in a fine veneer of moisture.

"Have you taken a break today?" I made sure everyone took a lunch hour at some point, but Henry set his own schedule.

He grinned . . . Henry actually grinned and shook his head. He was as happy as a pig in manure. Enrico stirred the large pots of chicken boiling in broth and twirled his ladle at me. It was a very jovial kitchen. I stepped back into the dining room.

"See the weather report?" Benny asked as he polished the soda taps.

"Not really," I said, scanning inventory sheets—the final delivery for the rehearsal dinner had been made an hour ago. I usually made a point of watching the Weather Channel in the morning, but lately I'd been a little preoccupied.

"A tropical storm is due to hit the Outer Banks this afternoon. It might turn and move north tomorrow morning. Could end up being a nor'easter."

I looked up. Hurricane Sandy's anniversary was coming up soon. I got nervous whenever there was a hint of stormy weather this time of year. Luckily, New Jersey had been spared a full-blown hurricane since Sandy, but a robust tropical storm could do a ton of damage as well. "You're kidding. I hadn't heard."

"Could put a damper on the rehearsal dinner. No pun intended," Benny said, and grimaced.

Just when things were moving along so nicely. "Maybe we'd better plan for the worst. There's extra doormats and some umbrella holders in the pantry, and let's get another coatrack for rain gear."

Carmen and Gillian appeared and began to set the tables. A trickle of patrons scooted in the door, windblown from gusts that had dropped the temperature and scudded clouds across a darkening sky.

To take my mind off the impending weather, I tapped Brianna's cell phone number and waited for her to answer. The phone rang. One, two, three, four . . . and then her voicemail clicked on. Brianna's not available. Blah blah blah.

I hesitated for a second. "Hi, Brianna. This is Dodie. I said I'd let you know if there was any new information on Antonio's death. I'm not sure if you heard, but the medical examiner found arsenic in his bloodstream." I waited a beat. "I know this must be startling news." I waited another beat. "I'll be in touch. Bye now."

* * *

Last night I'd set two alarms to guarantee that I would be up and dressed by seven thirty. I threw on a hoodie and worn jeans since I would be crawling in and around furniture on the stage; I had plenty of time to change later for the evening's event. I fixed a cup of coffee, transferred it to my travel container, and stepped onto my front porch. The sky threatened to pummel the town with rain. Well, nothing I could do about it; I resolutely climbed into my Metro.

I drove to the ELT and unlocked the front door. The theater was eerily quiet as I felt for the wall switch that flooded the house with light and spilled onto the stage, where the security lamp provided shadowy illumination. It would have to do, since I was not about to tackle the dimmers on the light board that controlled the Fresnel and ellipsoidal lights. I'd gotten familiar with theater lighting this past summer when I volunteered a few hours to help prep the stage for a guest gig by a dance company. Mostly, I held lighting instruments until the designer was ready to hang them on battens.

No matter. I was ready. I'd brought my camping lantern that shot out a substantial circle of light. I faced the stage and decided on a plan of action. To my left was the front door of the set, with small, lace-curtained windows and sconces on the wall. To my right was the infamous window seat—from which dead bodies would presumably be removed—adjacent to a large window through which actors could crawl. It was curtained in deep red brocade to complement the wallpaper. There was a door upstage-left that led to the interior of the house, specifically the kitchen, and a door upstage-right that led to the basement. Between the two doors were shelves chock-full of tchotchkes: books, china ornaments, dishes. Behind the shelving was a staircase that led to a hallway for the upper floor. Scattered around the set were a table and chairs, a sofa and side table, and a stuffed chair and ottoman. I lifted my lantern in a wide arc. Framed pictures and light fixtures dotted the walls and an aged Oriental rug covered the floor in the center of the room. The scenery was topped off with a period chandelier. Wow, JC had gone all out for this show. Must have broken the ELT budget; of course if the show sold out, that would be a moot point. *If* it sold out.

By the end of the first hour I had explored the exits—both on- and offstage—drapery, staircase, and furniture, feeling around door frames, curtain rods, sofa cushions, and the inside of the window seat. I came up empty. Next, I confronted the shelves, scrutinizing every book and prop. Nothing. It was ten o'clock. I had about thirty minutes left. I stood at the edge of the stage and scanned the entire setting. Where would I hide jewelry, likely in a bag of some sort? The door to the kitchen opened onto a fake hallway; the door to the basement likewise revealed a wall that provided offstage cover. I glanced upward. That left only the staircase to the second story.

I climbed each step carefully, checking for a loose board or an opening in the carpet tread. At the top, JC had built a hallway that ran six or seven feet and emptied onto an escape stairs. I was halfway down the escape when a wash of light flooded the scenery.

"Who's there?" an anxious voice rang out. Carlyle.

I was caught. I had no choice but to reveal myself. I scrambled down the rest of the stairs and stuck my head through the kitchen door. "Hi," I said with my brightest smile.

Carlyle glowered. "What are you doing here? You can't be backstage."

I ignored his reprimand. "JC did a spectacular job, didn't he?"

"Are you looking for something?" He was suddenly all suspicion.

"Looking for something? No."

"Then what are you doing here?"

"I'm . . . meeting Lola. We have a meeting." I paused. Best defense was always a good offense. "What are *you* doing here so early?"

His face closed down. "I have some work to do before the tech." He tapped his foot impatiently.

"How's Tiffany taking the news?"

"Huh?" he asked.

"The medical examiner's report that there were traces of arsenic in Antonio's blood."

Carlyle's bravado took a nosedive. "How do you think? She's upset. We're all upset."

Who was the "all"? "I'm sure. It seems clear someone intended to murder Antonio."

Carlyle threw back his shoulders. "Walter told me about you."

"He did? Well, that's—"

"That you consider yourself an amateur detective. Poking your nose in other's people's business."

I felt my face redden. "I don't consider myself an amateur anything. In fact, last spring, if it wasn't for me 'poking my nose' into the death of an ELT member, Walter might have—"

"Dodie?" Lola took a few tentative strides down the center aisle. "Hi, Carlyle."

We both swung our heads in her direction.

He nodded. Barely.

"I told Carlyle that we had a meeting."

Carol walked into the theater behind Lola. "Dodie, did you find anything?"

I gritted my teeth. *Geez.*

Lola took Carol's arm to head off any further indiscretions as they moved down the aisle. "Let's go to the dressing room."

Carlyle remained in the house, watching the three of us trek across the stage.

"I don't trust him," I whispered, after we'd shut ourselves in the women's dressing room and closed the door. "He said he had work to do before the tech, but I don't know."

"*Did* you find anything?" Lola asked.

"Like jewelry?" Carol added, breathless.

"No. But you two have to keep that to yourselves," I said firmly.

"Oops. Sorry." Carol's curly locks shook to and fro.

"I covered every square inch of the set and there was nothing." I felt stressed and frustrated. Not to mention annoyed at Carlyle's characterization of me as an amateur. *But I am, aren't I?*

"I'm sorry, Dodie. You've searched everywhere. I think we have to accept that if he did have stolen property, Antonio hid it someplace else."

Carol nodded.

"I have to get to the Windjammer. Good luck with the tech tonight," I said, dejected.

Lola crossed her fingers. "Good luck with the dinner."

I wore my little black dress. It hadn't been out of the dry cleaner's bag for a year, but back when the rehearsal dinner was the only good news on the Windjammer's horizon, I'd decided that the staff needed to dress for the occasion. Honey and Carmen in black skirts and white blouses; Benny and Enrico's cousin—on board to help out tonight—in black slacks and white shirts. All of them wore black bow ties. And me in my Jimmy Choo knockoffs, looking pretty hot, I'd say.

I'd scrounged up some painted screens from the ELT scenery stock and we'd arranged them artfully around the long table accommodating Rita's party. It gave them the feel of a private room. The place settings were gleaming, and fresh flowers in Rita's colors of purple and pink adorned Honey's boxy centerpiece, which she spent a half hour photographing for her packaging portfolio. Her favors were a pleasant surprise for Rita's party, even if the appearance of rice at the rehearsal dinner was confusing.

We even piped in some music, gentle classical stuff that wouldn't clash with Rita's tattooed persona but would compete vigorously with the sounds of the other patrons. All in all, the Windjammer had risen to the occasion. If only the weather had cooperated. It had started drizzling about noon, and by midafternoon had developed into showers. Still manageable. But the weather reports—delivered every five minutes by Benny—were growing dire. Downpours and squalls expected.

I smiled and ignored the consequences. The party had arrived at six thirty, on time, damp but game to have a good time. Rita was startlingly striking in a sedate purple dress, hair in an updo, compliments of Carol. I fervently hoped the storm would be gone by the wedding tomorrow.

The baby greens with walnuts and goat cheese went over well, and Henry began to relax. Benny kept the group lubricated, and I flitted back and forth from the party to the dining room. Carmen had just begun to serve the entrées when two actors hurried into the restaurant accompanied by a draft of wet air. Bringing the storm inside was enough to stifle the crowd for a moment. But I secured the door, turned up the music a smidgen, and smiled. And smiled some more.

"How's the tech going?" I asked one of the actors, in his period suit. Chrystal would have a fit if she knew he'd left the theater in a costume.

"Still in Act One. Slow, boring, and wet," he said, and paid for the coffees that Benny had prepared and rung up.

"Wet?"

"There's a leak in the roof over the stage. Walter put a bucket in the center of the room, but it's in the way and Abby kicked it over."

He tucked the bag of coffees into the crook of his arm. "The tech could take all night. If we don't get flooded out first."

Poor Lola, poor Walter . . . forget Walter. He called me an amateur.

"Want the latest update?" Benny asked.

"Don't tell me . . . rain?" I said.

"Smarty pants. Actually, it might be letting up. Depends on which way the wind blows."

Doesn't everything? I glanced behind the screen. Carmen had the table in hand. Across the way, Honey was chatting up Mildred and her husband, advising them on the most effective way to package their leftovers.

I sat down at the bar to check the weather. Maybe we should shut down as soon as the rehearsal dinner ended. The door opened and a gust of wind blew in, rifling a stack of menus. Again, silence for a moment, and then everyone reengaged with their dinner. Bill strode across the restaurant, his eyes clouded over, disturbed. His police slicker was shiny black and rain dripped off his cap and ran down one cheek. I stood up and handed him a napkin. "Wet one, right?"

He opened his mouth to answer and then seemed to really see me. He took in me and my dress, head to toe. "Very nice."

"This? Just something I had hanging around—"

"I need to speak with you. Can you . . . ?" He scanned the dining room.

I nodded. "Benny, cover for me?"

"Will do," he said.

I led Bill through the kitchen, where Henry and Enrico were congratulating themselves on the successful evening, and into the pantry. The only quiet and semiprivate place at this hour.

"Okay?"

He shook his head. "I received the rest of the ME's report. The substance that he couldn't identify? He ran a more sophisticated tox screen and, well . . ." He took a scrap of paper out of his pocket. "Succinylcholine."

"Huh?"

"It's a deadly chemical that, with an overdose, can kill in minutes. Usually delivered by syringe. The ME said he hadn't run across the drug outside the operating room. It's an anesthetic."

My stomach flip-flopped. I swallowed. "Someone delivered a dose of this stuff to Antonio at the food festival?"

"It looks that way. Whoever was responsible wanted a quick, tidy death that could be mistaken for a heart attack."

"Have you found Regan Digenza?"

"Not yet. I have an APB out on her and her place staked out. I'm posting a squad car at the theater. Suki will be on duty there all night. Once this storm passes tomorrow, I'm calling in some support from the Creston PD. Meanwhile, watch out and call me if you see anything unusual next door."

It was the Etonville Little Theatre. Everything was unusual.

"Where will you be?" I asked.

"There's flooding down by the highway. We might need to close off the road."

"Thanks for the heads-up."

He leaned into me and I smelled his aftershave mingled with coffee. "Someone's not messing around. This is serious. I'll be in touch later tonight."

"Can I have that?"

He handed me the fragment of paper and left.

I returned to the dining room. I'd only been away five minutes, but in that time, the world had tilted on its axis. Traces of arsenic somehow seemed possibly accidental, more familiar. But this other drug was a different matter altogether.

27

Everything was calm, so I picked up the notebook computer and headed to my back booth. I had just settled into the seat when the lights went out. A collective "Ah" from patrons, followed by a babble of concern. I hopped to my feet and made my way to the center of the room. "Please remain calm," I called out. "The emergency generator will kick in." Truth be told, the candles on the tables created a warm, romantic halo in the restaurant. I wouldn't have been unhappy if the lights had remained off.

Enrico emerged from the kitchen. "Miss Dodie, Henry is—"

The electricity flashed back on, the lights glowing. I nodded to Enrico and moved around the room, reassuring customers that all was well. I knew that Henry had installed a backup generator after Hurricane Sandy, but this was the first time we'd had to use it.

"Close one," Benny said, and checked his cell.

"Everyone okay at home?"

"Yep." He glanced out the window. "Only the businesses on this side of the street are without light. The wind might have knocked out a transformer."

Yikes. That meant the ELT was dark.

"Let's close the kitchen," I said to Benny. "But keep the bar open. I wouldn't be surprised if actors show up any minute." The door whooshed open and half of the cast of *Arsenic and Old Lace* trooped in. "See what I mean?"

Abby, Romeo, Penny, Edna, and a few others stripped off wet outer clothing and plunked them on the hooks on the coat tree, jostling each other to get a place at the bar. The drinks—hot and cold—soon flowed and soothed the frustration level of the cast.

"Why doesn't Walter get an emergency generator?" Edna.

"Too expensive. We can barely afford the sets." One of the policemen characters.

"He's going to have to cough up some bucks for the roof." Edna.

"Are we going to tech the rest of the show?" Romeo.

"Maybe he'll cancel the opening tomorrow." Abby.

And finally from Penny: "Duh. If you can't stand the heat, get off the stage."

The cast shook their heads. Edna's cell binged with a text. "We got a problem by the highway. The chief needs Ralph down there. I'm going to have to go on dispatch." She lowered her voice. "Suki's still on patrol at the theater. I was going to bring her some coffee."

"I'll take care of it," I offered.

Edna hurried away. Meanwhile, behind the decorative screens, Carmen served pastries and Enrico's cousin poured coffee. Only a half hour to go. I slipped off my shoes, massaged my feet, and returned to the notebook. I typed in "succinylcholine" and waited. A list of links appeared: The drug is a muscle relaxant used during surgery or when a patient is placed on a ventilator. It can cause paralysis of facial or breathing muscles, especially if the patient is given too much. It is administered through injection by a health care provider, and, with the right dose, is fast acting. I rested against the seat back. I still couldn't get over it. Someone had injected Antonio during the festival.

I continued to read about safety information, side effects, and overdoses. Then it stared me in the face: "... severe reactions ... tightness in the chest, irregular heartbeat, difficulty breathing, flushing ... has been associated with cardiac arrest." Why would the murderer use two separate poisons to kill Antonio?

I felt a tingling on the back of my neck. Bill had said succinylcholine was usually delivered by syringe, and the medical examiner hadn't run across the drug outside the operating room. I racked my brain. What had Pauli told me? *She was a nurse and worked in a hospital ... and for this doctor, and then there was this problem ... fired.*

I texted Pauli: WHAT DID REGAN DIGENZA DO TO GET FIRED?

The ELT crew wrapped themselves in outerwear in preparation for combating the wind and rain, Rita's fiancé paid the bill for the rehearsal dinner, and Carmen and Honey cleared tables. We'd made it through the night. Sort of. I knew I had at least another hour before I could take off my Jimmy Choos for good.

With the restaurant nearly empty, I poured myself a cup of coffee and set to work. Coffee! I'd promised to get some to Suki. A steaming hot liquid would go down easy on a night like this. I found a thermos in the pantry, filled it to the brim, changed out of my dress and back into a pair of jeans, a sweatshirt, and sneakers and slipped on my raincoat.

"Leaving already?" Benny asked.

"I'll just be a minute. I want to run this next door. Then you can go."

Benny stretched. "It's a deal."

The staff had worked hard and well tonight. Even Honey. I was proud of them!

On the sidewalk by the ELT, wind gusts whipped my coat open and a blast of rain soaked the front of my sweatshirt. I had a flashback to Hurricane Sandy, the storm that changed my life and sent me north. I still had occasional nightmares about that time. Ferocious winds, churning water, and crashing waves destroying the boardwalk and Bigelow's, the beach restaurant I managed, as well as all of the other businesses nearby. Once Bigelow's closed there was little to keep me down the shore. My parents had already moved to Florida, my then-boyfriend Jackson had exchanged his charter fishing boat for a job selling farm equipment in Iowa, and a fifteen-foot elm had landed on the roof of the house I rented. I packed my Metro and headed north across the Driscoll Bridge. I never looked back. Well, maybe only once or twice a week.

I grabbed my camping lantern from my Metro, and scanned the street. There was no sign of a squad car on Main. I figured Suki was either cruising around the block or on duty in the alley behind the theater. I switched on the lantern and hurried to the walkway that ran alongside the theater building. I hunkered down into my coat; the last time I'd trod this footpath, I'd gotten knocked out.

Ahead in the alley I saw the police vehicle, lights off. The entire area was pitch-black, with no electricity and a heavy blanket of clouds. My cell binged. I had a text message from Pauli: MISSING DRUGS. So Regan Digenza née Rottinger was a nurse who had an illegal history with medicine. Suki needed to get this information to Bill ASAP.

I pulled the hood of my rain slicker over my head and approached the squad car, ready to rap on the window. I lifted my lantern and peered inside. The police scanner was lit up and there was a sheaf of papers on the front seat. But other than that, nothing. Maybe Suki had had to use the ladies' room. I retraced my steps to the front of the theater, used Lola's master key to unlock the door. I paused, dripping on the lobby carpet. "Officer Shung? Suki?" The silence was deafening.

Next, I poked my head in the bathroom, but it was empty. Puzzled, I felt my neck hairs stand at attention. Something was wrong. I swept my lantern over the lobby again. The door to the theater was slightly ajar. She must have gone into the house to check on things. But the house was just as dark as the lobby, except for the red EXIT lights that had battery backups.

"Suki?" I yelled, my voice bouncing off the walls and scenery. I started to sweat inside my rubber slicker. I moved my light from left to right, taking in the whole house and stage areas. Out of the silence, I heard a soft, low whine like a puppy. Of course, there was no puppy in the Etonville Little Theatre, right? I followed the sound as it pulled me down the aisle to the front of the stage. I leaned down to check the floor, and gasped.

"Mmmm!" Suki, stuck between the first two rows and securely bound and gagged, was struggling against the heavy-duty rope.

"Suki!" I dropped the lantern and the thermos and reached for her gag. "Who did—?" Her eyes grew as large as saucers at something behind me. I turned to see a body dressed in black move toward me threateningly, a gun in its hand. I ducked and turned away as its arm curled above my head. I stuffed myself under a theater seat, one leg stuck out to defend myself, the other twisted under my rear.

"Let her go," a smooth, resonant voice commanded. Then to me. "You can come out now."

My heart pounded out of my chest. I glanced at Suki, whose black eyes were usually so serene. Now they had narrowed, furious. It was going to take a lot of meditation for her to forgive and forget this night. I eased out from under the seat and got to my feet, picking up my lantern on the way. I directed it to the voice facing me. Even in the dim light I recognized her. Regan Digenza. Her deep brown hair with streaked highlights hung damply to her shoulders.

I tried bravado. "What are you doing in here? Untie Officer Shung immediately."

A dark-clothed man stepped forward, grunted, and pushed me into a seat. I recognized him from his picture in the *Creston Enquirer*: Johnny Bilboe. Out on bail! He appeared every bit as threatening as his mug shot in the newspaper. "Reg, let me take care of her."

"No." Regan sneered. "We might need leverage later tonight."

"At least untie Suki's feet," I said. "Let her sit on the floor."

Regan laughed, her expression contorted. "Helpful, aren't you?"

Surely someone would notice how long I'd been gone and come to investigate. Then I thought: distraction. "I can't imagine what Antonio saw in you. Why he married you," I scoffed. "Especially after Brianna. But I can understand his leaving you for Tiffany."

Her eyes glinted for an instant, then went dull again.

Regan opened a bag and withdrew a long, narrow object. "Smart *and* helpful." She snatched the flashlight from Johnny Bilboe's grasp and trained it on her hand. "So smart you probably know what this is."

I gulped. It was a syringe.

Her laugh was brittle. "And you know what it can do. So behave yourself."

"But why kill off your partner? I know for a fact that Antonio was good at what he did. Trapping older victims into believing he was selling them security systems. You needed him."

I had no idea whether the ring of thieves needed him, but the atmosphere altered. Suki had stopped wriggling in her bindings and Regan nodded her head in acknowledgment.

"Yeah. We needed him. Until he lied and tried to double-cross us."

"Took the jewelry, right?" I said.

Suki slid her eyes in my direction.

"So why not just finish him off with the arsenic? Why use the succa . . . succin . . . succyl . . ."

"Succinylcholine." She took a beat. "Arsenic? What are you talking about?"

Johnny Bilboe was impatient. "We gotta get to work." He picked up a sledgehammer.

"Wh-what are you going to do with that?" I stuttered.

Did he intend to bash our heads? My life was about to pass in front of my eyes. Johnny heaved the hammer at me and I flinched. He smirked.

Regan climbed the steps to the stage. "Tie her up, too. And stick a gag in her mouth. Then get up here."

He had no intention of attacking us. Johnny's objective had to be the set. Regan threw a few pieces of furniture around, looking underneath the sofa and ottoman and the cushions. They had come to the same conclusion as I had. The jewelry was hidden onstage. I panicked. Never mind that my life—and Suki's—were in danger; I couldn't imagine the pandemonium that would ensue if the *Arsenic and Old Lace* set were destroyed. No opening, no box office, maybe no ELT, no theme food—my mind whirled. "You don't need to tear up the set," I said as Johnny moved from tying my hands to tying my feet. "I can show you where the jewelry is hidden." He stopped and Regan rotated on one heel and squinted.

Suki's eyes were trying to speak to me; probably saying *Are you out of your mind? You have no idea where the jewelry is or you would have turned it over to Bill . . . you would, right?*

"I was searching in here this morning," I said.

"So where is it?" Regan demanded.

"Untie me and I'll show you."

"Yeah, like that's going to happen."

I slouched down in my seat and tried for tough. "Never mind. Find it yourself. But time's running out. You may think the Etonville Police Department is just a small-town operation . . ."

Suki closed her eyes.

". . . but they were responsible for breaking the case in Creston."

Regan hesitated, then she gestured. "But leave her hands tied."

I prayed as fervently as I ever had that someone next door would miss me. Even Honey. I stood up, wobbled a little, and found my balance. As I turned to exit the row of seats, I peeked at Suki. She'd relaxed a bit, her brow smooth, her eyes encouraging. Neither Regan nor Johnny could see what I saw. Suki had loosened the rope around her legs; she had an inch of wiggle room.

Johnny took my arm and pushed me onto the stage. "Well?" He flung the sledgehammer over his shoulder. "Where is it?"

I needed an advantage. Walking up the staircase to the second level of the set would allow me to stall. "Up the stairs." They exchanged looks and Johnny shrugged.

I stepped around the bucket onstage that held rainwater from the leaking roof, half-empty since Abby had spilled the contents earlier and left the Oriental rug sopping wet. I felt as if we were marching to the guillotine, me slow and careful, Johnny tramping in work boots, the hammer knocking against his leg. I knew the escape stairs led off the hallway. I'd stuffed my cell phone in my pants pocket. If I could disrupt Johnny's timing and catch him off guard, maybe I could fly down the stairs, run through the green room, and call 911. Even a butt call would help. I paused in the middle of the hallway.

Johnny poked me. "Keep going."

"I need my hands to reach for it," I said, raising my tied wrists.

"I'll reach it."

"Hurry up," Regan yelled, now out of view.

I stood in the corner where the upstairs hall met the escape stairs.

Johnny shined his flashlight ahead of me and flipped it over the unfinished walls. "So?"

I looked up at the unpainted lumber where JC had marked the sheets of plywood to indicate which piece went where. There were arrows pointing to hinges and a scribbled "Slow Down" to remind actors that the route offstage could be dangerous in the dark.

I crammed my tied hands into a narrow gap on the back of a canvas wall where the triangular corner block was attached to the bottom rail. I pretended to stiffen. "It was in here this morning. Someone must have—"

Johnny pushed me aside and stuck his own eager fingers into the empty space. Then he grabbed me by the collar of my coat and forced me to move back down the upper-level hallway. "Either she's lying or somebody else is a double-crosser."

"Of course she's lying," a female voice said in the dark.

Regan waved her flashlight and snarled. "Where've you been?"

Brianna stepped into the circle of light. My mind reeled, lurching from my visit to her floral shop to our meeting at the Windjammer. I tried to put the pieces together. How did she fit into all of this?

Johnny stuck the sledgehammer into my lower back. "Let's go." He shoved me down the staircase.

I shuffled forward until I was in Regan's light and could see Brianna's face, cool and collected. My mouth dropped open. Even her jeans were creased and she had her fists in what looked to be a Gucci gabardine raincoat. What the well-dressed thief was wearing this season.

"Hello, Dodie," she said softly. "Sorry we have to meet like this. But you are too curious for your own good."

I struggled to find my voice. "I can't believe . . . you seemed so broken up over Antonio's death . . . how could you stand by and watch Regan kill him?"

Brianna laughed. "Stand by? I don't think so."

The truth hit me square between the eyes. Two poisons in his blood. "You gave Antonio the arsenic and Regan gave him the succa . . . succyl . . ."

"Succinylcholine," Regan shouted, aggravated. "What arsenic?"

"That's why he had to see the Chinese doctor," I hollered.

Both Brianna and Regan stared at me.

"Knock it off," Johnny yelled. "We gotta find the jewels *now*. And get outta here. Tie her up with the cop and I'll take care of these walls." He lifted the sledgehammer and pointed at the hallway.

"Wait!" I shrieked.

"No more stalling." Johnny swung the sledgehammer in an arc and crashed it into JC's delicately sculpted spindles that propped up the railing that led to the second floor.

I ducked as half a dozen of the vertical shafts shattered and the splinters of wood sailed everywhere.

"Stop!" I cried. "You can't destroy the set. The show opens to-morrow night!"

"Tear it all down," Brianna ordered, taking Regan's flashlight and sweeping it across the walls on the second story.

Regan grabbed Brianna's arm. "What's she talking about?"

Brianna was unruffled. "Let go of me."

I saw my chance. "Brianna tried to poison Antonio with arsenic. The medical examiner found traces in his system. That's why he had stomach issues and had to see the doctor in Bernridge."

Johnny's hammer was suspended in mid-swing. "What the—?" He stopped and glowered at the two women.

Regan's face was distorted. "We had a plan. What were you try-ing to do?"

Brianna growled. "*We* had a plan. Antonio only brought you in because he felt sorry for you."

"He loved me."

"He put up with you." She shrugged. "The arsenic was backup."

Uh-oh. There was nothing more infuriating than unrequited love. Might as well stir the pot. I cleared my throat. "Antonio had no feelings for either of you. He loved Tiffany." I had no idea *who* Antonio really loved, but claiming this bought me time.

"He was going to divorce her and remarry me!" Regan screamed. "Until he changed his mind about that little loser."

Brianna yelled back, "You're a pathetic fool! The only thing Antonio loved was his wallet."

I was caught off guard by the bitterness in Brianna's voice.

"He wasn't going to get off so easily this time," she said.

"Enough!" Johnny screamed. The ex-wives' heads swiveled in unison as he targeted the upstage wall. His first swing ripped into JC's beautiful wallpaper. The second blow exploded the glass globes on wall sconces on either side of an imitation period portrait. Shards of glass rained down, along with a shower of bracelets, rings, necklaces, and earrings.

The three of them gawked, frozen. I decided to take advantage of their shock and ran for the stairs, but Johnny had other plans. He seized my legs and dragged me back to the stage, my head banging on the floor before he deposited me in a seat next to Suki.

"Reg, get rid of these two. Brianna, the jewelry!" Johnny ordered. He attacked the rest of the sconces on the upstage wall and two on either side of the front door, sending torrents of jewelry cascading to the ground.

As if awakening from a trance, the two women went into action. Brianna crawled around the set with total disregard for her chic clothing; Regan juggled a gun and pulled the syringe out of her bag.

"You d-don't want to do this," I stammered. "Two more murders?"

Johnny scrambled to help Brianna just as Regan aimed her syringe for my neck. Suki kicked out a freed leg, Regan fell backward, and the houselights burst on. Adjusting from the dark to the bright light took a moment and I closed my eyes for a second. When I opened them, Bill was onstage with his weapon trained on Johnny and Brianna; Ralph was standing over Regan, dangling handcuffs. Suki slipped out of her bindings. She leapt up, her hands chopping the air in a karate stance.

I breathed deeply, trying to calm my racing heart.

* * *

The red and blue blazing lights of the police cruisers—two from Etonville and two from Creston—had attracted attention. Etonville was as nosy as ever and Ralph had his hands full with crowd control, once the threesome were safely tucked away in the Creston squad cars. The rain was irregular now and the wind had died down considerably. With the lights back on, the lobby of the Etonville Little Theatre was blazing with energy. Only some of it was the electricity; the rest was generated by Lola, Walter, Penny, and Carlyle, all talking and flapping their arms.

Lola stepped outside and joined me in front of the Windjammer, where Benny, Honey, and Henry peered out the front window. "Are you okay?" she asked and put an arm around my shoulders.

"Fine. Little sore from being bounced around on the stage." I rubbed my wrists where the rope had left red, rough marks that would be black-and-blue by tomorrow.

"Some mess in there," Lola said.

"But at least we're both alive." When I hadn't returned to the Windjammer after delivering coffee to Suki, and she hadn't checked in with the police department dispatch, Benny and Edna got suspicious and contacted Bill. I nodded toward Suki, who talked on a cell phone. She was the consummate professional. You'd never know that she'd spent part of the evening bound, gagged, and stuffed between two rows of seats. Probably how the ELT audience felt from time to time.

"I can't believe I didn't know about Antonio's criminal activity," Lola said.

"But he was also a serial husband who kept marrying younger. Hard to tell whom he really loved, but the first two hadn't gotten over him," I said.

"Is that true?" Lola asked.

"Regan thought she was running the show, but Brianna was the brains between the two of them and good at manipulating Regan. And me." I shook my head. *Maybe Carlyle was right. Maybe I am an amateur.* "I almost began to think of her as a friend. I guess she thought establishing a relationship with me would give her access to information." I sighed. "She fooled me."

"And both Brianna and Regan were fooled by Antonio."

"Looks like it. Until they discovered he tried to swindle them out of the jewelry."

"You know, Antonio was a good director," Lola mused. "When he showed up to work." Walter beckoned Lola into the theater. "We've got to get a crew together and repair the scenery. It'll be a long night." She glanced at her watch. "We have twenty hours till curtain!"

"Good luck."

She hugged me. "Thanks."

"For what?" I asked.

"You solved the murder."

She ran off. I glimpsed a cluster of officers by the squad cars. Besides the Etonville force, there were two others—a Creston officer and the brunette I'd seen Bill with twice before, looking fresh as a daisy in Versace. Bill shook hands with the officer and smiled that crooked grin at the brunette, giving her a pleasant squeeze. The Creston officers drove off.

Bill turned, inspected the crowd, frowning. Then he found me.

"Can't let you out of my sight," he said, pretending nonchalance. A catch in his voice gave him away.

"Just another night in Etonville. Break-ins, robbers, murders . . ." I kidded.

One side of his mouth crept up. "I told you to be careful."

I corrected him. "No. You said you'd be in touch later."

"Well, the highway flooding was worse than expected."

"And poor Suki got tied up," I said.

He paused and grew serious. "You did a good thing here. Staying on the case until the criminals were caught. Following your instincts."

"Thanks." I felt warm despite the dropping temperature.

"Anyway, Creston PD was relieved," he said.

"I could see that. The officer and the woman . . . ?"

Bill coughed and ducked his head, smiling. "Pia."

"Is that her name?" I asked as indifferently as I could manage.

"My old Philly partner. She works Special Crimes for the state police."

"Your . . . police . . . partner?"

"Her husband and I went to school together." Bill scratched his chin.

"Her *husband*?"

Bill turned his head forty-five degrees to avoid my face—which was one part chagrin and two parts "yippee"—and to hide his grin. "I've got to go do some paperwork."

"Have fun," I said.

Bill pulled a strand of hair off my face and tucked it behind one ear. "I still owe you an after-dinner drink."

Yikes! "Anytime."

28

The referee blew his whistle and eleven Tigers from Etonville's Youth Football League adjusted their helmets, tied their shoes, wiped their noses, and trotted onto the field for the final five minutes of the game. Etonville was losing by only ten points. I tilted my head back to let the morning sun beat down on my face. The temperature hovered around sixty, not a cloud on the horizon. It was a great day for football.

Bill tugged on the visor of his Buffalo Bills ball cap and clapped his hands. "Okay, Tigers, let's go. Let's see some tackling!"

The boys nodded, their helmets slipping forward and backward.

"Come on Tigers!" I yelled from my front-row seat on the metal bleachers.

The stands were full for this last home game, parents, grandparents, and siblings in orange clothing, cheering. The Banger sisters had organized a contingent from the Senior Citizens Center, who fluttered homemade signs and pennants. The Tigers hadn't won a game all season, but hope sprang eternal in this town's heart.

I was just happy to have the morning off. Henry had Honey covering lunch—it would be packed with the post-game crowd—because she was assuming more responsibility before her grand exit from restaurant management to return to the hallowed halls of packaging. Ever since Antonio's murder had been resolved, the Windjammer had regained its status as Etonville's only three-star eating establishment; as opposed to La Famiglia, its four-star rival. Commerce was thriving. The Banger sisters critiqued Henry's homemade soups, Edna made daily runs for the Etonville Police Department, and the ELT crowd stopped in for dinner before the show. Which went on. On time.

Lola had been right. The Etonville Little Theatre had pulled an all-nighter. Everyone pitched in and repaired the set of *Arsenic and Old Lace*. Unless you walked on the stage and touched the wet paint on the walls and tacky varnish on the staircase, no one could tell that, hours before, Johnny Bilboe had used a sledgehammer to hunt for the stolen jewelry. Which was now in a property lock-up in Creston.

The loose ends had been tied up. Brianna and Regan ratted on each other. Two ex-wives eager to rekindle a relationship with Antonio, even joining his den of thieves. But when he greedily double-crossed them, they had agreed to take him down. Former nurse Regan had managed to get access to succinylcholine: a quick end to Antonio's life. But Brianna didn't trust Regan and had formulated her own plan: slow death via the arsenic. Hell hath no fury like women scorned. Brianna and Regan admitted Antonio had come to town expressly to set up the burglaries in Creston; directing at the ELT provided a convenient cover. When the police searched Brianna's home, they discovered additional stolen property as well as plans for a getaway, complete with a chartered plane waiting for them at the Atlantic City airport.

As for Tiffany and Carlyle, they skipped town as soon as the show closed, and didn't bother to send a postcard. They'd both been deceived by Antonio.

Arsenic and Old Lace was a hit and sold out its run—as much because folks wanted to see where the thieves had been captured as they were eager to watch the dysfunctional family goings-on: death by elderberry wine, romantic high jinks, psychotic siblings.

Dysfunctional families reminded me of Walter's insistence that the theater was a family and Bill's speech to his team about the football family. Even the Windjammer felt like a family on Henry's good days. I'd been displaced from the Jersey Shore and my beloved beach, but I'd found a family in Etonville. It wasn't just the sun that could make me feel warm all over.

Mildred touched me on the shoulder and pointed. "Dodie, that's my nephew Zach," she said, as the Tigers' offense took the field and ran two plays.

I smiled. "I think he has promise."

"Do you?" she asked.

"Well, he's young yet . . ." Only ten years old. "But someday . . ."

Lola appeared on the sideline. "Scoot over," she said, and sat down. "What's the score?"

"Thirteen to three. Three minutes left to go."

"I guess we're past intermission?" she asked.

Lola would never get the lingo straight. "Halftime. Yeah."

Bill hurriedly gestured to the official. "Time out!"

He ran a hand over the stubble on his chin, collected his players, and directed their next moves before he sent them back on the field. He took his job seriously.

"Bill's looking good," Lola said, and poked me in the ribs.

"I don't know. Maybe *I* should take a time-out. Refocus my romantic life. I met a nice guy last summer at the shore, and if I—"

Everyone rose to their feet and the bleachers erupted in noise. Lola and I jumped up to see what had happened.

"That's my nephew. That's Zach!" Mildred screamed.

I stood on the bleacher and watched the kid run fifty yards for a touchdown. It didn't matter that the Tigers would probably lose this game, too. They had actually scored a touchdown!

"That's good, right?" Lola asked breathlessly.

"That's great!"

Bill ran to me, his eyes shining. "Did you see that?" He slapped his cap against his leg and threw his arms into the air. Then he grabbed me in a bear hug and planted a kiss on my lips, his bristly beard scraping my cheek.

Lola stared openmouthed and I gasped. "Yay!" I yelled.

He plunked his Buffalo Bills cap on my head and draped his arm over my shoulder.

OMG.

ABOUT THE AUTHOR

Suzanne Trauth is a novelist, playwright, screenwriter, and a former university theater professor. She is a member of Mystery Writers of America, Sisters in Crime, and the Dramatists Guild. When she is not writing, Suzanne coaches actors and serves as a celebrant performing wedding ceremonies. She lives in Woodland Park, New Jersey. Readers can visit her website at www.suzannetrauth.com.

A DODIE O'DELL MYSTERY

SHOW TIME

ETOVILLE

LITTLE THEATRE

ROMEO & JULIET

FIRST IN A
NEW SERIES!

SUZANNE TRAUTH

CPSIA information can be obtained
at www.ICGtesting.com
Printed in the USA
LVOW11s1026130317
527017LV00001B/27/P